Acknowledgments

As it takes a village to raise a child, it seems to take one to birth a book, as well!

Our heartfelt gratitude to all who were involved in the conception of Sirens! With a special thank you to our sensitivity readers, Kesha and Mal, and to our wonderful publishers, editors, cover designers, and above all, to our fantastic readers! The neuro-divergent weirdos among whom we belong. The small-town book clubs. The big city conference goers. To those who take Townsend Harbor on vacations, and those who curl up at home. Thank you for joining us in this magical place.

All our love,

K & C

KERRIGAN BYRNE
& CYNTHIA ST. AUBIN

OLIVER-HEBER BOOKS

ONE

In the weeds

WHEN SOMEONE IS SO BUSY—OFTEN
OVERWHELMED—THAT THEY CAN'T CATCH UP
AND SERVICE QUALITY TAKES A HIT

MAGGIE MICHAELS STARED BLANKLY AT THE BACKLIT array of bottles, desperately trying to remember what the hell actually went into a Long Island Iced Tea.

Which was kind of ironic, because wasn't obliterating your memory kind of the point of a Long Island Iced Tea?

Or was that just a thing at Kelly's Irish Pub back in Boston?

After several stymied moments drumming her long, elaborately painted nails on the old wood bar, all she could recall was a beverage that tasted vaguely like its refreshing, lemony namesake, and had frequently resulted in the loss of her keys, several items of clothing, and a shit-ton of pride.

And hell, just about any combination of the mood-enhancing elixirs in front of her would do that, right?

Grabbing a glass from the rack, she dumped in a shovel of ice and began tipping in healthy glugs of everything but eye of newt. Next came a blast of cola, which turned the drink something kind of like the right shade. She topped it off with a chunk of lemon that could only be described as a wedge by someone who was excessively kind or legally blind.

Whatever. It was at least worth the "Four-dollar mixed drinks!!" advertised on the happy hour chalkboard propped near the entrance.

Happy hour.

If Maggie had a time machine, she'd zap herself back to find whatever asshat had come up with the concept and punch him in the neck meat.

Okay, first, she'd zap herself back to 1880s London to have tea and *Tea* with infamous madam Marry Jeffries, *then* she'd punch happy-hour guy—because it was surely a guy—in the neck meat.

Or the dick.

"Is that mine?"

Speaking of...

Maggie turned on her heel to find Kurt, whose fingers she might have to bend into a pretzel if he didn't stop snapping them at her every damn time he shoved a new slip of paper into the already overloaded drink ticket carousel, looking at her expectantly.

"Sure is." Maggie slid the glass across the bar just hard enough to send a tiny amber wave tipping over the Kurt-ward side.

"What is it?" he asked, eyeing the glass.

"A Long Island Iced Tea."

Kurt's thin lips pursed into a judicious pout. "It doesn't look like a Long Island Iced Tea."

"It's from South Shore," Maggie said, parking a hand on her hip. "You got a problem with that?"

It was almost refreshing, letting the East Coast burr of her youth flirt with the syllables of her question after years spent carefully training it out of her voice.

Kurt wisely decided he didn't.

He gave her a beleaguered sigh and mopped the glass with an already badly used towel before shuttling it off to one of the many packed tables.

Maggie sucked in a lungful of air carrying a cocktail of scents as odd as the one she'd just mixed. Briny air gusting in the second-story deck where patrons fought the seagulls for their battered fries. The earthy pong of the deep-fat fryer responsible for said fries. The roasty undercurrent of beer that said fries were being washed down with.

And beneath it all, Sirens Pub itself.

With its nautical kitsch of real fishing nets draped across the ceiling and faux portholes on the walls, this joint really knew how to beat a theme to literal death. Because: mermaids. Mermaids on the menus, mermaids on the taps, a massive mural behind the bar featuring a mermaid squeezing her excessively perky, titanic tits.

Definitely painted by a man.

Pausing to massage a sympathetic pang in her lower back, Maggie turned back to the wheel of tickets.

Two vodka sodas with lime—thank God, something relatively easy.

One gin and tonic also with lime—her raw cuticles already hated her, but whatever.

One Raven Creek stout—she might just live through her first day yet.

And...a Ramos Gin Fizz?

The fuck was that even?

Maggie covertly slipped her phone from her apron pocket and consulted the search engine. Her eyes got as far as the second ingredient when she slapped the ticket on the margarita-salt-confettied counter and whipped through the other five drinks while she ignored the sixth on principle.

The very idea of egg whites in a beverage that didn't also contain wheatgrass and/or protein powder... Who the hell had decided that egg whites had any place *near* a cocktail?

Probably the French.

"Will my RGF be arriving any time before the heat death of the universe, Mads?"

Acronym-happy *and* an unsolicited nicknamer.

Oh, they were just going to be the very best of friends.

You're not here to make friends.

The thought appeared spontaneously in her head in a voice that made her heart give a painful little lurch.

Mark Kelly. Her best friend.

The one whose idea it had been for her to haul her ass all the way across the country to Townsend Harbor in the first place.

The one whose younger brother, Gabe, had called in several favors to get her this job.

That she was obviously spectacularly unqualified for.

Which proved just how well Mark Kelly knew her.

Ever since Gabe had bounced from Boston and landed smack in the middle of a friggin' Hallmark movie, Mark had been convinced that Maggie ought to follow suit.

She'd mostly blown him off until the clever bastard had to go and drop a trump card on her.

Madame Katz.

Townsend Harbor's very own Victorian villainess. Rumored to have had a hand—among other body parts—in the disappearance of thirty plus men.

Basically, perfect podcast fodder wrapped up in a homicidal bow.

Despite her swan dive down a research rabbit hole, she could find surprisingly little about either Madam Katz or the sailors she'd supposedly seduced into her brothel then conveniently vanished.

Which was when Mark's suggestion that she do some on-site research in Townsend Harbor started to sound a lot more seductive.

Because if there was one thing Maggie couldn't resist, it was a mystery.

Even if it meant subjecting herself to the low-grade torture of slinging drinks in the hopes of unraveling it. Because booze made people more likely to talk, and after the feverish research she'd done online, Maggie knew she needed a certain person to do a lot of talking about a certain topic.

But that certain person had yet to show as Gabe promised he would, so instead, Maggie had to keep pumping everyone's face holes with one of the last legal toxins and listen to the mostly meaningless bullshit flooding out of them.

Which wouldn't have bothered her, per se. God knew she had an impressive collection of name tags under her belt already. But her ineptitude reflecting on the Kelly brothers after the mess they'd already helped her clean up in Boston? That bothered the shit right out of her.

"Coming right up!"

Your ass.

Kurt propped his pristine tray against his also-pristine apron rather than resting it on Maggie's not-so-pristine counter to wait.

After a blur of pouring, spilling, swearing, shaking, squeezing, and more swearing, she handed Kurt a drink that *almost* looked like the bougie Orange Julius she'd glimpsed ahead of the seventeen-page-long story that preceded the recipe.

And Kurt looked—dare she say it—mildly impressed.

Without so much as disapproving snort, he set a cocktail napkin on his tray and whisked it away.

Spattered with an unholy slew of booze and mixers, Maggie excused herself under the guise of restocking her garnish caddy and slipped into the walk-in fridge.

The stainless-steel door was cool against her forehead, the sudden insulated quiet like a little pocket of heaven after the chaotic jazz of clinked glasses and conversation.

She was so. Damn. Tired.

And not just because this was the first job that required her to stand on her feet for hours at a time since working the Sabrett hot dog stand at Jones Beach the summer after her sophomore year of high school. At least then, she'd had sixteen-year-old cartilage and ready access to funnel cakes.

No.

Maggie was mentally exhausted from trying to remember drink orders and bartending techniques she had learned on the fly. Emotionally pulped from being in a new place after hastily leaving behind everything familiar. Even if that familiar wasn't especially pleasant.

"Mads?" Kurt shrilled through several layers of metal and insulation.

Right on fucking cue.

Maggie thumped her head on the other side of the door. "Yeah?"

"The customer at table twelve sent his RGF back. I'm going to need you to remake that *on the fly.*"

Acronym happy, unsolicited nicknamer, *and* a kitchen lingo dropper.

If this guy were any more determined to sabotage her, she'd be tempted to date him. He seemed to be her type.

"Oh, and I just put in an order for three Old Fashioneds and a Lemon Drop when you get a sec."

When you get a sec. As if someone was wandering around handing out buckets of unoccupied time.

Fuck. That.

Reaching for a bottle of seltzer from a nearby crate, Maggie knocked the cap off on one of the shelves and took a swallow. The aggressive bubbles made her eyes water, but successfully banished the dangerous clench at the base of her throat. She stashed it behind a bin of lemons and shouldered her way through the door.

"Where is he?" she asked.

Kurt blinked at her, his sad little soul patch dipping as his mouth formed the perfect O of a Christmas card angel.

"Who?" he asked.

"The guy who sent this back," she said, snatching the drink from Kurt's hand.

Even now, the condensation-kissed glass looked serenely

golden, the pillowy cloud of heavy whipping cream and egg white atop it as fresh as new-fallen snow.

It was ethereal.

Celestial.

Goddamn it, she had even *measured*.

"That's him," Kurt said, inclining his head toward the water-view side of the dining room. "In the yellow shirt."

Maggie nudged in beside Kurt's bony shoulder, peering through a rack of kitchen tools to locate her target.

And promptly had to steady herself against an industrial-sized whisk.

The man was...*perfect*. A goddamn *GQ* ad cut from the fabric of the universe and pasted into this chaotic everyday scene.

Most males of her acquaintance "got dressed." This dude put together a whole-ass *ensemble*. The kind she could easily see one of those Ken-doll-perfect mannequins wearing in a display window on Fifth Avenue.

Crisp, tailored shirt. Expertly cut trousers.

But it wasn't just the clothes. It was the way he wore them. Like they were the elegant but totally unnecessary wrapper of a ten-course meal, and the rest of the world would be lucky to get a single bite.

Which, judging by what she could see of his body, was an empirical fact.

Mr. GQ didn't just *work out*. He had a *regimen*. One that made his shoulders just the right kind of broad, his torso the perfect sort of cut to fit a tux he'd be wearing to swagger up to a roulette table on the French Riviera. Probably sit his equally perfect ass down across from a Bondian super-villain with an intriguing characteristic scar, eyeing him cooly across the green felt.

No wonder he was so goddamn picky about his drinks.

"Not today, James."

Maggie hadn't realized she'd spoken or that she'd begun

moving in GQ's direction until Kurt's hand clamped around her wrist, panic plain on his features.

"What are you doing?"

Maggie attempted a mild smile. "I'm going to go talk to him."

"Talk to him?" Kurt's eyebrows and voice lifted simultaneously. "Why? Why would you do that?"

"Because I'd like to know what he finds so objectionable." Maggie slipped past him, only to have Kurt leapfrog back into her path.

"Can't we just assume it's everything?" he asked.

Several acidic replies burned their way up her throat but were promptly neutralized by the chance glimpse of the antique mermaid masthead mounted on the wall, hair very nearly the same shade of scarlet as Maggie's, a secret smile playing about her painted lips.

The kind of smile that might advertise to lonely nineteenth-century sailors arriving in Townsend Harbor from ports across the known world that convivial companionship might just be on offer—for a price.

"The sooner I get this little conversation out of the way, the sooner I can get back to making the rest of your drink order," Maggie said.

"You know he's"—Kurt's words snapped off mid-sentence—" one of our regulars, right?" he said, speed-walking to catch up with her. "And kind of an important one at that. Please don't piss him off."

"Piss him off?" Maggie snorted, rolling her eyes. "What on earth would make you think that I'm going to piss him off?"

"Maybe the Manhattan you managed to dump into the fire chief's lap earlier?"

A fresh wave of irritation heated Maggie's skin at the memory. "That was an innocent accident and had absolutely nothing to do with the fact that hairy-knuckled letch spent almost an entire hour ogling my cleavage."

"I mean, it's kind of hard not to."

Maggie stopped so abruptly that Kurt clipped her shoulder. "And what do you mean by that?" she asked.

A single bead of sweat slid down Kurt's forehead as his eyes tried—and failed—to find a safe place to land.

Ever since hitting puberty, Maggie had been blessed—cursed? —with very large, very real breasts that had her confined to beige boulder slings when the rest of her middle school classmates were flitting around the PE dressing room like fairies in their delicate lace bralettes.

Galvanized by the memory, Maggie tugged down the neckline of her fitted Sirens t-shirt to reveal a whole extra inch of cleavage before fixing Kurt with a smug look. She marched past him and directly up to Mr. GQ's table, where she cleared her throat and waited for him to look up from his paper.

And then he did.

And then she died a little.

Because he *wasn't* perfect.

But he wasn't perfect in the most devastatingly attractive ways.

When those obscenely beautiful lips parted in a smile, they revealed the tiniest gap between his perfectly straight, perfectly white teeth. And when that smile reached his leonine eyes, a slim, dusky scar slicing his left eyebrow gave the lid a sleepy, sexy squint. Like a never-ending wink.

When that wink made him cock his head to look up at her, the last rays of coastal sunset revealed another scar just under his meticulously shaved jaw.

And when that jaw flexed in preparation to speak, Maggie felt her knees go all buttery.

"Hey," he said, flicking the briefest of glances toward her name tag, "Madison."

And the sound of it was so warm, so friendly, she almost forgot that Madison wasn't even her real name, just what happened to be on the name tag bestowed on her by Chris, Sirens' tough-as-nails and twice-as-practical owner, who didn't want to go the trouble of having a new one made—a process that clearly involved a wood-burning tool on a mermaid-tail-shaped plaque—since Maggie had no intention of being a long-term employee.

"I go by Maggie," she said for reasons she couldn't fathom. "And you are?"

"Trent," he said. The smile deepened, and so did the odds of Maggie/Madison wobbling on her totally adorable if not totally practical Vince Camuto booties. "But everyone around here calls me McGarvey."

"Trent," she repeated, then stood there frozen in the tractor beam of his smile for a span of time she was afraid to calculate.

Only when a staccato cackle of women's laughter drew his eye toward the bar did Maggie find the presence of mind to continue. "I would like to know what you find so objectionable about this drink." She set the glass down on the table, only to notice that in the time that it had taken her to walk from the kitchen, the foam had all but disappeared, and the contents separated into something that now resembled spoiled milk.

A crease appeared in the center of his smooth, brown brow as he considered the glass, then looked back at her.

"Taste it," he said.

Maggie swallowed hard, alarmed by the odd flutter developing behind her apron. "I don't need to taste it," she said, her voice lacking anything even remotely resembling conviction. "I know it's right because I followed the recipe."

"Recipe." Trent chuckled as he leaned back in his chair, the movement releasing the olfactory equivalent of a pheromone freight train. "Recipes are fine if you're baking a cake or mixing concrete. But *cocktails...*"

Was it her imagination, or had he placed just the tiniest hint of extra emphasis on *cock*?

"Cocktails are a sensory experience," he continued. "Temperature. Flavor balance. You have to develop a sense for it. And you can't develop a sense for it if you don't use yours. *Taste it.*"

Maggie saw his gaze flick toward her fingers as she reached for the glass, one corner of his mouth curling as he registered her nails. His eyes tracked her hand as she lifted it toward her lips, meeting hers above a rim lacy with the remnants of egg-white suds.

Milliseconds before she put her mouth where his had been, she spotted a shock of expertly styled salt-and-pepper hair in a clump of patrons gathering near the door.

Bingo.

The pilot light of her curiosity flared into urgency, burning away the magnetic hold this Trent *Whateverthefuck* had over her.

"Look, you don't like the drink, try ordering something off the menu next time," she said, adding an extra dash of South Shore sass.

Trent leaned forward, his dark eyes boring into hers. "Fine. I'll have a Manhattan, then."

Maggie opened her mouth, but no retort came. The crowded room rose in temperature by twenty degrees.

"Coming right up." She felt his gaze on her as she made her way back to the bar might have worked a little extra swing into her hips as she slid behind it.

Her hands trembled with a brew more potent than any she could craft as she reached for the bourbon, her attention fixed on her target as he made his way through the crush. Shaking hands. Slapping backs. Bestowing veneered grins of the proper self-depre-cating wattage.

Until, at last, he parked on the stool she'd done her utmost to ensure remained empty for his arrival. The fact that she'd had actual provocation to unceremoniously evacuate the fire chief had just been an added bonus.

"Hello there." Maggie slid a cocktail napkin across the bar and gave him what she hoped was a winning smile. "What can I get for you, handsome?"

His overly manscaped brows shot toward his surgically perfected hairline as an embarrassingly pleased smile stretched across his face. "Well, hello there. You must be new."

"How'd you guess?" she asked, batting her eyelashes.

"It's my job to know everyone in Townsend Harbor," he said, pronouncing the tiny coastal town's name with an extra flourish of pride. "I'm—"

"Oh, I know exactly who you are, Mr. Mayor." Maggie winked at him.

And soon, the 37,000-plus listeners of Maggie Michaels' Murderous Victorian Madams podcast would too.

Especially since—according to at least one contemporaneous source—Townsend Harbor's mostly ornamental political figurehead happened to be living in the mansion that once belonged to one Madame Katz during the height of her rumored dirty dealings.

"But you don't know my usual drink?" Mayor Stewart gave Maggie an extra-toothy grin.

"Give a girl a break," she said, leaning forward just enough that her breasts brushed her forearms. "I've been in town for all of five minutes. Let me finish memorizing Townsend Harbor's most influential citizens, and I promise I'll get their drinks licked."

The mayor's Adam's apple bobbed above his starched collar. His lips parted to issue what she assumed would be a lame-ass retort when his cell phone vibrated on the bar.

He glanced down at it and frowned. "Will you excuse me?"

"Of course."

The smile he gave her as he slid from his stool was tighter. Less polished.

Maggie watched him weave through the tables and out into the hallway, the phone pressed to his ear. She was still watching him when she registered a shape moving toward the mayor's still-warm barstool in her peripheral vision.

"Seat's taken," she said.

"Not anymore."

Had her head whipped toward the voice any faster, Maggie might have slipped a cervical vertebra.

Again.

Trent McGarvey leveraged his impressive wingspan to reach behind the bar and grab a towel, keeping his eyes on hers as he breeched a barrier that felt far more sensual than it should.

Maggie watched, open-mouthed as he efficiently wiped a stretch of the old wood clean before setting down his leather messenger bag and plopping down on the stool.

"Now," he said, pinning her with a killer smirk. "How about that Manhattan?"

TWO

McGarvey Highballer

SPEEDING MOTORIST DUCKING THE COPS

TRENT LEANED AGAINST THE POLISHED OAK BAR, HIS elbows pressed into a countertop so old the Virgin Mary might have given birth on it.

He glanced at the familiar menu with the Thursday specials of fish and chips, marionberry cheesecake, or jambalaya.

On Thursday, he read through emails and approved Deputy Probable cause statements over a much-needed cocktail, sometimes ate the jambalaya (decent for this far north), then turned in before the live music at nine thirty.

Tonight, though, his eyes refused to follow anything but the incredible curves of the terrible bartender's body as she made a mockery of her profession.

He was a sucker for a woman possessed of so many round cheeks. And she was *killing* him with her red hair pulled back in a bouncy ponytail, revealing the damp, downy skin of her neck and the adorable curve of her stubborn jaw.

Trent felt a twinge of guilt as he watched her, knowing that he should not be admiring her so openly, but he could swear to every god that her V-neck wasn't pulled *that* low a minute ago.

He glanced around to find something less seductive to focus on. Suddenly the glass vases in the windows took on incredibly feminine curves, the drink menu now seemed to offer only sexy liquors, and the décor?

Forget it.

Why did mermaids always have their perfect tits out? And the mermaids with red hair? Was that a thing, or one of those Disney visuals that just hung out in the general mythos?

Due to the immortal poetry of that sainted knight, Sir Mix-a-Lot, people always assumed he was an ass man.

Which...he was.

But Trent McGarvey's kryptonite? Big, soft, natural breasts.

The lady in question winked as she walked past him, her chest flushed pink with exertion. He felt a foreign surge of heat that emptied his mouth of all moisture. He cleared his throat and tried to think of something to say, but she and her swinging ponytail bopped away before he'd landed on a sufficiently pithy comment.

Her confidence was magnetic, even if he didn't want to admit it. He was *gone*. What that meant? He wasn't sure. All he knew was...

No other woman in the room existed.

She acted coy, like she didn't notice him watching her, avoiding eye contact as she wiped down glasses and restocked limes.

Trent wasn't fooled—the surreptitious glimpses she stole from beneath her lashes and the faint glow to her cheeks gave her away.

He couldn't help but notice that Maggie also kept glancing toward the door with expectancy, her green eyes flickering with an almost palpable sense of anxious anticipation.

Was she waiting for someone special? An enemy? A long-lost family member?

A love interest?

Trent winced at a pang of curiosity and, if he were honest with himself, a touch of jealousy.

He wasn't a detective *yet*, so he should cool it with the hyper-awareness.

"Barkeep!" bellowed Myrtle Le Grande, everyone's favorite pansexual septuagenarian, as she helped her wife, Vivian "Vee" Prescott, onto a barstool. "I'll have the slipperiest of nipples and my lady, here, will have her usual pitcher."

Trent had to squint against Maggie's megawatt smile. If anything, she needed to register that thing as a weapon of mass *distraction.*

"Pitcher of what?" Maggie asked, grabbing a few glasses from beneath the bar.

"Scotch," Vee moaned in her stolid British accent before dramatically resting her forehead against her hands.

"It's been a day," Myrtle explained, before whispering behind her hand, "She'll take a half and half with Newcastle and Raven Creek Nitro Stout, please."

"Still in a pitcher?" Maggie asked.

Vee groaned again.

"A bucket, if you got one," Myrtle translated.

"I'm on it."

Trent's mouth twitched as he counted the sixth time Maggie turned to the dark corner behind the hanging speakeasy lights to Google a cocktail recipe.

Slippery Nipple. Irish Cream, Sambuca, Grenadine. Sweet, slick, boozy, and should coat the tongue with a silky layer of cream and sugar. A favorite of drunk coeds on spring break and... apparently stressed-out lesbians.

"Want to talk about it?" Maggie asked the pile of Vee's silver-streaked hair as she placed the pitcher beneath the nitro stout tap.

Don't tell her. Do. Not. Tell her that she should be pulling the lighter ale first, as it would settle on the bottom beneath the stout!

Trent bit down hard on his tongue so the mansplaining didn't fall out.

Myrtle watched Maggie with all the one-eyed speculation of an old-timey prospector panning for gold. "You're new here."

"That obvious?" Maggie flashed that smile again. The one

that would be considered indecent in some countries and probably the entire Bible Belt.

A trainee. She'd never been a bartender before, that was for fucking sure.

"No, I mean you're not a local yokel, or I'd know ya." Myrtle threw her knitted leopard-print beret on the counter and began to take off the matching fingerless gloves. The woman always looked like she'd stepped off a stage during Fashion Week, but not in the good way. In the *WTF, no one would ever wear that* way. Today's ensemble was something Trent would call Golden Girls Chic, where the leopard print was rainbow colored and somehow there were palm leaves on her pink shirt and sequins on her sunglasses and three-inch platform sandals.

He checked the windows just to make sure it was still February.

Yup. And raining.

"The fuck?" Myrtle grimaced after one sip of her drink and slid it back across the counter at Maggie. "No offense, honey, but this Slippery Nipple tastes like licorice-flavored lighter fluid! Here, try this." She shoved the drink toward Trent. "One sip and tell me it's not like a butterscotch suicide-bombed a Twizzlers factory."

Curious, Trent reached for the stem of the glass only to be cock-blocked by Maggie.

"Oops!" She relieved the woman of her glass and poured the abomination into the sink. "Must have gotten your drink and someone else's mixed up in the middle."

"Or...accidentally traded Irish cream for butterscotch, which..." Trent offered to Maggie beneath his breath with a shudder.

Drink probably tasted like cough syrup.

Maggie blanched. "Then what even makes it extra slippery?"

"The grenadine." He couldn't help but grin. "Amaretto if you're feeling sassy."

Trent bet himself his next paycheck that she'd add the amaretto and

When proximity roped him into the conversation, he did his best to follow Vee's warbly tale of woe regarding a missed shipment of monster-themed dildos to her sex-positive, vagina-oriented boutique. Much as a story including Vee's Lady Garden made for a good yarn, his attention remained arrested by Townsend Harbor's newest character.

Trent was pleased to see that Maggie nailed Myrtle's drink on her second try, and his libido noticed that she'd poured the amaretto in his line of sight.

She *wanted* him to know she was feeling sassy.

Message received.

"Are you a local lush, or just passing through?" Maggie returned to Trent when she noticed his glass was empty.

"Recent transplant," Trent answered, enjoying the lo-fi background music and intimate lighting. "Got soul weary in the city, trying the small-town life on for size."

"Oh yeah?" She scooped ice into two glasses for a classic G&T on the rocks. "What city?"

"You've never been there." He laughed, trying to picture her ginger skin beneath the unrelenting Southwest sun.

She snorted and tossed him a look full of attitude. "I've been just about everywhere, you don't know—"

"Albuquerque."

Her mouth tipped down. "Okay. Yeah. Never been there," she mumbled with a self-deprecating laugh.

Trent was a big fan of not saying *I told you so* when it was obvious, so he basked in the unspoken victory, enjoying her discomfiture more than he ought to.

Why was it *so* sexy when someone could laugh at themselves?

"Okay, smarty-pants," she challenged, leaning over the bar in a way that deepened her cleavage to indecent levels. "Any more words of wisdom before I make your next Manhattan?"

"Actually, yes," he retorted, feigning seriousness. "You can shake a martini, fine. But never shake a Manhattan without asking. I prefer my vermouth unbruised."

"Fuck off, you can bruise alcohol?"

Trent almost did a spit take of his last sip but wrestled the unappealing brew down his gullet. "Do you have blackmail on Chris?" he asked, wondering why the fuck Sirens' owner would hire such an obvious newbie at the town's favorite watering hole without more extensive training.

Sure, she was an oasis of sexiness in the desert that was Townsend Harbor's under-fifty dating pool, but her bartending —if one could call it that—couldn't be good for business.

Maybe she was kin?

He eyed Chris, the owner, a sparkplug of a thin blonde with a dark tan and darker eyes. If she and Maggie were related, he'd claim Ed Sheeran as a sibling.

Maybe she had a good sob story? Needed a quick job out of desperation?

Frowning, Trent studied her, looking for any victim vibes and not exactly sensing them from her. Didn't mean anything, per se. He was proud of his investigative instincts, but he wasn't a damsel-in-distress divining rod or anything.

"Hey, how about a round of flaming rim shots for my friends here?" a customer called out, breaking the tension.

Maggie glanced at Trent, who raised an eyebrow.

"Sure thing," she said, grabbing shot glasses and filling them with tequila. "Just remember, I'm not responsible for any bad decisions made after these."

"Fair enough," the customer agreed, clinking his glass against hers before downing the shot. "Think you could be one of those bad decisions?"

The smile she flashed him was flat as day-old soda. "Trust me, neither of us wants that."

Trent sucked some air through the gap in his teeth, a habit when chewing on a problem. Something about her just set off his spider-senses.

"Hey, hot stuff, how about a refill?" Bernie Crowder slurred, eyeing Maggie's cleavage a little too long for Trent's comfort.

"How about you sip some water instead, Bernie?" She slid him a glass, unfazed. "Gotta stay hydrated. The night is young."

Trent was impressed with her perceptivity, though Bernie was not deterred.

"The night is young and so are we, sweetheart," the sixty-year-old crab fisherman brayed, his overalls catching on his rain slicker as he peeled it from his briny layers. "Tell me when you get off your shift and I'll be waiting to get you off again."

A few men laughed.

No women did.

Maggie's face drained of any remaining color, but she squared her shoulders at the man, jutting her jaw forward in a stubborn refusal to show fear.

"Maybe you can answer me a question, Crowder," Trent chimed in, pulling his cuff links below his suit coat in case he had to unlatch them in order to hand this old white perv his own ass. "Men like you have a tendency I can't figure out... You walk into a place like this looking like you just quit your shift beneath a bridge terrorizing the local children, and you hit on the prettiest young woman you can find as if your dick were dipped in gold. Is it? Is your dick dipped in gold, Bernie Crowder?"

The scowling seaman ran a hand over what sweat-greased hair he had left before mumbling, "No."

"Does a world exist where a woman that young and fine goes home with you?" Trent gestured to an open-mouthed Maggie, who startled when the beer she pulled overflowed, drenching her hand.

Bernie's beard sank below his clavicles as he bowed his head. "No."

"Then maybe sit the hell down and stop harassing the servers, yeah?"

"Yes, sir."

The atmosphere was heavy with a pregnant pause as the customers waited for permission to breathe again.

Trent gave it by ordering his third and final drink.

"One for the road?" He tipped his empty glass toward Maggie, who was looking at him with an odd fascination.

"Anything you want." Something in her heavy-lidded eyes caused everything south of his belly button to melt...then harden.

"I just have to light this on fire for these guys first."

"You have to do what?"

Maggie grabbed a bottle and two shot glasses. As she reached for the matches to flame the shots, her hand knocked over a display of cocktail napkins, which tumbled to the bar in a messy pile. Unaware, she struck the match and touched the flame to the rim of the shot glasses, which ignited dramatically.

But as Maggie placed the flaming shots on the bar, the trailing edge of her sleeve grazed the flames, and then the pile of napkins, setting a corner of the bar on fire.

"Shit!" she yelped, shaking her arm fast enough to smother her sleeve. But the flames spread quickly across the napkins.

Trent leapt up, grabbing a pitcher of water.

But Maggie was faster. She snatched the soda gun and doused the growing fire before it could spread.

For Sirens, it was a near miss.

For Kurt, it was a direct hit to the vitals, drenching him sternum to knees with freezing soda water.

Trent wasn't that mad about it. Kurt was one of those assholes who hid their true nature behind burlap shirts and waxed hipster mustaches.

"Oh no, I'm so, so sorry," Maggie said for what had to be the thousandth time that night.

"It's fine," said Chris as she relieved an astonished Maggie of the soda gun through her giggles. "Go home and change your panties, Kurt—I'll cover your tables."

Maggie sputtered at her boss. "I promise, I—"

"No worries," said Chris with the laid-back demeanor of a woman who'd seen it all happen within these walls. "I don't mind a mess if you take it on yourself to clean it up as you go. Besides," she whispered as she leaned in with a conspiratorial smirk, "Kurt needs a good douche every so often. Keeps him from getting too big for his britches."

Maggie let out a shaky laugh as she swept the soggy napkins into the trash. But Trent noticed her hands trembling slightly as she took the bleach rag and wiped beneath the patient bar patron's glasses and took their good-natured ribbing with genuine humor.

When she reached Trent, he couldn't stop staring at the peach blush spreading beneath her light freckles.

A natural redhead, then.

Fuck. He couldn't know that.

"Hey, you handled that like a pro," he encouraged her. "Might have a future at the fire department."

Maggie snorted. "Might have...but I dumped a drink on the fire chief an hour ago, so I think that vocational avenue is closed for good."

"What? Why'd you do that?" Trent asked with a laugh.

"Because that pervy old goat grabbed my ass and pretended it was an accident."

Trent shook his head, his expression turning serious. "Someone should do something about that problematic mother-fucker. You want to press charges?"

Maggie gave him a small smile that snaked through his insides with a slick desire. "It's okay. I handle assclowns like him a *ton* in my line of work. But thanks for having my back."

Trent lifted his glass in a mock toast. "What is your line of work, anyways?" he asked, only half teasing. "We both know it's not bartending."

Maggie chuckled, but the mirth didn't reach her eyes.

Because anxiety flared there.

Interesting...

She was saved from giving him a reply by a customer at the other end of the bar.

Trent turned back to his tablet, promising himself he could go five minutes without glancing at her.

And he did.

Well, four minutes.

All right, three minutes and twenty-seven seconds...

...was his record over the next hour and the extra Manhattan he'd ordered to wash out the flavor of the one before it.

How the hell was she getting *worse* at her job as the night wore on?

Every time Trent looked up at her, she was watching the door, her shoulders tense until they drooped in disappointment when she didn't recognize the face.

"Expecting someone?" he finally asked around a sip.

Maggie's head snapped up, her cheeks flushing slightly. "What? Oh, nope. No one special."

Trent raised an eyebrow. "You sure about that? You've been watching that door like a hawk all night."

"Pfft, how would you know?"

"Because I've been watching you all night," Trent murmured.

The flirt was out before he could call it back, landing with an extra swoop of her butterfly-wing lashes.

He couldn't call it back, but he could stuff it down and smooth it over. Smooth was his calling card. His specialty. His motherfucking descriptor.

"Watching you commit multiple offenses against Townsend Harbor's post-dinner drinks crowd." *Clearly* he shouldn't have had that fourth awful drink. It was giving him equally awful ideas.

Oh damn, he was a sucker for a woman who could laugh at herself, and her laugh wasn't just infectious—it imbued every smile within its blast radius with an extra glow. "Well, so long as you don't turn me into the authorities."

"Please, I *am* the authorities."

"And humble, too."

His entire vocabulary abandoned him as a familiar feminine expression darkened her eyes from jade to forest and her gaze set fires of appreciation to all the right places. Not just the fit of his suit over his more sculpted parts...

She checked his empty ring finger.

Twice.

He liked that. She was ethical. Or...at least careful.

Trent McGarvey from Albuquerque's fifth precinct would have pulled some stupid show-off shit with the maraschino cherry stem and had her screaming his name before midnight.

But that wasn't him. Not anymore.

Trent McGarvey of Townsend Harbor had this village tucked in by ten on a school night and did nice things for dangerously pretty, mysterious ginger women without any of the moves from his player's handbook.

"Listen, I have all day tomorrow free and an apartment down the block and around the corner. How about you come around to my place and we can go over a few bartending basics?"

Her hesitation was almost as offensive as her mixed drinks. Eyes darted just about everywhere as an entire conflicted conversation splashed across her ultra-expressive features.

"You're asking me to your place?"

"Yup."

"In the middle of the afternoon."

"Uh-huh."

She tucked an invisible hair behind her ear. "Like...a date?"

"Like...an intervention." He softened his tease with a wink, and she choked on her next inhale.

"I work the lunch shift tomorrow," she warned with a licentious quirk of her lips. "I don't get off until five."

"Then come by afterward," he offered, fully aware that he'd said it far more casually than he meant it.

Something about her sent every instinct he had into overdrive. This wasn't just an intervention, it was an investigation.

Nah, not that serious. Not *assigning it a case number and establishing a file* kind of serious. More like...an exploratory expedition.

Because Maggie wasn't what she was claiming to be...and to him, she'd just become a person of fucking interest.

Even though the only crimes thus far had been against their livers.

"Are you sure you want to risk teaching me?" she asked playfully, her voice laced with sarcasm and a little bit of sin. "I mean, I *did* just almost burn down the pub."

"I'm not scared," Trent lied, more nervous for the damage she could wreak on his taste buds, liver, and carpeting than anything.

Maggie snagged the little plastic skewer of maraschino cherries from the dregs of his glass and slid them past her plump, glossed lips with a smile that could have set the devil on fire.

"You probably should be."

THREE

Muddle

TO MASH INGREDIENTS WITH A MUDDLER, A
SPECIAL TOOL FOR GRINDING AND CRUSHING
INGREDIENTS INTO THE BOTTOM AND SIDES OF
A GLASS

THIS WAS A MISTAKE.

Maggie had known it when she accepted Trent McGarvey's invitation for a crash course in cocktails.

She'd known it when she reached for her lacy La Perla bra and matching thong instead of her comfortable cotton crotch covers.

She'd known it when she fibbed to Mark Kelly about her plans for the evening.

She'd known it when she'd given Roxie—her blind, bipolar Peekapoo—an extra scoop of kibble and promised to be back early.

She'd known it with every step that carried her from her temporary sublease two blocks down Water Street.

And she knew it now, standing on the second-story landing outside the door to McGarvey's place with her knuckles poised to knock and the damp chill of a February evening still clinging to her coat.

It wasn't too late. If she turned around right now, she could slip down the stairs and back out into the night. Send an apologetic text message. Promise to do it another time.

And then what?

Now that Maggie's hopes that her first day as a lackluster bartender would be her *only* day as a lackluster bartender had been thoroughly dashed, her options were limited.

Option one: scrap the bartending gig, even if it meant blowing her chances of getting information from Mayor *Spewart*, as she now knew several of the locals called him.

The very idea made her stomach clench like a fist.

Gabe had said Townsend Harbor's famously douchey first dude was a talker once moderately lubed, and she *needed* him to talk. And just because the mayor had bounced nanoseconds after arriving yesterday didn't mean he'd do that every time.

Ergo, option two: stick it out at Sirens a little longer.

Which raised another important question: wouldn't it be a good idea to actually learn a little bit about the art of cocktail making so as not to completely alienate Chris's clientele?

Damn straight it would.

Sucking in a deep breath, Maggie took a moment to arrange herself for the all-important first look. Fluffing her hair. Reaching inside her coat to wiggle her underwire back below her boob crease. And last but certainly not least, wrestling the overly enthusiastic elastic band of her waist-snatching body shaper back over the soft swell of flesh that had escaped its confines on the walk over.

Then, and only then, did she square her shoulders and raise her hand to knock.

Only, the door swung away before her knuckles could make contact with the wood.

Trent McGarvey stood there looking unfairly handsome in a crisp white dress shirt and tailored slacks of a deep navy, a bemused grin tugging at one corner of his lips.

"Did you want to come in, or were you planning on loitering in the hall all night?"

Loitering. Implying that he knew she'd been standing there for some length of time.

Implying that—

"Motion sensor camera." McGarvey's voice, deep and smooth, caught her off guard.

Christ on a slice. He'd *seen* her?

Imagining McGarvey watching while she wrestled her chub back into the spandex cincher slowly cutting off the circulation to her ankles, Maggie wasn't sure whether to be annoyed or aroused.

Unfortunately, her body had already decided for her.

"Just making sure the building is equipped with fire extinguishers," she said, giving her head a playful toss.

"Smoke detectors, too." Trent nailed her with a swoon-worthy smile and stepped back to grant her entry.

"Glad to see everything is in working order," she said, giving him a stiff nod as she breezed across the threshold into an *Architectural Digest*-worthy foyer.

"Take your coat?" he asked, closing the door behind her.

My coat. My panties. My firstborn...

"Sure." Maggie made quick work of the buttons and shrugged the classic, figure-flattering trench down her shoulders.

McGarvey's eyes flicked toward her nails as she held it out him. "I don't know how you do anything with those."

Maggie suppressed an eye roll. If she had a dollar for every time she'd heard that, she wouldn't have to haunt the sample stands at Costco on weeks when her nails and stomach both needed a fill.

Not that that would be an option in Townsend Harbor unless she took the ferry back to Seattle.

Still, she'd already wrangled a brunch invite from the two adorable, ruckus-raising late-in-life lesbian life partners who'd made her evening infinitely more tolerable after the mayor had fucked off.

And women over fifty almost always sent you home with leftovers, in Maggie's experience. Probably she'd be able to put off a grocery run for at least a few days after this weekend.

"Carefully," she said belatedly. Her standard, if totally untrue, answer. Mostly she accidentally punctured things and swore a lot.

Trent's grunt sounded less than convinced as he opened a closet door and plucked a black velvet hanger from the rail. "I have a purse hook too if you want to offload that." He tipped his chin toward the Prada clutch dangling from her forearm.

A purse hook? In a bachelor pad?

Oh, this guy was *good*.

"Thanks," Maggie said, clipping open the buckle to extract her phone. McGarvey's eyes followed it as she tucked it beneath her bra strap below the neckline of her sweater.

She couldn't afford to miss Gabe's call. Not after what she'd learned about the Palace Hotel.

Namely that, like the mayoral mansion, it was owned by Mayor Stewart, but had ties both to Madame Katz *and* the Townsend family. Who, Maggie was quickly learning, were balls deep in just about every account of this picturesque Pacific Northwest hamlet's history.

History that was proving to have some rather interesting inconsistencies, depending on whose version of it you were reading.

Which was why she intended to make Ethan Townsend—Townsend Harbor's golden boy, according to Gabe—her next target.

"Do I need to take my shoes off?" Maggie asked, pointing to the orderly rack beside the door.

Trent's Adam's apple bobbed above his crisply starched collar. "Your call."

Glancing down at the creased cuffs of his pants, she noted the Gucci slides on his socked feet.

His indoor shoes—she'd deadass bet her Neumann U 87 Ai Set Large-Diaphragm Condenser Microphone on it.

Maggie stepped out of her heels and placed them in one of the available spots in the pristinely ordered rows, grateful she'd had the foresight to wear toe panties, but wishing she'd had the presence of mind to get a pedicure.

Not that she'd had that kind of time.

In the twenty-four hours since she'd accidentally lit the ancient bar at Sirens ablaze, she'd had to fill out a small mountain of paperwork, speak with an insurance adjuster, and sit through a millennia-long meeting with a Jurassic gasbag from the Townsend Harbor Historic Development Division accompanied by one Caryn Townsend.

Who, Maggie had decided, would vastly benefit from either a decent dicking down or a solid elbow to the hinge of her jaw. When Gabe had informed her that the platinum-haired former first lady actually used to be much worse, Maggie had crossed herself and pretended to shove a head of garlic down her shirt.

For such a small town, Townsend Harbor was proving to be a hotbed of rather sizeable egos.

"The kitchen's this way."

Maggie followed McGarvey down the hallway and couldn't resist—not that she tried overly hard—stealing a peek at his ass, which was even more perfect than she'd imagined.

And she'd imagined real hard.

So hard, in fact, that she'd had to pick up an extra pack of batteries for the only self-care device she'd bothered to bring with her when she hurriedly left Boston.

But in exactly none of her feverish fantasies had she anticipated that McGarvey's decorator-ly sensibilities would rival his fashion sense.

Maybe even outstrip them, she thought as he led her past a rustic wooden table adorned with a fresh bouquet of flowers, and into a serene living area that would make Martha Stewart weep rivers of Lancôme mascara down both buttery cheeks.

Maggie's gaze swept the room, taking in the tasteful minimalist décor and impeccable mid-century modern furniture. The bookshelves held an array of titles that Maggie suspected had been selected more for their size and color variation than for content.

Unless McGarvey harbored a secret obsession for *Mykonos*, *Dali*, and *Fifty Dresses that Changed the World*.

No family pictures. No college wrestling trophies or B-movie posters. No gym bag with boxing gloves or a lucky basketball. Not even a junk bowl to collect mail, keys, or pocket contents.

Well, this is no help whatsofuckingever.

Getting to peep McGarvey's landing pad had been the deciding factor in accepting his invitation. A chance to scour for clues as to who the hell he was and, thereby, what it was he wanted with her.

Because after confirming that Trent McGarvey's living quarters were just as perfect as the man himself, she knew for damn sure it wasn't a conquest.

"You could have *at least* run a vacuum around the place," Maggie teased, trying to sound casual as they entered the spacious open-concept kitchen. It was just as immaculate as the rest of the apartment, with gleaming stainless-steel appliances and neatly arranged utensils.

"I just need to grab a couple things from the pantry," he said, pointing down a hall off the kitchen. "Be right back."

It was all the invitation Maggie needed.

Fueled by the same investigative instinct that had led her to peer into windows as soon as she was tall enough to reach them, Maggie began easing open McGarvey's cupboard doors, glancing at the contents, mentally cataloging anything about him she could glean.

It was, in effect, the same insatiable curiosity that had initially led her to internet sleuthing and, ultimately, starting her podcast.

She just had to *know*.

"You should see my sock drawer," McGarvey said, opening the double-door fridge with a smirk. "It's a work of art."

Maggie whirled around, her heart doing the flamenco within her chest.

"Easy, my guy," she said in a voice far breezier than she felt. "I never look at a man's sock drawer on the first date."

"Date?" asked McGarvey from behind the fridge door. "And here I thought I was pretty clear that I just wanted to show you how to make some cocktails."

For the first time since he'd extended the invitation, Maggie actually believed him. Because he seemed like exactly the kind of dude who was so picky about his shit that he'd even be willing to offer free instruction and consider it doing the Lord's work.

Damned if that didn't make her feel... What?

Messy. Lazy. Sloppy. Careless. Impulsive. Reckless. Thoughtless.

Words her army drill sergeant father had welded to her when, as a teenager, she'd lost interest in following the rigid structures he'd set forth like an eager shadow.

Fuck.

"And here I thought you had at least a passing familiarity with sarcasm," she shot back after a pause several seconds too long.

A symphony of muscles flexed beneath his shirt as he set down a food-blogger-worthy charcuterie board on the polished granite counter. Piled high with gourmet cheeses, meats, and olives, the spread made her stomach rumble on sight as her salivary glands splooshed their metaphorical panties.

Please, God, don't let him have heard that.

"Hungry?" he asked

Thirsty, more like. In every sense of the word.

"I'm good for now, thanks." Another oft-repeated and totally inaccurate answer. "Maybe in a bit."

McGarvey's broad shoulders jerked upward in a *suit yourself* shrug as he cut his eyes toward the bar. "Shall we?"

"After you," Maggie said, hanging back a couple of steps for maximal gluteal admiration.

McGarvey brought the tray, goddamn him, sliding it onto the bar's counter before swinging around behind it. "I'd offer to make you a drink, but..."

"That would defeat the purpose of my being here," she finished for him.

"You catch on quick, rookie." His wink shot a bolt of heat straight through her middle.

Had any other man called her that, Maggie would have been tempted to introduce his gonads to his epiglottis by way of her knee. But somehow, Trent McGarvey pronounced it with a casual affection that made her feel like the loose cannon in every buddy cop comedy ever.

Movies she'd gladly watch over a rom-com every day of the week and twice on Sunday. It was one of the few things she and her father had ever done together that didn't end with him volubly critical and her silently seething.

"Well?" McGarvey asked expectantly.

She blinked at him. "Well what?"

"You're on the wrong side of the bar for bartending," he said.

"Oh," Maggie said. "Right. I knew that."

She joined Trent behind the expanse of sleek black marble and polished cherry wood, the limited space forcing them to stand hip to hip.

Her hip to his thigh, anyway.

As she was absent her heels and stood a thoroughly average five foot four, the crown of Maggie's head barely grazed McGarvey's chin.

Or would, if he were to, say, fold his massive arms around her shoulders and pull her in for a long, lingering lip lock.

Maggie shoveled the unhelpful thought onto the growing pile and pushed the sleeves of her clingy cashmere sweater up her forearms.

"So, what are we doing first? Slicing lemon wedges? Making those ridiculous zest curls?" Maggie reached for the bowl of sunshine-yellow fruit on the counter but was arrested by a gentle grip on her wrist.

"Wait." His fingers were long and dexterous, adorned with a simple silver pinky ring. She imagined those capable hands gripping her waist, moving lower to—

Open a cabinet and withdraw an apron. One of those old-fashioned jobbers with big pockets and a pithy message that always said something like "Kiss the Cook."

"Can't have you getting anything on that cashmere."

Maggie held her breath as he walked around behind her and looped the halter strap over her head. His warm fingertips brushed the sensitive skin of her nape as he lifted her hair to adjust the fit. Goosebumps cascaded down her torso and arms when he captured the ties on either side of her hips and knotted them behind the small of her back.

His hands lingered for a moment before finally retreating back into his own space.

"Not bad," Maggie said when her lungs remembered how to process oxygen. On the rare instances when she'd had occasion to don an apron, her tits had typically ended up playing peekaboo with the panel of fabric meant to cover the average chest.

And Trent McGarvey's chest was a good deal broader than hers, if not quite as convex.

A fact he seemed to also notice as he followed her gaze, then cleared his throat.

"What should we start with?" he asked, consulting the array of bottles. "A rum and Coke?"

Maggie arched an eyebrow at him. "I'm pretty sure I know what goes in a rum and Coke."

"But do you know how *much of* each goes in it?" he asked. "Because Myrtle was three sheets to the wind after two of yours, and I've personally seen that woman drink lumberjacks under the table."

"I knew there was something I liked about her," Maggie said, accepting the bottle of Bacardi McGarvey held out to her.

Their fingers brushed during the exchange, sending a jolt up Maggie's arm that nearly made her fumble the bottle. Her nails clicked ridiculously against the glass as she nearly dropped it.

"Careful, rookie," he said. "A bartender who can't hold her liquor isn't going to last long around here."

"I can hold mine *and* yours." Maggie planted the bottle on

the counter with a satisfying thunk. "How'd you get to be such a cocktail snob, anyway?"

"Snob?" Trent chuckled and began arranging cocktail tools on the polished countertop. "That sounds like a judgment."

"Not a judgment," Maggie said. "An observation."

"So you like to watch?"

Maggie's cheeks grew warm as the suggestive words hung in the air. He was close enough now that his breath stirred the hair at her temple as he leaned in to snag a bottle of simple syrup.

"Sometimes," she admitted. "What about you?"

Trent's eyes flickered to meet hers before he turned back to the counter, his movements slow and deliberate as he set various implements on the gleaming counter. "All the times."

Maggie's heart took a header into her nether regions.

She knew what he was insinuating, and truth be told, she suspected she'd rather enjoy it. But this shit here was a disaster waiting to happen. Townsend Harbor was bent to be equal parts recovery ward and hidey-hole. As geographically distant from the life she'd led in Boston as she could get while remaining in the same country. And for reasons she didn't want to think about while standing this close to the man who occupied this pristine palace of solitude, she needed to.

Maggie cleared her throat, trying to ignore the heat that was pooling low in her belly. "You didn't answer my question about the cocktail snobbery."

He looked thoughtful for a beat.

"Spent my twenties focused on quantity," he said, his voice low and smooth. "My thirties are about quality."

She wondered if that maxim had applied to all of his appetites.

"I enjoy the artistry of it," he continued. "And how that art rewards precision."

Precision. Artistry. Order.

Oh, this man was *so* not her type.

So, what was it about the way he moved, the way he talked,

that made her feel like someone had buried a live coal behind her sternum?

"Fair enough," she said, hoping to distract herself from her own thoughts. "Which precision-rewarding drink will we be starting with?"

McGarvey gestured to the array of components on the counter. Fresh mint. Limes. A glass jar of raw sugar. "How about a mojito?"

"Fine by me," Maggie said. "The mint goes in first, right?"

"Right," McGarvey said.

Maggie twisted off a small bunch of leaves and dropped them in the glass before reaching for the wood pestle.

McGarvey's jaw flexed.

"What is it?" she asked.

"Go ahead," he said, shaking his head. "Let's see your technique."

Looking at the pestle with its long, thick wooden shaft and blunt head, Maggie had a sudden flash of inspiration. Her skill set might just overlap with this particular activity after all...

Wrapping her fingers around the handle, she began to work it up and down within the glass. In the suddenly oppressive silence, Maggie would have sworn that she could hear the individual plant cells rupturing.

"What?" she demanded.

"Nothing," he insisted.

"Look, you might as well tell me before that vein in your forehead bursts and you stroke out."

McGarvey swept in like a man relieving an inept copilot of an airplane's instrument array and quickly added a slice of lime and a spoonful of sugar.

"Gives you a little extra friction and helps release the zest's essential oils," he said.

"God forbid we don't maximize the essential oils," Maggie muttered before resuming her task.

Not even ten seconds had elapsed when she heard a muffled sound of dismay.

"What now?" she asked.

McGarvey's toffee-colored eyes cut to the pestle. "May I?"

"Seeing as it's that or listen to you aggressively grind your teeth, I'm going to say you may." She stepped aside as much as the compacted space would allow and watched as his large, long-fingered hand wrapped around the blunt-ended wooden implement.

But it was her thoughts that were becoming muddled as her gaze strayed from the green pulp in the glass to the smooth ridges of muscle flexing in his forearm as he began to work the pestle.

"We're just trying to open up the mint," he explained, "not punish it for the sins of its ancestors."

Maggie didn't quite manage to stifle her snort, but his teasing only made her more flustered. Each time he gently corrected her, it set her freckled cheeks aflame.

"There," McGarvey said, aiming the rim of the glass toward her so she could appreciate the perfectly pummeled contents.

"So *that's* what they mean by bruised?" she asked, despite already knowing the answer. If her years of investigative reporting had acquainted her with any truth, it was that men were always willing to teach you something.

"It's all in the wrist," he said, setting the pestle aside.

Yeah it was.

"So, what's next?" she asked briskly, eager to move things along. "Do we add the bourbon now?"

Trent's grin wilted.

"Kidding," Maggie insisted. "I totally know bourbon doesn't go in a mojito." As of the last thirty seconds. "It's rum, right?"

"Right," he said, looking immeasurably relieved. "I like to add it first so the liquor can draw out the oils before we add more acid with the lime juice."

"Makes sense." Maggie grabbed the rum and unscrewed the lid.

McGarvey slid a double-sided silver jigger between the bottle and the glass. "We'll need one and a half ounces."

"What is it with men and measuring?" Maggie poured out what seemed like an exceedingly stingy amount of the clear liquid and upended it into the glass.

"Now you'll want three-quarters of an ounce of lime juice." McGarvey handed her another wooden implement with what looked like a rudimentary drill bit at one end.

Because *of course* he expected her to juice the limes herself.

Maggie grabbed one from the bowl and plopped it onto the cutting board for dissection.

"Can I show you a trick?" McGarvey asked.

"Several, I'd wager."

"What?" he asked.

"What?" she repeated.

Placing his wide palm over the fruit, McGarvey began to roll it on the cutting board in smooth strokes. "Releases the juices," he explained.

Boy, does it ever.

Scarcely had the tip of Maggie's knife pierced the gleaming green skin than a little spurt shot up.

"Oops," she said, proceeding with a modicum more caution. "I usually get a little warning before that happens."

McGarvey's warm chuckle allowed her shoulders to sink away from her ears as he placed a small wire strainer over the glass measuring cup. "Disembowel at will."

This, at least, Maggie did with enthusiasm, stopping when the pale green liquid nudged the one-eighth cup notch on the cup's side.

"Perfect," he said. "Toss it in."

Maggie decanted the juice into the glass.

"Ice," McGarvey said. Leaning down below the counter, he pulled on a handle that revealed a slim freezer drawer. Inside, Maggie saw several varieties of ice in all shapes and sizes, from oversized Old Fashioned cubes, to delicate spheres with slices of lemon and orange suspended in their perfectly transparent centers.

"Wow," she said, her eyes widening. "I thought only those OCD TikTokers actually did this shit."

McGarvey gave her that knee-softening grin as he pulled out a metal tray. "OCD TikTokers and motherfuckers like me from the Southwest."

"Becaaause heat stroke?" she guessed.

"Because sometimes air conditioning and a cold beverage is all that stands between a you and a desperate act."

Maggie narrowed her eyes at him in exaggerated scrutiny. "Is this where you pull out an ice pick and make vaguely menacing comments?"

One of McGarvey's dark brows lifted as he pressed a tab on the side of the tray that made the iconic cracking sound.

"Oh," Maggie said, pulling the tray toward her.

"About five cubes ought to do," he said.

"Really?" she asked. "Exactly five?"

Heat radiated from McGarvey's broad chest as he turned his torso to face her. "That ice is going to turn into water, and the amount of water it adds to the drink is as important as every other component we've added."

He had a point. Maggie really hated it when that happened.

Using the wickedly pointed tip of her nail, she pried out the appointed number and slid them into the glass. "So Albuquerque, huh?" She would *not* have pegged that. Austin. Phoenix, maybe. "How'd you end up out here?"

"Work," McGarvey said, his answer as artfully casual as her query had been. "All we need now is some soda water."

The condensation-kissed bottle hissed as Maggie opened it. "How much?"

"Just top it up."

Maggie fluttered her lashes and dramatically swept her fingertips to her chest. "You mean, I get to...to...*eyeball* it?"

Speaking of eyeballs, McGarvey's seemed to have fixed on the spot where Maggie's nails fanned across the swell of her breasts.

"Don't make me regret it." But something darker and deeper had sanded away the teasing edge to his voice.

Maggie swallowed hard as she streamed in the soda, the bubbles making it necessary to pour even slower so she could stop when it kissed the rim of the glass.

"Beautiful," McGarvey said. But he wasn't looking at the drink. "Go ahead and give it a stir."

Plucking a metal straw from the container, Maggie slipped it into the glass and swirled.

"*Gently*," McGarvey said. "The bubbles are part of what makes it so refreshing."

Having completed several painstaking revolutions, she slid the beverage toward him for final approval.

"Not bad," he said. His gaze flickered up to meet hers. "Want to taste?"

Lord, do I.

Maggie nodded, her mouth already watering as the tangy, minty flavor exploded on her tongue, savoring the coolness that spread through her middle.

"Oh wow," she said, opening her eyes to find him watching her intently.

"Good?" he asked, his voice low and husky.

"Really good." She offered him the drink, praying the single sip would somehow cool her nerves.

Trent took it, his eyes staying fixed on hers as his lips wrapped around the straw where hers had just been. Maggie felt a delicious shiver race through her veins at the casual intimacy of the gesture.

"Not bad," he said, setting down the glass.

"Not bad?" She snatched the drink back again and downed an additional gulp, as much for the alcohol's mood-enhancing effects as to dispute his noncommittal flavor assessment. "This is fan-fucking-tastic. Probably the best mojito I've ever tasted."

"You drink a lot of those on Long Island?" McGarvey asked.

But before she could respond, McGarvey stepped closer. "Or was it Boston where you became such a connoisseur?"

Maggie's heart began to thump like a rubber mallet against her sternum, her mind racing as McGarvey's lips curved into a slow, wicked smile.

It wasn't like she'd made a secret of the fact that she knew Gabe and his family, so Boston was a pretty logical leap. But Long Island? Maggie knew for a *fact* that the only person who'd even heard her mention anything remotely adjacent was Kurt. And even then, in a totally offhand way when McGarvey was on the other side of the bar.

Which could mean one of two things. Kurt had been running his incessantly smirky yapper...or McGarvey had been doing some research.

Neither option felt like a good thing, considering what there was for McGarvey to find.

"Neither," Maggie said, arranging her lips into a smile that felt several sizes too tight. "I went on a booze cruise for my birthday last year."

She took another sip of the mojito and offered it to him again, her fingers brushing his as she handed it over.

"From Boston?" His voice held a teasing lilt that made her second-guess herself.

"Why do you want to know?" Maggie met his gaze, refusing to be the first to break eye contact.

He was so close now that she could make out the individual filaments of his ridiculously long lashes. "Maybe I find you intriguing. Maybe I want to know what a woman like you is doing in a town like Townsend Harbor."

Maggie tensed. This was the moment she'd been dreading.

"Just looking for a change of scenery, I guess." Not *technically* a lie.

"And decided to take a job bartending at Sirens?"

She shrugged. "They had an opening. I needed to make some money. Seemed like a pretty easy solution."

"Even though you don't know the first thing about mixing drinks?" Trent raised an eyebrow. "I'm sure you're a woman of many talents."

She leaned into him, damage control mode now her sole focus. "You have no idea," she said.

The tension that had been simmering just below the surface since the moment they met was rapidly reaching its boiling point.

Their lips were a hairsbreadth apart now. The playful banter had shifted into something far more dangerous. Maggie knew she should pull away, but her body refused to cooperate. She was drowning in the intoxicating nearness of him.

And in no hurry to be saved.

Her eyelids fluttered closed, a brazen invitation to end this topic.

Any moment now, she'd feel that first brush. His lips on hers. Danger of discovery seared into oblivion by the very real heat between them.

"What did you do?" McGarvey's question ripped through the haze of desire.

Maggie took a steadying breath, searching for an anchor. "In Boston? Oh, all kinds of stuff. Waitressing, data entry—"

"No." Trent's expression turned serious, sending a jet of icy alarm spilling down Maggie's spine. "You left Boston and traveled all the way across the country just to take a job as a bartender despite knowing nothing about mixing drinks and having a temperament terribly suited to the service industry. So, I'll ask again," he said, his breath warm on her lips. "What did you *do*?"

IT WAS BAD.

Whatever she'd done was unspeakable. Illegal, probably.

While Trent prided himself on having a keen investigative mind, he found it in no way necessary to apply his training. The evidence was in the way she grabbed his face and mashed her mouth to his to avoid the question.

And...if the intensity, passion, and skill of her kiss was any indication of her guilt, she'd probably done something worth twenty-five to life.

Yet Trent couldn't pull away to save his skin.

Or anyone else's.

Shit, someone could have been robbing the wine seller across the street, complete with an *Equalizer*-style shootout, and he wouldn't have noticed or cared.

Because Maggie Michaels kissed like the act was an Olympic sport and she was defending her gold medal.

Which was usually his thing. He had a formula, one wherein he applied hard-earned skill to turn a woman's knees to quicksand and her insides liquid.

Then he'd *really* start trying, his every movement thought out and controlled in order to make certain the evening went the way it was supposed to, and she left singing his praises.

But tasting Maggie was like drinking a fine wine or a perfect cocktail, and Trent found himself helpless to do anything but savor every note and nuance.

Christ, she was sweet...but not cloying. Warm but not scalding. With a hint of liquor and an aftertaste of lime. He sampled it all. Her mouth, the slick glide of her tongue. The sweetness of her breath.

The world outside his open window melted away. The smell of fresh rain dampening pavement, the sound of a lone motorcycle engine growling in the distance, and a car door slamming shut. Who could mark those things when they were busy learning what desire tasted like?

He swore he could hear the blood throbbing in her veins. Could make out the individual twists and whorls of her fingerprints as she softened her touch against his face and charted the angles of his jaw with questing fingers. For a moment, Trent forgot everything else. Forgot about his job, his responsibilities, his own identity. All that mattered was the woman in front of him, the way her lips moved against his, the way her body pressed closer to his. It was a dangerous game they were playing, but Trent couldn't bring himself to care.

Couldn't summon the terror that truth should have wrought.

How could he when she was a balm and an irritant all at once?

His blood felt like warm honey, but his skin was on fire. His hands would tremble unless they splayed over her abundant curves. The curve of her back, her waist, the swell of her ample ass.

Holy Christ, he was in trouble.

And he loved how trouble tasted.

The moment was as perfect and slow burning as a summer night. The air around them felt heavy and heady, like the prelude to a storm. Trent pulled Maggie closer and moved his lips against hers reverently, tasting her in ways that had nothing to do with sex.

Her response set him on fire. She pushed herself up onto her toes, pressing her body even closer to his own. Her hands moved up from his face to his chest, testing the dips and swells of muscle.

Trent groaned into the kiss and knew that there was no going back now. He wanted this woman in ways that were both primal and poetic all at once. Without breaking contact, he led Maggie over to the couch.

She sank down. He followed, settling into the cradle she made with her gorgeous body.

The kiss only intensified, their hands exploring each other while their mouths spoke words too profane for language. It was something out of a dream—pure bliss wrapped up in an embrace so tight it felt like it would be this way until one of them finally conceded ground so they could remove the clothes that dared keep their skin from touching.

With their mouths fused, she clawed at his shirt, undoing a few buttons below his neck while he slid her zipper down.

Damn, his mouth was watering violently.

"Psycho Killer" by Talking Heads started blasting from her phone.

"Gah! Balls."

It was the first time that word had been spoken *into* Trent's mouth.

Maggie performed some improbable jujitsu roll and unfolded from beneath him to her feet, snatching the phone from her bra.

He could do nothing but pant like a man who'd run a marathon and watch her while still balancing on one knee in the world's most awkward I *almost had sex but the phone rang* position.

How could she pick it up?

Not that he thought himself that good. Well...he did, but that was only half the problem. Not only did she answer the phone like it might be the lottery calling, she'd done it after sexing him up so completely he'd forgotten what a phone even *was*.

He watched her expressive face light up as she unceremoniously wiped the gloss of their kiss from her swollen lips.

"Uh-huh... Fuck yes... Uh-huh. I'll be there."

After the shortest phone call in the history of ever, Maggie was stuffing her phone back in her purse and grabbing her keys with a self-satisfied glee that made him shrivel.

"Sorry, Trent," she said with a smirk, "I gotta go—it's an emergency." She winked as she turned away from him, as if she didn't know it would be painful to follow her with what was going on in his pants.

She suddenly wouldn't look at him, and every investigative sense he had began to steal some of the tingle from his more engorged parts.

Was she feeling awkward? Shy?

Guilty?

"Everything okay?"

She swallowed hard and flashed him a grimace that was meant to be a smile as she stumbled on her way to the door. "Oh, yep.

Yeah. Just got some news I've been waiting for, and it's...time sensitive."

Didn't she have work in an hour?

"Well, um... We should..." Her eyes darted to where he was unfolding from the couch. "Thanks for the...the lesson. I'll see you!"

"Maggie, wait—"

The door slammed behind her.

Trent collapsed on the couch, his legs splayed and his veins still throbbing as he scrubbed his hands over his face.

He'd dodged a few bullets in his day, but if he wasn't careful, Maggie Michaels just might be the end of him.

FOUR

Nightcap

A DRINK CHOSEN FOR THE END OF THE NIGHT

MAGGIE'S CHEEKS BURNED LIKE THE EMBERS OF A summer bonfire as she climbed the steps of Vee's Lady Garden, her heart still fluttering like a nervous bird from the lingering taste of Trent McGarvey's lips. The kiss had left her in a state of delicious disarray, and she struggled to compose herself as she pushed through the door for her rendezvous.

"Lord Almighty, honey," Myrtle said, her eyes widening behind her oversized, red-framed glasses as she took in Maggie's flustered appearance. "You're redder than a lobster's ass."

Myrtle, on the other hand, looked like a burglar from a vintage heist movie, complete with black leggings, black turtleneck, black beret, and, of course, black fingerless gloves.

"You look very fetching," Maggie said, setting down her bag and shrugging out of her coat.

"Darling, I'm just embracing my inner femme fatale." Myrtle winked, striking a dramatic pose.

"We were starting to worry about you," Gabe said, rocking back in the velvet vulva-shaped lounge chair in the corner. "Thought maybe you'd changed your mind about our little adventure tonight."

"Me?" Maggie laughed a little too forcefully. "What would make you think that?"

Gabe's massive shoulders bunched in a shrug. "You just sounded a little weird on the phone. Kinda out of breath." He pinned her with a knowing smirk. Like his brother, Mark, he'd proven annoyingly adept at reading people.

"Aw, honey," Myrtle cooed, patting Maggie's hand reassuringly. "There's no need to be nervous. I've been sneaking in and out of places since Obama was in diapers. And besides, I'm stealthy as a panther."

In her enthusiasm, Myrtle demonstrated her feline agility by throwing an impromptu ninja chop at the air with a theatrical "Hi-yah!"

Unfortunately, the blade of her hand caught a display on the counter, sending a wave of red, purple, and neon-green silicone butt plugs skittering across the floor like rubbery bowling pins. A few even bounced into the corner, where a life-sized cutout of Fabio adorned in fairy wings and a glittery fig leaf stood.

"Huh," Myrtle said, papery skin creased in confusion. "That almost never happens."

Maggie and Gabe shared a tense look.

"You got the blueprints?" Maggie asked.

Gabe reached into the messenger bag beside his engine-oil-spattered work boots. "Gemma wanted me to tell you that you owe her a drink. She had to do some seriously fast talking to borrow these without the Townsend Harbor Historical Society or the city council knowing."

"If this works, she can have free drinks on me for life."

Maggie stared at the blueprint of the Palace Hotel spread out across the table in the dim after-hours lighting.

"All right," Gabe said, tapping the building schematic. "Myrtle says the best time to hit it is at exactly eleven p.m."

"Oh really? Why's that?" Maggie asked, hoping the question wouldn't insult the mission's self-appointed matriarch.

Myrtle reached into the pocket of her turtleneck and pulled

out a small packet of chewy caramel candies. Unwrapping one, she popped it into her mouth, chomping down with a satisfied sigh.

"You know Caryn Townsend's nephew, that Jenkins boy? The one who can't stop tripping over his own feet? He's the only security guard they've got for the night shift." She paused to suck on the candy thoughtfully before adding, "Poor guy has narcolepsy, and the second he sits down in his Corolla for a lunch break, *pow*. Out like a light for at least a good hour."

"What about security cameras and the alarm system?" Maggie asked. "Were you able to learn anything about the setup?"

"Oh, there are cameras, all right, but they're not actually *on*," Myrtle said, crumpling her candy wrapper and sticking it in her pocket. "Seems Mayor Tightwad thought just having them there would be enough to scare people off."

Gabe shook his head disgustedly. "This fuckin' town."

Myrtle arched a penciled eyebrow at him and cleared her throat.

"—that I've dearly come to love with my whole heart," Gabe quickly added, scooting off the chair to begin gathering the butt plugs. "How much time do you think you'll need once we're inside?"

"If the accounts I read online are accurate, Madame Katz's room should be on the fourth floor on the side facing the water. As long as there are no obstructions blocking off the stairwell, I'd say fifteen minutes tops?"

"No problem." Gabe grinned, flexing his tattooed arms. "I can disable the security system for at least that long."

Yet another skill he'd picked up from his infamous family.

Maggie took a deep breath, trying to steady her nerves. "All right, then," she said, determination surging through her veins. "I guess it's a go."

"Let's get a move on," Gabe said finally, rolling up the blueprints and tucking them into his messenger bag before slinging it over his shoulder.

Deciding it would be best to avoid parading conspicuously down Water Street, they exited through the back door of Vee's Lady Garden and picked their way down the alley.

The moon was high in the sky, casting an ethereal glow over the Victorian brick buildings. Shadows danced along the uneven cobblestones, giddy with their nightly freedom. The air was heavy with the mingled scents of ocean brine and damp earth, punctuated by the lingering aroma of garlic from Waterfront Pizza.

Just ahead, the sharp edges of the Palace Hotel loomed ominously against the star-splashed canvas of night. The ivy-clad walls seemed to shimmer in the spectral light, lending an almost otherworldly quality to the grand old dame.

Gabe fell into step beside Maggie, giving her a friendly nudge with his elbow.

"So, where were you when I called earlier?"

Maggie hesitated, feeling the heat rise in her cheeks as she remembered the kiss she'd shared with Trent McGarvey not half an hour before.

Lie?

No good. Probably at least five people had seen her, and the way gossip circulated in this town, Gabe would probably find out anyway.

"Uh, I was at Trent McGarvey's," she admitted reluctantly. "He offered to teach me to make some cocktails."

"I'll bet he did," Gabe teased, waggling his eyebrows.

"It's not even like that," Maggie protested.

But...wasn't it?

Wasn't it *exactly* like that?

A dizzying flash of sensations produced a rollercoaster flip in her middle.

"Just be careful, Mags," Gabe said, slowing as they approached their destination. "You know I'm not tryna crawl up your ass or nothin', but if living here has taught me anything, it's that getting involved with a local is a one-way ticket on the gossip train."

"I'm not getting involved with anyone, Gabe," she said. "Promise."

And she meant it.

Because even in the wake of the searing uncertainty their impromptu clinch had caused, Maggie already knew one thing with perfect surety.

Women like her didn't end up with men like him.

The thought spilled over her like a bucket of ice water, unceremoniously washing her back to the present. She shivered as the looming silhouette of their destination came into view.

The Palace Hotel, its once-grand Victorian architecture now a mere shadow of its glorious—if somewhat scandalous—past. The darkened windows stared down at them like hollow eyes, the scaffolding that clung to the building looked like a skeletal beast, its metal limbs stretching upward. A deafening silence hung around the deserted construction site, magnifying each scrape of their shoes on the gravel as they cautiously approached.

"All right," she said, taking a deep breath. "Let's unpack the essentials." They rummaged through their bags, her for her handheld HD camera, Gabe for lock-picking tools, and Myrtle for a... road flare?

"What's that for?" Maggie asked.

"In case I need to create a diversion," Myrtle said with a wink.

Considering Myrtle was pretty much a walking diversion, Maggie was reasonably confident she'd excel on this score.

"Ready?" Gabe asked.

Maggie nodded.

"I'm going to try the windows first." He worked his way down the back of the building, trying each one in turn. Finally, he grinned triumphantly when one slid open with a soft creak. "Bingo," he declared, motioning for Maggie to follow.

She approached the narrow opening, her stomach tightening into a cold ball. "Unless you've got some Crisco and a crowbar, there's no way you're getting this ass through that narrow gap. Or your shoulders, for that matter," she pointed out.

"Ahem." Myrtle stood behind them, fingerless gloved hands perched on her narrow hips. "What am I? Chopped liver?"

"I think maybe Gabe should just try picking the door lock," Maggie suggested, catching Gabe's eye with a pleading look.

"Why do that when I could just *open* the door from the inside?" Myrtle asked.

"She does have a point," Gabe said. "I'd probably have better luck disarming the security system that way too."

"All right," Maggie acquiesced. "Just be careful."

Myrtle merely grinned, her eyes twinkling in the dim light. She stepped up onto a precariously wobbly milk crate, and for a moment, Maggie was certain the elderly woman was going to tumble off and break something vital. Like her neck.

But then, in one fluid movement, the older woman gracefully somersaulted through the narrow opening, leaving a flabbergasted Maggie and Gabe gaping at each other in stunned silence.

Moments later, the door creaked open and there stood Myrtle, fingerless gloves gripping the doorframe, beaming at them like she'd just done an encore at Madison Square Garden.

"Used to be a gymnast." Myrtle flashed a smug smirk over her shoulder as she stepped aside to grant them access. "Couldn't roundoff worth a damn, but my Full-Twisting Shaposhnikova once made one of the judges weep."

"Thanks, Myrtle," Maggie said gratefully as she stepped into the darkened hallway.

She paused for a moment, as much to let her eyes adjust as to steady herself against a powerful wave of déjà vu.

The air was thick with the scent of dust and mildew, the old wood floor groaning its protest underfoot. Maggie flicked on her camera as they approached the stairs, determined to capture every detail—the layers of peeling wallpaper, the dilapidated curtains and antiques.

"Watch your step," Gabe warned as they reached the third floor, where the boards seemed even more precarious. "Last thing we need is to fall through."

"Amen," Maggie whispered, her heart pounding in her chest.

Reading about this place and seeing pictures online had been one thing. Being here was a whole-ass other.

It was a feeling she knew well, fascinated with historical sites ever since sixth grade, when she'd talked (translation: whined) her parents into stopping in Salem, Massachusetts on their way to visit her grandmother in Danvers.

Despite the touristy veneer that had since been layered over the old homes and cobblestone streets, Maggie had practically *felt* the vibration of all that had happened there radiating from the very walls.

Just as she was now.

The fine hairs on her arms lifted as she reached for the brass doorknob, a frisson of adrenaline shooting through her as she turned it.

The door to Madame Katz's boudoir swung open with a creak. Through the camera's eye, Maggie drank in the grayscale-moon-silvered details. The ornate canopy bed, the stately armoire.

The secret passage.

"That's got to be it," she breathed, floating over to the closet where the historic building schematic had shown a connecting corridor.

"Let me look first," Gabe said, shouldering in front of her in the pushy, brotherly way she'd come to secretly love when she first met the Kelly boys after her move to Boston.

Maggie hung back, allowing him to open the narrow door and disappear into the pocket of inky dark behind it.

"Holy shit," he said.

"What?" Maggie asked, pulse leaping high in her throat. "What is it?"

Gabe's dark head reappeared, a smirk sharpening his features. "A really fucking tiny closet."

Shaking her head, Maggie followed him, blinking against the glare in her lens as Gabe fired up the flashlight and pushed the false panel aside.

There, embossed on the brick wall at the top of a narrow set of stairs, was a mermaid.

Maggie broke out in a full-body shiver as a tsunami of déjà vu spilled over her.

She could swear she'd seen one just like it somewhere else.

A tremor sizzled through her fingers in time with her heart as she reached to touch it...just as the ear-piercing shrill of an alarm shattered the thick silence.

"Shit!" Maggie blurted, panic seizing her chest. She and Gabe exchanged wide-eyed glances, his face mirroring her own fear.

Without another word, they raced back down the rickety stairs, the urgency of their escape underscored by the relentless wail of the alarm.

They'd barely made it to the ground floor when the unmistakable strobe of red and blue lights danced across the peeling wallpaper.

Myrtle stage-whispered the totally fucking obvious through cupped hands: "It's the fuzz!"

"Fucking perfect," Maggie muttered, cursing small towns and their infuriatingly quick response time. Her mind raced, scrambling for a plan.

"Look, both of you should get out of here," Maggie insisted. "You both have businesses in town. You have so much more to lose than I do."

Myrtle snorted, a hint of defiance flickering in her eyes. "Fuck that. I'm no coward."

"Same here," Gabe chimed in, his jaw set with determination. "We're in this together."

"All right then," Maggie whispered, steeling herself for the inevitable confrontation.

Flanked by Myrtle and Gabe on either side, she pushed open the hotel door and stepped out into the cool night air.

To her astonishment, there stood Trent McGarvey.

Trent McGarvey...in a *uniform*.

"Deputy McGarvey," Myrtle drawled, offering him a saccharine smile. "What brings you to this fine establishment on such a lovely evening?"

Deputy McGarvey?

"Evening, Myrtle. I could ask you the same thing," McGarvey replied, his gaze flicking from Myrtle to Maggie and Gabe. "Seems like an odd time for a stroll on private property."

"Odd time for a patrol, too, wouldn't you say?" Myrtle shot back.

"Actually," Trent retorted, his voice firm but not unkind, "I received a call about a possible break-in. And lo and behold, here you all are."

As Trent's gaze locked on to Maggie's, she could feel the heat rise in her cheeks. She tried to sink into some well of inner calm but found only a nest of oily snakes. It 't help that the memory of their kiss lingered on her lips, making her wish they were anywhere but here.

"All right, folks," McGarvey finally announced, his expression somber, "I have no choice but to bring you in for trespassing."

"Are w-we under arrest?" Maggie stammered, a sick ache mingling with the growing dread in her gut. An arrest would mean an active warrant search...maybe a criminal record search.

And if he found that, he'd find—

"Right now, you're being detained pending a little chat at the station." His voice betrayed a touch of disappointment. "The quicker we get this over with, the faster Vee shows up with Lyra to bail Myrtle out and/or bully everyone out of pressing charges. Swear to Christ, those two have more lives than Kevin Costner."

"He's a cat," Myrtle explained.

"Huh," Maggie said as they followed McGarvey to his police car.

"Hey, uh...Trent?" Maggie ventured as he opened the back door of the cruiser, her voice soft with urgency. "Could we maybe talk about this for just a minute?"

"Sorry," he sighed, shaking his head. "Any further conversations between us will need to be officially documented."

Her gaze found McGarvey again as he opened the driver's side of the cruiser. His clean-shaven nape gleamed under the dome light, revealing a flawless stretch of skin that looked tantalizingly warm and touchable.

Suddenly the warmth of Trent's lips, the feel of his strong hands at the small of her back, and the intoxicating scent of his aftershave flashed in her mind, weakening her knees. The delicious intensity of it was almost enough to erase the memory of why the kiss had happened in the first place.

Because Trent McGarvey suspected she was running from something.

And he was right.

FIVE

JDLR

JUST DON'T LOOK RIGHT; EXPRESSION USED BY
POLICE OFFICERS WHILE VIEWING A
SUSPICIOUS CIRCUMSTANCE ON A HUNCH

TRENT FOLLOWED THE TRIO OF TRESPASSERS AS THEY
trudged down the walkway to where his patrol car hugged the
curb. He tried to keep his gaze anywhere but on Maggie Michaels,
as her abundant, distracting curves were hugged by skintight
black leggings and a t-shirt that could've been painted on. Beneath
the nearly full moon, she stood out like a siren against the hotel's
crumbling façade. Her fiery hair seemed to capture the moonlight,
a beacon of rebellion that Trent found both infuriating and intoxicating.

He allowed his gaze to linger for a moment before remembering he was on duty.

And she was on his shit list.

Myrtle, on the other hand, was making a spectacle, fluttering
around like a deaf bat who'd just discovered caffeine, while Gabe
leaned casually against the patrol car, his tattoos telling stories
Trent wasn't sure he wanted to read.

"Hey, McGarvey," Myrtle chirped, dramatically slamming
herself against his vehicle and assuming "the position." "There's
only so much frisking you can do in public, so—and I know this

is usually your line to say— keep your hands where I can see 'em and no one gets hurt."

Gabe snorted out an unhelpful chuckle. "You'll have to commit police brutality to get me to bend over for you like that."

Trent very carefully *did not* look toward Maggie, or his brain would produce an image he wouldn't ever be able to let go of.

"Come on, Myrtle," he said. "I'm not trying to frisk an old lady who broke into a construction site. What would you steal, drywall nails? What I need to know is what you three were doing there in the middle of the night."

Gabe's mouth tightened.

Maggie's dropped open as if to reply.

Myrtle beat her to it. "*Old lady?*" she screeched. "Do I smell old to you?" Reaching up, she peeled her top off and threw it at Trent, who caught it with his astonished face.

It smelled like peppermint and pralines.

Snatching it away, he blinked over at the woman in pure shock, relieved to find she'd dressed in layers on a freezing February evening, and still had a skintight thermal on.

"Ms. Le Grand, I really—"

"I smell like the taut, teenaged clavicles on those sparkly models in the perfume ads. Eat your heart out, Dior!"

"Who watches ads anymore?" Trent blurted before berating himself for being drawn into this ridiculous conversation.

Myrtle's sharp chin jutted out, disturbing her impressive wattle. "I don't know, Five-Oh, but I'm feeling a little less guilty when I think about what my generation has done to yours and the climate. I hope you die in a wildfire."

"Myrtle! You don't mean that," Maggie said.

"She doesn't," Trent replied. "Last week she threatened to melt me with holy water when she was caught stealing some from the Catholics."

"It was for science!"

"She turns Our Lady of Sorrows into Our Lady of Sassy Pants." Gabe's mouth remained unhelpful.

"You couldn't make it stick to me then, and you won't now, po-po!" Myrtle adopted a stance that Jet Li would have approved of.

"*Deputy* McGarvey?" Maggie cut in, one auburn brown raised. "I didn't realize you moonlighted as hotel security."

"I don't. This is what we call a bust."

"Oh, come on now, McGarvey." Myrtle turned to face him, fists planted on her tiny—and probably brand-new—hips. "We were just doing a little historical research."

"At midnight? Without permission?" Trent raised an eyebrow. "That's called *trespassing* at best, and possibly breaking and entering."

"Look, I'm really sorry about this." Maggie brushed back a lock of red hair, her green eyes earnest. "This was all my idea. I'll confess to you that I'm here in Townsend Harbor on business."

"What business is predicated on B&E?" Trent challenged.

"Investigative reporting on historical cold cases. Ever heard of Madame Katz?"

"Now you're just making up names."

Her brow pinched in an adorable scowl. "She's a local legend who died under incredibly mysterious circumstances. The story goes that she was involved in shanghaiing sailors from this old brothel-turned-hotel. I've been all over the records, and the original blueprints of the building don't show it, but there's a hidden passage I wanted to explore to help prove it for my...investigation."

Trent tapped his fingers against his bicep, wishing he didn't want to trust her when it was charmingly obvious she was feeding him the kind of bullshit Myrtle slung for a living. "Investigating what, an A&E special or a *New Yorker* article or something like that?"

"Something *exactly* like that," Maggie said with a coy smile.

Trent's gaze lingered a moment too long on the confident tilt of her chin, the playful defiance in her stance. And as the cool night pressed against them, he felt the warmth of curiosity blooming in his chest—not just about Madame Katz, but about the woman who planned to bring her story to life.

Did he trust her?

Did he trust anyone?

Gathering each of their IDs, he shook his head at the absurdity of what his job had become. "Am I going to find any warrants when I run these?" he asked, only half joking.

"None from this millennium, bucko!" Myrtle mouthed off. "But I've caught charges older than your tight little butt."

Gabe only lifted his shoulder and ran a surprisingly steady hand through his close-cropped dark hair.

Maggie adopted a faux-innocent look that fooled exactly no one.

Trent ducked into the driver's seat and squinted at the glowing laptop screen, his fingers flying over the keys as he ran background checks on his midnight marauders.

Gabe's record popped up first: a mosaic of car theft and youthful defiance splattered with Boston's grit. "No surprises there," Trent muttered, eyeing the mechanic whose tattoos told stories darker than the night sky.

Myrtle shocked him with a rap sheet that unfurled like a scroll of ancient parchment. "Myrtle... You were quite the uh, green thumb in your day."

"Reefer madness! Wait until you get to my civil disobedience decades!" the woman crowed proudly. "In the sixties and seventies, I looped all the holes, stuck it to the man—and a few women if they wanted it—fought for civil rights and women's rights, and for it all I've spent eighty-one total days in the pokey and am banned from the St. Louis airport, most of Russia, Texas, Florida, and all the Offices Depot." She turned to Gabe. "Don't ask now, but I'll show you a cool trick with a hole punch and a rolling chair later."

"Fuck yeah, Myrtle." She and Gabe shared a gentle fist bump that made Trent's eye twitch.

But it was Maggie's file that had him genuinely taken aback—

a blot on an otherwise spotless record. "Breaking and entering, South Temple, Mass?" he said, disbelief shading his tone as he glanced at her. "Resisting arrest? Obstruction of justice? You're a repeat offender."

"Only when history calls for it," Maggie fired back, her shoulders squared. "That arrest was for a similar investigation of mine, and the officer was like the Count of Assholvania, and because I'd broken into a federal building, he reported me to the FB-*fucking*-I and it was a whole-ass thing." She threw her arms up as if she couldn't believe the gall. "I almost caught federal charges. What a crock."

"Yeah, you snuck into a federal building."

"It was a library, not the Pentagon." She rolled her eyes.

Trent felt like a Karen when he muttered, "Still. it wasn't right. It wasn't the honorable thing to do."

"Honorable? What is this, Feudal Japan?" She snorted.

"No, but we're a civilization with laws, and one of those laws is people stay off your property."

Instead of rolling her eyes, she tossed her entire neck in a circle of tantrum. "God, you sound like one of those septuagenarian retirees that just want everyone to get off their lawn."

"Paradoxically, you're trespassing in the middle of the night like a teenaged hoodlum."

"*You're acting like a teenaged hoodlum,*" she replied, mimicking him.

To his surprise, his temper flared. "Now you're just being childish."

"And you're being a prick." She stuck out her tongue to punctuate her point.

Trent's radio chirped in his ear, startling everyone. It was Judy, the dispatcher, following up on the call. "All's well, Judy," he said. "Just some trespassers."

"Mayor Stewart owns the hotel building and isn't answering his phone," Judy replied. "We've sent someone to wake him up, but you'll need to bring the perps in for now."

"Ten-four, we're en route to booking." He glanced back to the unlikely trio, whose faces had become comically grave.

He glanced at Gabe first. The guy was a little taller and a little leaner, but his knuckles and nose told tales of a past where they'd have been enemies. But since the Southie ex-con opened a body shop and moved in with his girlfriend, Gemma, he'd been a model citizen in Townsend Harbor.

Mostly.

Until now.

To his surprise, Gabe turned around and tucked his knuckles behind his back like a man who'd been cuffed one too many times. "It's procedure." The Bostonian sighed. "I know."

Trent clicked them on without tightening them too much and helped Gabe into the back of the car. "You want to ride shotgun, Myrtle?" he asked.

"Aren't you arresting me, too?" she groused.

"I don't think we need to just yet," Trent said. "I'm detaining you on suspicion of trespassing—"

"Then why is Gabe in cuffs?" she demanded.

Trent squeezed at a headache blooming behind his eyes. "It's protocol, Myrtle—it's for both our safety."

"Don't try to shovel shit at me and call it mud. Shit is my stock in trade, kiddo! You don't think I'm dangerous?" Myrtle put up her dukes like a Victorian pugilist.

"I think you're a seventy-year-old woman."

"Ha! You say 'tomato,' I say you're an ageist jackhole. I could take you out." She threw a few practice jabs into the air between them. "When women go bad, they go all the way. They won't just go to war with ya, they'll take away your birthday *and* your will to live. They'll ruin you and your namesake before they allow you the sweet, sweet release of the abyss and—"

With a beleaguered sigh, Trent reached for his second pair of handcuffs and dangled them in front of Myrtle.

"That's more like it!" she crowed, shoving her excruciatingly tiny wrists at him.

Trent slapped on the cuffs and even made a show of protecting her head while gently "pushing" her into the back seat with a grinning Gabe.

Despite himself, Trent chuckled before he addressed Maggie. "I'm out of handcuffs—are you gonna be good, or should I call for backup?"

It shouldn't have frightened him that she didn't answer, but he found himself taking a stabilizing breath.

She slid into the front seat of the patrol car and Trent settled in beside her, catching a whiff of her perfume—something exotic and spicy.

"Listen, *Deputy McGarvey*," Maggie started, her voice urgent, "we weren't just fooling around in there. We found something."

"Found something?" Trent repeated as he started the engine, its purr a stark contrast to the tension inside the vehicle.

"A passageway," Maggie said quickly, "hidden chutes and all. Not on any updated blueprints, but they were in the original ones —ones that never got filed with the city."

"Hidden chutes?" Trent raised an eyebrow, trying to keep his professional composure despite the nonsense of it all. "What is this, Clue?"

"Look, I know how it sounds, but hear me out," Maggie insisted, leaning forward as if to bridge the gap between disbelief and possibility. "Madame Katz, she had this reputation, right? And if my hunch is correct, she shanghaied at least thirty-three sailors back in the late 1800s. Smuggled them right out of her brothel through these secret passages and sold them to ship captains. Poor men just fell asleep after paying for a little sex and woke up on a ship halfway to Shanghai."

"Right..." Trent drawled, the corners of his mouth twitching. He found himself intrigued despite his best efforts to remain detached. "And you uncovered all this playing Nancy Drew at midnight?"

"Need I remind you," she replied, the ghost of a smile touching her lips, "it's investigative journalism."

"The press," Trent muttered, half impressed, half exasperated. "When I moved to Townsend Harbor, I didn't think I'd be policing journalist sleuths with a penchant for trespassing."

"Technically, we're not sure if it's trespassing yet," Maggie shot back, her eyes gleaming with a mix of defiance and excitement.

"Technically, you have the right to remain silent..." The three occupants of the car bitched and booed as he recited the Miranda rights for the body camera...okay, and a little bit just to kick the hornet's nest.

"Come on, McGarvey," Maggie pleaded, her gaze locked on his. "Can't you see this is bigger than a slap-on-the-wrist midnight escapade? We're talking about history here. About justice too long denied!"

"Plenty of historians aren't charged with high crimes and misdemeanors," Trent countered, though the edges of his resolve were starting to fray like well-worn denim.

"Hardly *crime*." Maggie waved him off, dismissing his concerns with a flick of her wrist. "Think of it as...an educational field trip that was just a little less...authorized than others."

"Field trip or not," Trent grumbled, pulling out of the parking spot, "you can't break into a building that isn't yours."

Maggie scoffed, rolling her eyes. "You're such a cop."

"And you're such a...what, a renegade historian? Indiana Jones or Lara Croft?" Trent quipped, feeling the strange pull of her enthusiasm and the heat of her proximity.

"I mean... I don't hate it," Maggie said, a smirk playing on her lips. "It's a sexy job, and someone's gotta do it."

"Sexy doesn't get you out of consequences," Trent pointed out, but even he had to admit, there was something about this whole night that felt less like routine police work and more like the opening scene of a rom-com he'd accidentally stumbled into.

Sexy heroine included.

"The hell it doesn't!" Myrtle said. "How do you think I escaped prison time after clocking those mounted police at

Columbia University? Fascist pigs didn't seem to mind that I'd burned my bra that night!"

Trent swallowed a laugh and did the safest thing, which was ignoring Myrtle altogether.

"Did you find anything in this alleged secret passageway?" he asked, putting the car in drive.

"Alleged?" Maggie grimaced at him. "*Someone* dragged us out of there before we could explore the whole thing. The original blueprints show it leading from Madame Katz's bedroom down to the basement, with an exit to the alley. But it's not on the new plans."

"And you think Katz used it to, what, smuggle sailors out of her brothel?" Trent glanced at her skeptically.

"Exactly! It explains how she could abduct them without anyone seeing. The harbor was just a block away." Maggie's green eyes shone with enthusiasm.

Trent frowned. "Seems like a stretch."

"I know it sounds crazy. But I'm telling you, something sinister was happening there. Katz had a lot of blood on her hands."

Despite his reservations, Trent felt his curiosity stir. A hidden passage and a killer madame from the 1800s? It was quite a story. An investigation that had every one of his senses keyed up.

And Maggie herself was proving even more fascinating.

Trent snuck a look at her animated face and cascade of red hair. She was a troublemaker for sure...but he was having trouble remembering why that was a bad thing.

Maggie's phone buzzed in her pocket, and she pulled it out, her expression shifting from playful to worried as she read the message. "You can't take me in. I haven't made it home to give Roxie her medications."

"Roxie?" Trent raised an eyebrow, momentarily distracted from their standoff.

"My Peekapoo."

"Please tell me that's not a Pokémon or something."

"My dog is old as balls and has special needs," Maggie explained, the worry lines around her eyes deepening. "Narcolepsy, partial blindness, deafness... Without her medication, she could have seizures."

"McGarvey will feed her, wontcha?" Myrtle volunteered for him. "Since it's your fault the poor thing will be alone all night."

"*My* fault? How is it *my fault* when you're the one who broke the law?" he asked.

"Because you should know the difference between what is legal and what is right, young man, or have I mistaken you?" For the first time in a while, maybe ever, the woman looked dead serious.

Goddammit.

Driving up to the jail booking annex, he handed his suspects off to Deputy Edna Dancewater, a Salish grandma with thirty years on the force and the best aim in three counties.

"Okay." Trent sighed, rubbing the back of his neck. The thought of the helpless dog waiting anxiously for its owner tugged at something inside him. "Hand over the key. I'll make sure your pooch gets what she needs."

TRENT FOUND HIMSELF PAUSING AT THE DOORWAY TO Maggie's apartment to once again read the litany of care instructions Maggie had jotted down in the jail booking area while rapid-firing the info at him like her brain was on fully automatic. For someone who struggled with drink recipes, she sure could remember a complex dog food regimen.

"Fluff her food," he grumbled, wondering how his night had gone from patrolling the sleepy streets of Townsend Harbor to drug dealing to a disabled designer dog.

Unlocking the door, he stepped inside.

"Jesus Hoarding Christ," he muttered, surveying the piles of clothes strewn across the floor, dishes piled high in the sink, and shoes. So. Many. Shoes. In a pile by the door. Kicked off at the foot of the couch. Discarded by the fireplace. The bathroom counter was an explosion of makeup and hair accessories, with blush dusting the surface like a light snow dusting over fallen comrades.

This place was his actual nightmare.

The coffee pot sat half-full, a bitter aroma clinging to the air, a testament to a hasty exit or an indulgent morning.

The place looked like the aftermath of a Fashion Week tornado, yet amongst this whirlwind, designer brands gleamed and winked at him with silent luxury, seemingly abandoned by their owner who didn't care enough to cherish them properly.

The shoes were Gucci. Armani. Manolo Blahnik, the bags Kate Spade, Prada, Valentino.

And she just tossed them around like they'd come off a clearance rack at Payless.

"Roxie?" he called, hoping the dog didn't do something unspeakable to all this luxury and good taste. He suddenly felt like an idiot, remembering the dog was deaf. And mostly blind. And easily spooked.

The combination was a recipe for disaster.

Trent found a bundle of off-white fluff curled on a tiny velvet bed next to the fireplace heater. He approached with the care he'd have shown the raptors in *Jurassic Park*, reaching two fingers out to nudge the warm little body out of torpor.

The tiny thing came up teeth first, and luckily missed his hand with her first chomp and decided to scream about it.

Not bark. Not whimper.

Scream.

The creature emitted a sound so unholy Trent shrank away and crossed himself like the lapsed Episcopalian his granddad had been, then made another older sign against demons taught to him by his Dominican Grandma.

A tiny furball of a dog came yapping fiercely at Trent's feet, but the old spell must have worked, because the little shit promptly keeled over on the carpet mid-yap.

Wait. That was bad.

"Fuck!" Trent rushed to scoop up the collapsed canine and exhaled in relief as the little body came to before long and began to squirm. Though, instead of needing an exorcist, the pup startled him by sniffing the hands that held her and greeting him with two swipes of her little warm tongue.

"Friends already? That was fast." He tried to sound gruff but couldn't suppress a hint of affection. Carefully setting down the five pounds of deaf dervish, he fetched her meds and pill pockets from the kitchen, his eyes trailing over the ridiculous gourmet dog food that needed "fluffing."

"All right, Roxie girl, let's see what *haute cuisine* you've got here." Pulling the bowl from the fridge, Trent eyed the contents with skepticism before attacking it with a fork, fluffing as instructed. "Your mom's a piece of work, you know that?"

No, he wasn't talking to a deaf dog with one milky eye... He was *not* doing that.

"What your mom *doesn't* know is that by giving me a key, she gave me permission to search the premises." A devious smile lifted his mouth as he took in the chaos that surrounded Townsend Harbor's newest addition.

For a moment, he stood there, contemplating the woman who could unravel sailors' secrets from centuries past and yet couldn't keep her laundry off the floor.

As if compelled by a force outside of himself, Trent lined her shoes up by the door and straightened a collage of periodicals with titles like *Serial Killers—A Psychological Model* and *Murder Manual*. He was about to meticulously search through Maggie's mess and see if he could come up with anything he could use.

"An investigative mind, a cluttered place, an ass that won't quit, and a dog that faints more often than a Southern belle?" He shook his head, chuckling despite himself. Trent McGarvey, deputy of Townsend Harbor, was knee-deep in something far more perplexing than any cold case file—he was wading through the layers of Maggie Michaels, and the waters were getting deep.

They became the fucking Mariana Trench when he found her living room.

Here was an oasis of organization in the chaos. Files stacked and consolidated and labeled alphabetically. Recording equipment gleaming and carefully maintained.

It unclenched the knot of disquiet building in his gut at the disorder.

Trent's hand hovered over an accordion file folder next to a box full of papers, his lawman's instincts warring with the personal intrigue that gnawed at his brain.

He should walk away, maintain that professional distance. Instead, his fingers betrayed him, flipping through the file marked "important personal paperwork."

He knew he shouldn't snoop, but the temptation was too great.

"Birth certificate, social security card...business paperwork for 'Murderous Madams with Maggie Michaels,'" he read under his breath. Nothing too surprising so far.

But then he found it—the official document on that special linen paper used only for such certifications.

Certifications such as the marriage of one Margaret Michaels to Charles B. Wiggins.

"Shit," he whispered, reeling from the implications. According to her driver's license and birth certificate, she was still a Michaels. Was she married and hadn't taken her husband's name? Were they separated?

Shit. Did he just kiss a *married* woman?

Trent's thoughts spiraled as he aimlessly tidied up around the apartment. He replayed their flirtatious encounters, the passionate kiss they had shared. Was he merely a flirtation while she was away from home on business?

Galvanized by his discovery, he began pawing through the

place, starting in the kitchen and finally ending up in her bedroom.

He very carefully did not start at the cluttered nightstand made a beeline for the dresser beneath the picture window looking out over Water Street.

All the drawers on the right were empty. And why wouldn't they be? She had one of the most expensive *floor*drobes he'd ever been privileged to see. And was that a—

"Oh no she did *not*." With more care than he ever showed the dog, he rescued a Chanel camisole from where it was wadded on top of the dresser and folded it, enjoying the play of the violet silk against the whorls of his fingertips.

Soft Maggie dripping in silk?

He adjusted what was going on in his pants and opened the top left drawer, finding an explosion of silk and lace that immediately overflowed whatever lady magic she'd used to shove it all into the one drawer.

Trent couldn't resist.

Was it an invasion of privacy?

Yes.

Was it illegal?

Not yet.

Was there any *official* reason for him to be color-coding thongs that would grace the glorious globes of her ass?

Only psychopaths did shit like that.

A soft sound escaped his lips as he held up a particularly daring pair of lacy panties, contemplating the woman who wore them with such unabashed confidence.

"Having fun there, deputy?"

The sound of Maggie's voice made him jump, and he hastily dropped the underwear as if it were on fire and whirled around. Vee, Myrtle, and Maggie stood in the doorway, grinning like Cheshire cats at Trent's obvious discomfort.

When was the last time someone snuck up on him?

Trent couldn't remember, it'd been so long.

"Mayor Stewart didn't press charges," Myrtle announced triumphantly. "He just gave us a warning to leave his building alone, so my wife came to collect us." She squeezed the Helen Mirren-esque lady next to her and kissed her shoulder.

"Great," Trent mumbled, flushing. He scrambled for a way to explain his presence in Maggie's apartment—and more importantly, in her underwear drawer. "I was just... Uh..."

"Doing my dishes?" Maggie raised an eyebrow, gesturing to the now-spotless kitchen counter.

The room fell silent, the tension thick enough to slice through like one of Myrtle's prized organic tomatoes. Maggie's eyes narrowed, scrutinizing Trent as if she were peering through the lens of a microscope, dissecting his intentions layer by layer.

"Deputy! Caught with your hand in the cookie jar." Myrtle cackled.

"Or should I say the panty drawer," her wife, Vee, added with a smirk.

Straightening up to full height and attempting to salvage his dignity, Trent reached for whatever his brain spit up as an excuse. "You granted me access to the premises. I was searching for probable cause."

"PSA, Deputy Pervy Pants," Myrtle replied, "but you don't usually find probable cause during a panty raid. I take one photo of you with my smart phone and you'll be canceled faster than an Armie Hammer dinner reservation."

Maggie went to the fireplace and scooped up her dog, who nestled into her warm neck with a sigh that made Trent unnervingly jealous. "Just what evidence are you looking for, Deputy Trent McGarvey?"

"I'll tell you what I found," he said, gritting his teeth against the defensiveness in his tone. "Why don't we have a chat, Miss Michaels... Or should I say, Mrs. Charles Wiggins."

SIX
On the rocks

SERVED WITH ICE, TYPICALLY IN A ROCKS GLASS

THE NEXT DAY

"Fucking Pacific coastline and its stupid fucking hills."

Maggie wheezed out breath as she trudged up the steep incline toward the highest point in Townsend Harbor, cursing the founding fathers for their poor urban planning skills with every step.

Stopping to rest a hand against the stitch in her side, she mentally calculated the distance between her and Mayor Stewart's lair.

Somewhere between ten yards and for*fucking*ever miles.

Her Chanel overcoat was now sticking to her back, beads of sweat trickling from her armpits down her ribcage like lazy insects.

"Why can't anything ever be fucking easy?" Maggie asked the universe at large, forcing herself to resume her uphill battle.

The blisters already forming on her heels stung with each step, mocking her choice in footwear. The worst part? Her black leather Jimmy Choo riding boots had been her favorite pair once upon a time.

A time before her dumb fuck of an ex—okay, *almost*-ex—had somehow managed to reach his pasty, trucker-tanned arms through the bars of Queensboro Correctional Facility all the way to this tiny tourist hamlet.

And onto the laptop screen of one Deputy Trent McGarvey.

Or should I say, Mrs. Charles Wiggins.

A hot flush crept up her neck at the flat, businesslike way McGarvey had pronounced the name that hung about her neck like a balding albatross.

Okay, so he knew she was *technically* still married.

At least he didn't know *everything*. And Maggie certainly hadn't felt compelled to offer up any extra details.

Like the fact that Charlie was about to be paroled after serving a four-year sentence for bribery and racketeering charges, along with eleven other members of the Long Island Local No. 200 Journeyman and Apprentices of the Plumbing and Pipe Fitting Industry Union.

Or that he'd taken her virginity in the back of his 1989 Cadillac Eldorado the night of the Sophomore Fall Formal to "Closer" by the Chainsmokers.

She shuddered as the sprawling Victorian monstrosity came into view, looming over Water Street and Puget Sound, its tidy garden and wraparound porch boasting an unobstructed view of the lighthouse beyond.

Maggie paused to catch her breath, glaring at the structure as if it were personally responsible for her discomfort.

And in a way, it was.

If only Mayor Stewart had shown up at Sirens' happy hour either of the last two evenings like he was supposed to, she wouldn't be fighting for her life while the town's native deer gangs silently judged her, their liquid chocolate eyes stoic as she aggressively sucked salty wind down her raw, hoarse throat.

On the upside, she'd had a chance to schmooze with Darby Dunwell, who had quickly become her favorite—okay, second favorite—person in Townsend Harbor. And that was only because Myrtle and Vee were a package deal.

Over cosmopolitans almost the *exact* shade of her hair, she'd served Maggie the tea about the Townsend-Stewart scandal that had rocked the small town to its core. While her lumbersnack of a man-piece slowly turned the color of an atomic beet.

Maggie supposed she might too if her mother had been out bribing officials and arranging Machiavellian machinations instead of sucking an endless succession of Newport 100's while using her one-year AA chip to molest Lucky Dog scratch-offs at the kitchen table.

The image opened an ache in her chest that propelled her the last few yards to the border of the mayor's property.

Dappled sunlight fell through a thick canopy of trees, casting playful shadows on the cobblestone driveway that snaked its way up to the grand façade. Illuminated beneath the flickering light, the mansion was simultaneously imposing and inviting with its ivy-scribbled walls, intricately carved gables, and the towering oak that stood sentinel by the small service gate entrance.

Which, thank fuck for small favors, was exactly as it had been pictured on Google Maps: concealed from the street by a hedgerow and on the other side of the formidable gazebo that stood between it and the rear veranda.

Maggie paused on the corner, midwifing her camera out of its carrying case and lifting it to her face to squint through the aperture.

Only, there wasn't one.

She blinked at the wall of black, confused until she pulled it away to examine the lens.

Which was covered by a lens cap that Trent McGarvey had helpfully put on it.

After he'd obviously wiped it down. Just as he had the rest of her cluttered hidey-hole of a home base before she came home to bust him pawing through her panty drawer.

A little shower of sparks sizzled through her center as she remembered the stricken look on his face.

And the not-inconsiderable semi in his trousers.

What followed was adorably awkward confrontation that ended with McGarvey sputtering something about verbal consent before he'd hightailed it out of her place like he was being chased with a blowtorch.

Still. The man was perhaps the only cop in existence who left the premises nicer than he found them after a search.

Never in her life had a man she was sharing a home with ever bothered to lift a finger to clean. Her father, for instance, had only ever contributed to household chores by mowing the lawn and carving the holiday ham. And the only thing that walking colostomy bag Charlie had ever lifted around the house was his left butt cheek to rip ass every time the Jets scored a touchdown on Sunday afternoons.

And now, there was McGarvey. Beautiful, responsible, infuriatingly meticulous McGarvey, who had not only navigated her labyrinthine instructions for feeding Roxie, he'd broken down the small mountain of empty Amazon boxes to craft a makeshift barrier to keep her everything-impaired rescue dog from getting stuck under the coffee table.

Again.

Speaking of Roxie, Maggie thought—the sooner she finished this unpleasant errand, the sooner they could curl up on the couch together with a bowl of 9 Pound Hammer and the Entenmann's Lemon Crunch Cake that Mark had been kind enough to send in her East Coast withdrawal care package.

True to Gabe's "nobody fuckin' locks nothin' around here" adage, she found the gate secured by only a basic gravity latch, which she easily reached through the wrought-iron bars to unhook.

Beyond the gate, a wild oasis of lush greenery stretched out before her, a stark contrast to the cookie-cutter lawns of Townsend Harbor. Century-old willows wept their tendrils over a stone path leading to a small pond surrounded by well-manicured rosebushes, seemingly transported straight out of an English countryside.

As she neared the back of the house, the unmistakable sound of sharp consonants and hissed whispers pricked the air with tension. Her curiosity piqued, Maggie sidestepped a marble statue of a cherub peeing into an ornate birdbath—Townsend Harbor's idea of tasteful lawn décor, apparently.

Peeking past its plump marble buttocks, she felt a jolt of shock as she saw Mayor Stewart talking to...*Ethan Townsend*?

Bracing a shoulder against the statue's base, she brought her camera up to her face, killed the flash, and began snapping photos.

Through the electronic aperture, she watched Ethan's broad shoulders stiffen as he turned to respond, his voice too low for her to make out except for a handful of words that kicked her heart into a gallop.

Not going to give up... no longer hide... founders... time they knew.

Whatever he'd said, it was enough to make the mayor's artificially tanned face darken to a raw-liver burgundy.

"As long as you remember that the Stewart family's reputation isn't the only thing that stands to suffer if the Palace Hotel's full history comes to light," the mayor said with the affected projection of a man used to cutting ribbons with ornamental oversized shears. "If some comes out, all comes out."

Ethan crossed his arms over his flannel-clad chest, giving the mayor a look that would have frozen molten lava. His ice-blue eyes narrowed, and his lip curled in distaste. "So be it."

With that, he turned on his heel, the gravel crunching under his boots echoing through the tense silence.

Maggie's face tingled as her mind raced, questions swirling in her mind like the plastic snow in the tacky globes her mother collected from places that had never seemed worthy of remembering.

How was the Townsend family connected to the Palace Hotel? Did that mean they were also connected to Madame Katz?

What had Mayor Stewart meant when he said "if some comes out, all comes out"?

Why was the stone structure she had been leaning against slowly disappearing from beneath her shoulder—

A gasp tore free from Maggie's throat, the thick strap around her neck jerking as the camera dropped from her hands and her arms pinwheeled out to regain her balance.

Only in grabbing the branch of a denuded Japanese maple did she manage to keep herself from going face-first into the drink.

The perpetually pissing cupid, not so much.

Mayor Stewart's eyes went first to the mess in the fountain, then rose to her, his face a mask of indignant fury. Maggie's breath hitched, and she felt an unwelcome flare of irritation spread through her chest and rise to her cheeks.

"This was a lawsuit waiting to happen!" she said, stabbing a dagger-like nail at the ceramic soup. "I could have been killed."

"Miss Michaels," he said, his voice soaked with contempt. "What do you think you're doing on my property? You're lucky I didn't press charges after your little stunt at the Palace Hotel."

Maggie took a step closer, narrowing her eyes at him. "Lucky?" she challenged. "See, I kind of thought it was super sus that you took your balls and went home so quickly. What is it about the Palace Hotel that has your taint in a twist?"

The mayor's face deepened to summer eggplant. "Apologies, but would you mind repeating that in plain English? With your quaint colloquialisms and your...accent, it's difficult to apprehend your meaning."

"I bet the readers of the *Townsend Leader* won't have any difficulty," Maggie said, using her nail to flick the flash back on before snapping a picture of the mayor's rage-creased face. "Especially accompanied by the pictures of you attempting to strong-arm Ethan Townsend into keeping quiet. You apprehend that okay, jackfuck?"

Mayor Stewart paled slightly at her words, though he tried to maintain his composure. "You have no idea what you're talking about, Miss Michaels. This is pure, rank speculation on your part."

Picking up on the subtle tension in his shoulders, she leaned in closer, her breath tickling his cheek as she whispered, "Is it, though? Because you have no idea what I was able to document before Deputy McGarvey came along the other night." She tapped the camera hanging around her neck. "And whatever secrets you're trying to protect, well... I've got all the evidence I need right here on this memory card."

The mayor's steely façade cracked for an instant, allowing Maggie a glimpse of the fear lurking beneath his arrogant exterior. He cleared his throat, obviously attempting to regain control of the conversation. "If you think this kind of sophomoric bluff will be effective on me, you're sadly mistaken."

"Am I?" Maggie replied, her heart pounding with adrenaline. "You tell me, Mr. Mayor. Are you willing to take that risk?"

The mayor lunged without warning, his lotioned grip surprisingly strong as it closed over her wrist.

Maggie clamped her fingers down on the camera strap just as Mayor Stewart made a grab for it, their hands brushing against each other in a tug-of-war for control.

"Let go of my Nikon, you pompous asshat," Maggie snapped, her knuckles whitening as she tightened her grip.

"Not as long as it contains unauthorized images of *my* property," Mayor Stewart retorted, his face reddening with exertion.

"You take your hands off her camera, or I'm going to take them off for you."

The sudden, unmistakable rasp of Trent McGarvey's voice had both of them freezing and whipping their heads toward him. He was standing by the wrought-iron entrance gate, his muscular arms folded across his chest and a stern expression on his face. At his side was one of the mayor's staff members, who had clearly been watching the confrontation unfold.

"Respectfully," McGarvey added.

"Officer McGarvey," the mayor said, releasing his grip on Maggie's wrist as if it had suddenly become white hot. "I find it quite concerning that, despite your assurances, I continue to be harassed by Miss Michaels on my own property."

Maggie clenched her fists, trying to suppress the urge to roll her eyes at the mayor's overdramatic response. She glanced at McGarvey, wondering if he could see through the mayor's theatrics just as easily as she could.

"Mayor Stewart," McGarvey said calmly, "I understand your concerns. However, that doesn't give you the right to take Miss Michaels's property."

The mayor's mouth twisted into a sour grimace. "If this is the kind of support the Townsend Harbor Police Department and County Sheriff provides, perhaps it's time to reevaluate the allocation of our municipal bonds."

"Sir," McGarvey responded evenly, "we take all investigations seriously, and I assure you, we're doing everything in our power to maintain order and safety within our community."

"Everything in your power?" Mayor Stewart retorted, raising an eyebrow. "Well, I'd hate to think what would happen if your department was any less capable."

"Actually," Maggie interjected, "it's the Townsend Harbor municipal law that gives me the right to be on this property."

Mayor Stewart raised an eyebrow, clearly unimpressed with her interruption. "Is that so?"

"Absolutely," she replied confidently, even though she was only half certain she was right. "So unless you want to have a lengthy discussion about civil codes, I suggest you let me continue my work."

"Fine," he huffed, gesturing dismissively. "You're welcome to leave so that those with the proper authority and qualifications can discuss this matter."

"You mean like a dick?" Maggie asked, folding her arms across her chest. "Because last time I checked, a penis isn't required to read civil codes. Or press releases, for that matter. Because I've got some contacts at the *Seattle Times* who would just cream their khakis to run a feature piece on the sordid sex worker scandal that Townsend Harbor was founded on. In fact, that reminds me. I'm supposed to meet Michelle for coffee."

Maggie's fingers danced over her phone screen, tapping out a message before she raised the device to her ear. The mayor shifted his weight from one foot to the other, trying to maintain his air of superiority even as his face betrayed his anxiety.

"Michelle whom?" he asked, his voice dripping with condescension.

"Michelle Thompson," Maggie replied, her smirk widening as she hit send and switched the call to speakerphone. "The editor in chief of the *Seattle Times*."

The ringing on the other end echoed through the tense silence, and Maggie watched with delight as a bead of sweat escaped the artfully sculpted shock of the mayor's silver hair. It traced a wet path down his spray-tanned, Botox frozen forehead, signaling his growing unease.

"Hey, Maggie!" Michelle's cheerful voice rang out from the phone. "What can I do for you?"

"Hi, Michelle," Maggie responded, keeping her eyes locked on the mayor's increasingly uncomfortable expression. "I was just thinking about that coffee date we've been meaning to set up. How does tomorrow sound?"

"Sounds great! You better have some hot goss for me!" Michelle—her nail tech—replied, blissfully unaware of the power play unfolding on the other end of the line.

"Perfect. See you then," Maggie said, ending the call and tucking her phone back into her purse.

Mayor Stewart's jaw flexed. "Very well, Miss Michaels," he said through gritted teeth. "You've made your point."

"You have no idea how delighted I am to hear it," Maggie replied, her smile never faltering.

"Now kindly remove yourself from my property. And be

advised that if you come within a hundred yards of me again, I *will* press charges for your recent trespassing offense."

"Are you serious?" Maggie interrupted, incredulous. "Townsend Harbor is so small it's nearly impossible not to be a hundred yards away from someone at all times!"

"Then I suggest you find a way to manage it." Mayor Stewart spun on his heel and disappeared back into the mansion, leaving Maggie fuming in the garden.

McGarvey placed a warm hand on the small of her back, gently guiding her down the hill. The unexpected touch sent a shiver up her spine and sparked that familiar flutter in her stomach.

"Can you believe that dickwrinkle?" Maggie vented, feeling the need to fill the silence between them. "Who the actual fuck does he think he is?"

"Um, the mayor," McGarvey replied, his voice tinged with frustration.

She hated it when he had a point.

As they reached the bottom of the hill, McGarvey removed his hand from her back, leaving her skin tingling from the loss of contact.

"Listen," he began, hesitating for a moment as if choosing his words carefully. "You need to be careful with Mayor Stewart. He may be an insufferable prick of the first order, but he's a well-connected one."

"Are you worried about me?" she asked, poking him playfully in the shoulder.

The moment they stepped out of the line of sight of the mayor's gawking staff, McGarvey spun her around and pressed her against the car, hovering a breath away from her.

"Tell me," he said, his voice rough and low. "When are you planning on going back to the Palace Hotel?"

Maggie's heart stuttered as she stared up at McGarvey, eyes wide, swallowing hard. "I have no idea what you're talking about."

Amusement danced in his eyes. "Give me a little credit, *Margaret*." His gaze dropped to her mouth, and heat flared in her belly. "I know you better than that."

Maggie pressed her palms against his biceps, but the gesture backfired magnificently. Rather than creating the space she'd hoped for, the feel of his mounded muscle in her grip made her stomach flip. "I don't have any plans to go back there. I got what I needed."

"Really?" he challenged, raising an eyebrow. "Because I could always call in a request for surveillance on the place. You know, just to make sure."

"Okay, fine!" she snapped, her resolve crumbling under the weight of his scrutinizing gaze. "I was thinking of going back tomorrow night. But if you think the fact that we tongue wrestled gives you the right to try to stop me—"

"Stop you?" he scoffed. "Hell no. I'm coming with you."

"The fuck you are," she said, sinking to the soles of her boots. "I don't need a babysitter."

"How about a bodyguard?" he asked.

"With all due respect, Deputy McGarvey," she purred, looking at him from beneath her lashes, "your body seems to be the one I need guarding against."

His eyes softened as they took on a sexy, sleepy, hooded look that Maggie found irresistible. "Tell that to your nipples."

But Maggie didn't have to glance downward to know that he was correct. She could feel the achingly stiff peaks brushing against her Judas of a bra.

She licked her lips, acutely aware of his hand still resting on her lower back, his touch burning through the thin layer of her dress. "I can take care of myself," she said, her protest somewhat lacking in conviction.

"Really?" he asked, his voice firm but gentle. "Because judging by your record, you're an absolute embarrassment as a thief."

Maggie stared at him, torn between arousal and exasperation. "It's like I told you—"

"Now I'm telling *you*," he said, his breath fanning warm over her cheek as he leaned in. "You've got a better shot of getting what you're looking for with me watching your six."

A delicious shiver ran down her spine at the implication in his tone. She swallowed hard, torn between suspicion at his sudden interest in her work and the desire coiling hot in her core. "What's in it for you?"

A low groan rumbled in his chest. His hands snaked down her back to cup her ass, dragging her flush against him. She sucked in a sharp breath at the feel of his arousal, hard and unmistakable, pressed to her belly. "Watching your six."

He flexed his fingers against her ass as his lips descended on hers, hard and hungry, stealing her breath and what was left of her resistance. Maggie melted into him with a soft sigh, her reservations burning away in the fire of their merged mouths.

She pulled back, breathless, and gazed up at him with a dazed smile. "All right, deputy. You've convinced me."

"Good." He chuckled, a low rumble that vibrated through her. His eyes darkened as he studied her kiss-swollen mouth. "Though honestly, I'm a little disappointed. I was hoping to have to persuade you a little harder."

Heat flooded her cheeks at the implication, and an answering ache coiled low in her belly. "Maybe I'm being agreeable for my own nefarious purposes. You don't know."

McGarvey's smile turned wicked. He slid a hand into her hair and tilted her head back, baring the line of her throat.

"Yes, I do." His lips brushed her pulse point, and she shivered.

Maggie sucked in a sharp breath at the scrape of his teeth over her skin. She clutched at his shoulders, her nails biting into the fabric of his shirt. "Well, when you put it like that..." Her words momentarily evaporated as she struggled to regain her equilibrium. "But you better not get in my way."

"Relax, Michaels," he said, pulling back enough to aim his perfect grin into her upturned face. "I'm just trying to keep you from adding a felony to your illustrious record."

His casual reinstallation of her maiden name despite his knowing full well she was still hauling around the balding millstone that was Charlie Wiggins did something to Maggie's insides. The warmth creeping into her chest spilled downward to augment the liquid heat pooling at her core.

"Very magnanimous of you."

"Just that kind of guy," he said.

The deep, mournful bellow of the ferry's horn shivered the air, tolling the official end of the moment. Glancing over her shoulder, Maggie saw the lumbering beast of metal and lights slowly sliding toward shore. She turned back to Trent, who was already relinquishing his grip. "Meet me at eleven below the dock next to the Palace Hotel," she said. "Wear dark clothing."

The corner of his mouth curled in amusement. "Should I come alone?" he asked. "Make sure I'm not followed? Maybe bring a suitcase full of unmarked bills?"

Maggie hauled back and punched his shoulder, uncertain her knuckles hadn't gotten the worse end of the transaction. "Smartass."

"Better than a dumbass any day." McGarvey peeled himself from her, discreetly tugging his pristine khakis as he opened the door of his cruiser. "Better yet, meet me at eleven *a.m.* on the sidewalk in front of the hotel."

Maggie blinked at him. "But what about Mayor Stewart?"

McGarvey hit her with the full force of his slow, sexy smile. "Let me worry about that."

Swallowing hard, Maggie nodded.

"Until tomorrow, then?"

Maggie's stomach flipped for the second time as he slid behind the wheel, releasing a heady current of his clean scent.

"Until then."

SEVEN

Leg bail

TO RUN FROM POLICE ON FOOT TO AVOID ARREST

IF YOU'RE ON TIME, YOU'RE LATE.

Trent's dearly departed Grandma Grace's idiom echoed like a mantra as he pulled to the curbside of the Palace Hotel five minutes before he and Maggie had agreed to meet.

He tugged at the collar of one of his more casual button-down shirts, the fabric suddenly too tight and warm even for a frigid February lunch hour.

Maggie was already there. Standing amidst the drab backdrop of gray stone, sawhorses, scaffolding, and plastic sheeting, she was an arresting sight, her curls a riot against the stormy renovation chaos, each one defying the notion of order that Trent held dear. She'd dressed *way* up for an afternoon tour through an active construction site. Trent's gaze lingered a moment too long, taking in her hourglass figure hugged by a vintage-inspired dress that seemed to laugh in the face of practicality.

"Thought I was early," he said, his voice betraying a hint of surprise mixed with a pleasure he wasn't ready to examine too closely.

"Early bird gets the worm, or in this case, the scoop," Maggie quipped, her mobile recording gear clutched like a shield of journalistic integrity. "Now let's do this—if I skip lunch, I get *real hunty*."

Trent frowned. "Don't you mean hangry?"

"No, I do not." Flashing him a mischievous smile, she turned on her heel and started off for the curtains of plastic sheeting protecting the edifice from the late-winter rain.

He palmed her elbow, gently detaining her for just long enough to snatch an implement off the scaffolding shelf.

"Hard hat." He thrust the yellow helmet at her, avoiding her gaze.

She giggled, the sound lifting the fine hairs on his body like some live feed ASMR. "You can't be serious."

"Rules are rules, Michaels. Safety first."

"We're the only ones here, McGarvey. The crew doesn't work Sundays." She shook her head. "There's no need for either of us to walk around looking like lemony dildos."

"It's code," he insisted around a snort of laughter. "I was granted permission for this tour, only if it's all on the up and up. So it's hard hats or hard luck."

"Jesus Christ, McGarvey, you're like a Hemingway hero but, like...less hilarious," she groused as she wrenched the helmet out of his hand and stuffed it over her curls.

She should have looked ridiculous rather than sexy.

He swallowed hard, heat pooling low in his belly at her teasing. "Don't hate. I don't make the rules, I just enforce them."

She rolled her eyes, jamming the hat down even further to keep it from slipping off her head. "Whose hat is this?" she bitched. "It smells like someone vomited it out of a roughneck ass factory. Can hats give you, like...scalp chlamydia? If I get scabies or leprosy or something, I'm coming to rub my *narsty*, peeling skin all over your anal retentively clean house."

"Fair," was all he said before donning a helmet and fetching the borrowed keys to the building from his pocket. "See? No need for a B&E if you know the right people and do the right thing."

"Ugh." She shoved past him into the gloom beyond the entry. "You're such a dork, I think my virginity grew back."

The last thing either of them expected was his boom of laughter that sounded too warm and too dark to be paraded out in the daytime. "From Albuquerque to here, I've been called many, *many* names, Ms. Michaels, but I think I was today years old before 'dork' was ever added to the litany."

"Well, add it and put an asterisk next to it, because I have receipts." Trent could swear she put a little extra *sash* in her *shay* before disappearing into the shadows of the building.

With a sharp inhale, he silenced the warning bells clanging from his head all the way down to his more sensitive bits.

Inside, he surveyed the grand foyer of the old hotel. Intricate woodwork, high ceilings with ornate crown molding, a spiraling staircase leading up to the mysterious second floor. Trent broke out his duty flashlight, the strong beam necessary even in the stormy gray light from the windows. By the time he'd blinked the daylight out of his eyes and adjusted to the dark wood interior, Maggie had flipped on her phone camera with an attached light and filmed her way up the staircase, her palm gliding along the smooth wooden banister. At the top, a long hallway stretched out before them, rooms branching off on either side.

"So...what exactly are you looking for?" Trent asked, peering into one of the bedrooms. A large brass bedframe, *sans* mattress, dominated the space, and the dusty velvet curtains hanging from an oval-framed window had long since faded to an indeterminate color.

"Best-case scenario? A smoking gun that solves the mystery of Madame Katz's disappearance and that of the thirty-three men who were last seen at her establishment. Worst case? Some kickass footage I can edit into whatever story unfolds." Maggie grinned at him, her eyes glinting with mischief.

"Without the proof, do you just take...creative liberties to tell the story?" he asked, idly testing the fortitude of a discarded bench and losing all faith in the structural integrity of anything nearby. Forget leprosy—they were in real danger of tetanus.

She whirled on him. "How very dare you question my journalistic integrity, sir," she said, clutching imaginary pearls. "The truth is often entirely too weird to water down with fiction. What's the point of telling a true story if you leave out the truth? Might as well make all the shit up and not lurk around haunted old whorehouses with a man so wholesome he's basically a sentient pile of quinoa."

"Hey, I like quinoa."

"I already knew that, McGarvey. *Everyone* already knew that."

Scowling, he followed her, ripping down spider webs and clearing detritus before she haplessly tripped.

"A cell camera makes for a bad navigator, Michaels." Trent almost killed himself kicking aside a metal pipe and slipping on dusty old papers strewn on the ground.

"You're doing the Lord's work, McGarvey," she quipped. "At least you're making yourself useful. Also, stay out of the shot—your butt is too distracting."

Trent didn't try terribly hard to fight off a self-satisfied smirk. "If I had a dollar for every time..."

"You'd still have to work for the government. Now go through those three rooms on that side and tell me if the light is any good for a wide angle, or if I need to come back during golden hour."

Trent set off to obey before he realized what the fuck she'd said and pulled up short. "This is your one-time access to this hotel, Michaels," he said with the appropriate amount of gravitas. "There is no coming back after this."

Not with you, she might have grumbled.

"What?" he said.

"What?" She peeked out from behind the camera to bat her Betty Boop eyes at him.

"I'm serious. If you're caught here again, you might actually do time."

"Don't worry, Dudley Do-Good, you won't *catch* me here again..." Her beatific smile hid a diabolical intent.

"It's Dudley Do-Right," he said without thinking.

"Oh. My. Gawduh." Flashing him a look that might have threatened to drown the *Calypso*, she pointed across the hall in silent directive. "I've never bullied anyone, but I want to give you the worst wedgie right now."

With a cheeky grin, McGarvey made himself scarce, surprised at how much he was enjoying himself. Each room whispered secrets of scandal, the faded opulence still clinging to the walls. Trent couldn't help but admire the intricate woodwork, the ghostly remnants of luxury, even as his mind kept wandering back to the woman exploring across the hall. On the labyrinthine second floor, he still felt tethered to her. To the sounds of her shoes on the old floor. The small exclamations she made to herself. The pauses she took to presumably touch something she shouldn't.

He couldn't readily blame her. The place begged to be explored through texture. The thick, lined wallpaper. The grit on the plaster. The over-sanded banisters and well-worn door latches.

"You know, Madame Katz was quite the entrepreneur." Maggie's call echoed through the gloom as if it were an old friend. "Story goes, she had her girls slip laudanum into the drinks of unsuspecting workmen. Next thing they knew, they were waking up at sea halfway to Shanghai, the prisoners of the ship captain and at his dubious mercy."

"Dubious mercy?" he mused. "I've never met anyone who talks like you."

"That isn't the flex you think it is."

Always with the comebacks, this one. It was like she was afraid to say something real.

"Each room was rented by the hour," she continued. "The madame ran a tight ship, let me tell you. She didn't tolerate any funny business. Her enemies had a way of getting what was coming to them."

"Funny business?" He arched a brow, a smile tugging at his lips despite his best efforts. "Wasn't that basically her... business?"

"Har, har."

"Shanghaied by seduction," Trent said, his tone even as he pondered the cruel fates of those men. His own path to self-sufficiency had been paved by a workaholic father with a service record that shamed most of the Southwest. All the while Thomas Trenton McGarvey instilled in Trent the same work ethic and tendency to chase advancement and excellence.

If you do something, you do it perfectly, or why even start?

It was a question that ricocheted around his mind every day.

"I wonder how Madame Katz selected her victims?" she wondered aloud. "Did she pick men she didn't like? You'd have to be pretty pissed to ruin someone's life so effectively."

Thoughts of men captured in ships and forced into work was just about the worst place his mind could go... "There's something about history's darker corners that's just...compelling. It's important that people don't forget. The past isn't romantic for everyone."

"That's why I do this. It's like peeling back the layers of a forgotten world." Maggie made her way across the hall to find which room he was inspecting. Her excitement was palpable, her energy infectious as she detailed every sordid tale she'd unearthed for her podcast.

"Murderous Madams" wasn't just a catchy title—it was Maggie's relentless pursuit of the truth, wrapped in the enigma of a past that refused to die quietly. He appreciated that about her, he realized. The fact that she didn't want to sensationalize history but preserve it. To tell the stories people would rather keep hidden.

"Imagine the stories these walls could tell," Trent said, running his fingers over a patch of exposed brick as if it might whisper its secrets to him. His gaze drifted to the skeleton of a bed, and he imagined Maggie spread out upon the sheets, her hair fanned across the pillows, creamy skin bare against the crimson velvet...

He shook off the vision, his face flaming. What the hell was wrong with him? He barely knew this woman, and here he was picturing her in some fantasy old-timey brothel he'd never even have been allowed into back in the day.

They continued their exploration, stepping lightly over the threshold of time, guided by the spirit of curiosity that seemed to bond them in a dance as old as the tales they chased. Trent found himself caught in a web woven of intrigue and attraction, spun by a woman who was as fearless in her search for truth as she was unknowingly adept at stirring his blood.

Trent couldn't help but snicker as he followed Maggie, listening as she recounted the horror stories of life at sea, touching everything that caught her eye. Old picture frames. Shredded molding. Peels in the wallpaper that might hide a secret cubby in the wall.

"Scurvy-ridden sailors singing off-key shanties? No thanks," he said, shaking his head. "You'll understand if I don't have a similar fascination with ships bearing cargo they ought not to."

"Fucking A," she agreed.

"Though I feel like HBO needs a show like *Shanghaiing Sex Workers in the Gilded Age Pacific Northwest*. I'd watch the shit out of that."

Their laughter echoed through the hallways as they moved from room to room, the derelict beauty of the place weaving an enchanting spell around them. Then, tucked away in the corner of what used to be a lavish bedroom, Trent's gaze fell upon an armoire, its wood darkened with age.

"Check this out," he called to Maggie, pulling open the creaky cupboard and drawers to find mostly dust bunnies and dead flies. After wrestling with the latch on the cabinet, he uncovered a stack of yellowed pamphlets, their edges brittle to the touch.

"Is that what I think it is?" Maggie asked, peering over his shoulder with wide eyes.

"Madame Katz's menu of...kittens and services," he confirmed, a hint of heat creeping onto his cheeks as he read the titles aloud. "'Miss Alice and the Privateer's Prize'? 'Miss Kitty and the Captain's Kiss'—they sound like bad romance novels."

"Or really good ones, depending on your taste," Maggie countered, arching her brow playfully.

They stood side by side, flipping through the pages, their amusement growing louder with each absurdly named act. "Oh, look—'Martha and the Mariner's Prayer.' And they have pictures! Do you think it's called that because she's on her knees?" She nudged Trent with her elbow and gave him the Groucho Marx eyebrows. "Look. Swallowing is a dime extra. A whole dime! Can you imagine the taste back then?" She made a face.

Swallowing.

Something Trent was no longer capable of doing.

Something he was absolutely not imagining her doing...

Oh fuck.

"'Ariadne's Anchor,'" he murmured, the whorls of his thumb smoothing over the rough, dusty vellum paper as he tried to think of something—*anything*—else. "Everything on this menu is five pennies to five bucks, but this one costs thirty dollars in the 1890s?"

"No helpful pictures or descriptions like the others... It must be some real hardcore kinky shit," she replied. "What do you think? Group stuff? Butt stuff? LGBTQ stuff?" Her eyes widened, and she shook his arm. "Do you think it's LGBTQ group butt stuff? Before I dropped out of college, I used to have these roommates that would pay to go to parties where they would—"

"Know what? I think that's probably a question for the Google gods," he said before she could say anything that further revved his libido.

He was a man. A man who had control of his own body and mind. He knew better than to act like a fool.

Think unsexy thoughts. Paperwork overtime. Morning wheat-

grass shots. My sophomore golf instructor, Mrs. Garcia, and her curly-haired neck mole.

Oh, good. It worked.

Kinda.

"Wouldn't surprise me if it came with a side of vitamin C to ward off the scurvy," Maggie said to herself, unable to resist the easy volley of innuendo between them. "If I were to pick, I think I'd do this 'Fanny's Feathered Slap and Tickle.' I don't know what it is, but I love a good spank, and feathers are fun."

Jesus H. Truman Capote Christ, he *couldn't* know that about her.

Where did I leave off? Mrs. Garcia's mole. That weird green color that happens to refrigerated cured meats. Open abscesses. Fox News anchors of any gender.

Whew. Boner dead again.

He placed the pamphlets back where he'd found them, making sure the edges of the decades of dust lined up as if they'd never been disturbed. What he needed was to move on. "Let's see what else—"

Maggie opened her Dolce leather tote and arm-swiped the entire paper stack into the depths. "Digging for oil and struck gold! Hell yeah. High five!"

"Hell no, as it happens," he replied, pointing at the now-empty cupboard and leaving her hanging. "You can't take anything from here. It belongs to Mayor Stewart. You'll have to put those back."

"Oh, come on, McGarvey, he's the kind of guy that docks his pet's ears and tails and says it's better that way, then goes home to eat his soup with a fork. Who cares? He probably doesn't even know they exist. It's basically garbage, and you can legally go through garbage."

Trent let out a wry sound of disbelief. "That's actually super illegal in almost every state."

"Is it?" Those damn Betty Boop eyes again. "Oh. Well... That's a thing I know now, and I have totally never broken that law. Anyways, onward!" She held her arm out as if it held a rapier and made to goose-step away.

"Hold on there, Napoleon—you have to put the pamphlets back." He caught her elbow and gently dragged her back.

She rolled her eyes so hard he actually worried they'd get stuck. "Hey, man, don't bust my lady balls, just look the other way. Pretend you're letting me off a speeding ticket and you can totally get me next time. Cuffs and everything. I'll even let you do the frisk." She bounced those eyebrows again and did a little shoulder shimmy.

Damned if he didn't actually find himself considering it.

At his stone-faced silence, she made a rude expression he hadn't seen since elementary school, dug in her bag for the papers, made a dramatic show of organizing them, and placed them back on the shelf with the same exactness he'd shown. "Man... Madame Katz might have killed thirty-three dudes, but she'd be impressed by how fast you can murder a vibe."

"We were all born with our own gifts." He grinned, noticing that she clutched her tote tighter, tucking it over her shoulder and the opening to the bag beneath her arm. Suspicious, Trent picked up the pamphlets and counted them, realizing he'd not counted to begin with so wouldn't know if the exact number had made it back onto the shelf. "Is this all of them?"

"Far as I can tell." She shrugged. "Let's do this."

"Show me your bag."

"Show me your warrant." Her chin jutted all the way forward, and for a second the teasing took on a serious edge.

If he pushed her, she'd push back. Or clam up and cut him off.

His entire life, he'd been trying to learn how to better pick his battles. Maybe now was a good time to put that into practice. With a sigh, he relented, shutting the cupboard and gesturing for her to continue.

Her smile outshone the beam of his flashlight.

"C'mon, McGarvey, which thing would you have ordered?

Lemme guess. 'Bertie's Backdoor Bob'? Or perhaps 'Leo's Lusty Cabin Boy' is more your speed?" Maggie teased, her voice dripping with faux innocence. "Oh, I know... It's 'Sally's Slippery Swab.' If that's not a cleaning kink waiting to happen, I'll eat my hat."

It wasn't that he was a germaphobe. It was just that he could feel just about every part of his skin crawling with the ick. "Only if it includes not having to swab the deck afterward." Trent matched her tone, leaning in closer as the air between them crackled with something more than humor.

Why did she make him forget everything he compulsively had to remember?

Their eyes met, and for a moment, the world outside the crumbling walls of the Palace Hotel ceased to exist. There was just Maggie with her fiery hair and mischievous smile, and him, Trent McGarvey, caught in the tangle of his own restraint and the undeniable allure of her laugh. The way her lips tasted when she was excited...

"Come on," Maggie said finally, her voice a soft challenge. "Let's find that secret passage before we get completely lost in"— she gestured to the armoire with a grin—"historical appreciation. Oh! And speaking of shady dealings," she added, her tone shifting to one of conspiratorial glee, "remember that secret passage I mentioned—the one you caught me sneaking around last time?"

"One of the weirder reports I've ever written."

"You're welcome." She laughed, then pointed toward the staircase that would take them back to the grand first floor. "Well, I never got to see where it leads. The schematics don't match up with anything in the archives. What do you say, deputy? Ready to go down the rabbit hole?"

"Lead the way, Alice," he replied, the prospect of undiscovered history momentarily outweighing the rational part of him that screamed about safety regulations.

She gathered extra footage on the way back down what was once a grand staircase. Their steps echoed through the empty foyer until she led them to the alcove he'd found them in a few nights prior.

"To the Batcave!" she said.

Trent's gaze followed the trail of Maggie's laughter, but it was her flushed cheeks that set his pulse racing. She was a siren in her own right, luring him into dangerous waters with just a smile. He shifted uncomfortably, turning on his heel under the guise of inspecting a nearby wall. As he adjusted the fit of his trousers, he missed the exact moment Maggie found the panel, but her triumphant cry snapped his head around.

"Look at this!" she exclaimed, pointing to the wooden wainscot panel marked with the darker brand of a mermaid. With hardly any effort, she unlatched it, revealing a hidden stairway plunging steeply into the earth below.

"Ah, the classic 'enter the creepy hidden tunnel' move. You know we're the exact kind of folks who get axed first in horror flicks, right?" Trent jested, peering down the ominous staircase.

"Please, if anything, I'm the plucky survivor," Maggie retorted, her grin undimmed by the eerie descent ahead. "I'll keep you safe, McGarvey. Horny old ghosts love me—I have the perfect body type for most of recorded history."

"Comforting," he deadpanned, though his chuckle betrayed his amusement. She had the perfect body type for now. For always.

For him.

"What kind of ghosts do you think live here?" he asked. "Horny ones? Or polter ones?"

"Probably both," Maggie replied with a wink, her earlier warmth returning in full force. "Now come on, let's find out where this little trip through time takes us."

"Um...the past is a bit kinder to some of us than others. I've never shared your fondness for it and most definitely don't want to visit." Also, he hated being underground—dirt floors, cobwebs, and standing water—but would eat all of his Baccarat stemware before he admitted it.

She grimaced, casting a sheepish glance up at him. "Super fair point. I can take it from here, *el jefe*—you guard the door and come running if I die." She tipped her yellow hard hat at a jaunty angle, gave him a two-fingered salute, and plunged down the stairs.

Goddammit.

He followed, if only to watch her backside—er, back.

With a shared sense of intrepid (or foolhardy) spirit, they began their careful descent. The earthen stairs were a claustrophobic hug, the walls pressing close as they made their way down. The air was thick with the scent of old wood and dust, a musty perfume that spoke of ages gone by.

Trent felt the weight of history here, a tangible presence surrounding them.

Maggie was like a torchbearer for the past, illuminating forgotten stories with her fervor. Trent admired that about her—the way she relentlessly pursued the truth, regardless of how uncomfortable or unflattering it might be. It was a stark contrast to the whitewashed narratives so often paraded before the public as unbiased truths.

"Most people prefer their history scrubbed clean and dressed in Sunday best," he remarked casually, watching her navigate the narrow steps with care. "But not you. You're not afraid to dig up the dirt and show the bones beneath. That's...impressive."

Maggie paused, looking back over her shoulder at him, and he could see the impact of his words flickering across her face—a fleeting vulnerability quickly masked by determination.

"Thanks. Someone has to remember these lives," she said, her voice echoing slightly in the tight space. "Did you know Madame Katz wasn't just running a brothel? She was teaching men how to please a woman—publishing manuals and everything."

"Enlightened for her time," Trent mused, picturing the formidable madame sharing secrets most Victorian men would blush to even contemplate. "Or maybe just good business sense."

He followed Maggie through the tunnel, their shoulders

brushing against the earthen walls that seemed to close in with each step. It was a narrow passage, barely enough for one person at a time, and Trent had to duck occasionally to avoid the low ceiling.

Their journey ended abruptly at a large iron door, rusted with age, yet still formidable. An image of a mermaid, now reduced to a faint outline of a tail, decorated its surface—a silent sentinel guarding whatever was on the other side.

Maggie tried the latch, and it turned, but something on the other side barred their entry. She glanced to him with a silent plea for help.

With a concerted effort, Trent pressed against the barrier. His muscles strained until, with a groan of protest, the door yielded to reveal a dark room beyond.

"Looks like we've hit the jackpot," Maggie said, her excitement palpable as they stepped into the dank space.

"Or...the Sirens storage room," Trent observed dryly, noting the muffled sound of music and voices from the lunch crowd on Sirens' restaurant balcony. "Which means we've tunneled under Water Street from one basement to another. Could this just be a way to move things across a busy thoroughfare when this was an active international port town?"

"Could be. But my instincts tell me there's more to this. Think Mayor Stewart knows about the tunnel?" Maggie pondered aloud, scanning the room. "This could be a gold mine for the history of the Palace Hotel when he reopens it."

"Good luck getting him to sit down for an interview," Trent replied with a chuckle. "He's more slippery than an eel in an oil spill."

"No lies detected."

Trent traced the faded tail on the now-open door. "Clever using the same symbol to mark the secret entrances. Not that many people would have recognized it for what it was."

"Exactly." She turned to face him, soft features a mask of excitement. "So why put it there if it's not meaningful? I'm going to ask Mayor Stewart at the first available opportunity. He's the kind of guy whose favorite book is *Where's Waldo?*—He won't be tough to outmatch in a game of wits."

"Well, if anyone can crack him, it's you." Trent gave her arm an affectionate squeeze. "You're nothing if not persistent. Just... don't give him a reason to call me, yeah?"

He didn't miss the fact that she made no such promises herself as she turned to investigate the carcasses of kegs of weekends past, a defunct deep freezer, several boxes of seasonal restaurant décor, the Valentine's Day box noticeably missing from its spot.

"At least it's organized chaos." She spread her arms. "Let's look for more symbols of mermaids or sirens. My gut says that's where the answers lie."

Trent nodded his agreement. "What else is your gut telling you?"

She stopped for a second as if listening. "That I'm having the chicken pesto on ciabatta and sweet potato fries with sriracha mayo for lunch after this."

Chuckling, he batted aside a few cobwebs hanging from old iron shelves, checking the wall behind for a siren guarding secrets. Trent couldn't help but think of the dual nature of such a place: a potential safe haven or a prison, depending on which side of history you stood. "Places like these... They could've been sanctuaries," he mused, touching the rough wall. "But with those heavy doors and solid earth? Feels more like a cage."

"I know what you mean... Were the doors built to keep people out? Or to trap people inside?"

Maggie efficiently started searching the other side of the room, lifting tarps and checking behind boxes. As she searched, bending over, squatting, and leaning into corners, Trent couldn't help but watch her movements. He grew more aroused by the second, cursing his body's reaction to her unintentional provocativeness. She was so engrossed in her search, oblivious to the effect she had on him—a siren unaware of her own song.

"Wouldn't it be hysterical if there was a body in this deep freeze?" she said, testing to see if the lock was engaged.

"If by hysterical, you mean horrifying, then yeah." Trent drifted over, waking a little differently to compensate for what was going on in his pants. "If you find a body in there, give me time to beat feet, because that's paperwork I don't want to do on my day off."

She'd opened the lid like a treasure chest to look down inside by the time he reached her.

Empty.

"It's not even plugged in." She pouted, then brightened. "Maybe it's here to hide something behind it."

Trent's brow furrowed. "I don't think—"

Bending over at the hips, she bent across the freezer to peek at the scant inches between it and the wall. "I need your flashlight," she called.

Need.

It slammed into him with all the invisible force of a hurricane. His vital oxygen swirled into a tornado of lust in his lungs.

The charged air seemed to crackle around them, the musty scent of earth and the faint sound of muffled voices from above forming a backdrop to the tension that stretched as taut as the zipper over his cock.

As he watched her wiggle and lean yet a little further, the way her back arched and her skirt hugged her form—

"Maggie." Trent's voice was husky, barely a whisper over the hum of his own racing pulse. "I swear you're doing this on purpose."

She glanced over her shoulder at him, an impish grin playing on her lips. "Doing what, deputy?" she teased, feigning innocence while straightening up.

"Killing me, slowly," he admitted with a rueful chuckle, closing the distance between them with two decisive strides. "We need to get out of here, or I'm gonna do something impulsive... like kiss you again."

Instead of stepping back or showing any signs of reluctance, Maggie set down her phone camera with deliberate care and faced him fully, her green eyes alight with mischief. Without a word, she closed the remaining gap and pressed her lips firmly against his.

The world outside the basement seemed to vanish as the kiss deepened, their breaths mingling, the taste of her sending every other thought scattering. The deep freezer became a mere prop in the devastation of their passion.

Devouring her delicious mouth, Trent had no trouble finding the curves of her hips as he lifted her onto the deep freeze. The act was a dance of control and surrender, one he performed with a growing hunger.

Maggie made a soft noise of approval, encouraging him, parting her legs instinctively. Trent slid his hands up, pushing her skirt to bunch around her waist, and kissed her fiercely through the thin barrier of her leggings and panties. The heat and damp-ness he found there sent a jolt of desire through him, so intense it bordered on pain.

Trent groaned, possessive need coiling hot and tight in his gut. He wanted nothing more than to strip her bare and take her right here, hard and fast against the wall. Bent over the freezer with that sweet ass high in the air. But he forced himself to slow down, to gentle his kisses and ease the grip of his hands.

He sank to his knees before Maggie, gliding his hands up her bare thighs to grip her hips. Her skin was silky smooth under his palms, and he groaned at the scent of her arousal.

"Trent," she whimpered, fingers gliding over his hair.

The sound of his name on her lips was his undoing. He buried his face between her thighs, licking and sucking at her clit until her moans rose in pitch and her hips bucked against his mouth.

He slid two fingers into her slick heat, crooking them just so, and Maggie came with a sharp cry that rang off the walls. Her inner muscles clutched at his fingers as her orgasm rolled through her in waves.

The silence of the room was quickly filled with a chorus of sighs and soft moans as Trent lavished attention on her with an eager tongue, tracing the contours of her desire with a reverence befitting the goddess beneath him. Each breathy whisper from Maggie echoed off the walls, creating an intimate symphony that felt sacred in the cool, musty air.

Maggie white-knuckled the edge of her perch as he rested her legs on his shoulders. She undulated, urging him closer, her hips rising to meet his mouth as waves of pleasure cascaded through her. The sound of her bliss, unrestrained and resonant, swirled around them, mingling with the scent of old wood and an age long forgotten.

Trent gentled his touch, laving at her until the tremors eased and her hands loosened their grip on the edge.

Only then did he raise his head, wiping his mouth with the back of one hand.

The sight of Maggie splayed out before him, chest heaving and eyes glazed with pleasure, was nearly enough to make him come in his pants.

As if reading his mind, she glanced down at his hips, her gaze widening and then glazing with a dark hunger.

Her questing fingers beat his own to his belt, wordlessly grappling with it.

Struggling for breath, Trent glanced over her shoulder and saw the one thing that could quell his lust faster than the ice bucket challenge.

Kiki Forrester stood in the doorway, one brow arched, arms folded over her chest.

Not only was the regal, forty-something indigenous woman the sheriff and his boss...

She was also the last woman he'd slept with.

EIGHT
Shake and Strain

TO POUR INGREDIENTS AND ICE INTO A SHAKER
TIN TO SHAKE AND DRAIN THE LIQUID OUT OF
THE TIN

"KIK—ER, SHERIFF FORRESTER."

Not since her senior year at William Cullen Bryant High, when Mr. Hill had busted Tony Bianchi getting a blowie from the marching band's student teacher in the woodwind closet, had Maggie seen someone get their pants buckled so quickly.

That it was McGarvey now behaving like he'd been caught with his hand—or other applicable piece of anatomy—in the cookie jar somehow made it considerably less entertaining.

That McGarvey was behaving this way while Maggie still sat with her knees wide enough to straddle a Clydesdale while a drop-dead gorgeous woman who looked like she might run triathlons for fun stood in the doorway?

That shit there brought a tsunami of scalding shame.

As McGarvey had done, Maggie quickly rearranged herself, willing the *I just came hard enough to permanently alter my brain chemistry* scarlet to recede from her cheeks.

"Finish waiting for the cable guy, did you?" Sheriff Forrester asked in a smoky voice that she could probably charge men $2.99 a minute to listen to.

"Yes—no—I mean, they rescheduled," McGarvey sputtered.

The sight of him, normally so composed and self-assured, tripping over his words like a teenager caught jerking it in the back row at church was downright unsettling.

Only when his tackle was fully stowed did McGarvey address her.

"Gotcha." Kiki wandered further into the basement, boots clicking on the concrete floor. "Now if I could only figure out what you're doing in the basement of this building despite not having the owner's permission or any understandable legal purpose, we'd really have something here."

Maggie glanced at Trent, who had sprouted a sheen of sweat on his smooth brown forehead. Surely, as they apparently had a working relationship, he would offer up some plausible explanation any second now.

Or minute.

Or—

"Mermaids!" Maggie blurted.

Both McGarvey and Sheriff Forrester turned to look at her— McGarvey concerned, Sheriff Forrester amused.

"That's right," Trent said at last, gesturing vaguely at the dusty shelves. "So, uh, I was accompanying Miss Michaels on a tour of the Palace Hotel for a journalistic endeavor that she's currently pursuing, documenting mermaid motifs in Townsend Harbor's historic buildings."

"I see," the sheriff said, the lines of her probably yoga-toned forearms flexing as she crossed them over her chest and made a show of looking around the basement. "I hate to be the bearer of bad news, but we don't currently seem to *be* in the Palace Hotel. And though I know Miss Michaels is an employee of Sirens, she's not currently on shift."

Maggie's heart began to thump harder, and clammy sweat coated her palms.

So, Sheriff Smoke Show not only knew who she was and where she worked, she knew her schedule as well?

Why this rankled her so when they'd never even met, she

wasn't certain. But she suspected it *might* have something to do with the fact that the woman standing before her had the power to turn McGarvey into a stuttering, foot-shuffling schoolboy.

McGarvey lifted a hand and scratched the back of his neck.

"Yes, well—" Trent shifted his weight, avoiding Kiki's gaze.

"What's it to you?" The words snapped from Maggie's mouth like the crack of a whip, sharpened by the edge of the East Coast burr she'd tried so hard to lose after leaving Deer Park for Boston.

McGarvey's head swung toward her, his eyes telegraphing something like censure. Or panic.

Which only served to augment Maggie's irritation.

The sheriff, on the other hand, remained cool and even, authority radiating from her carefully neutral expression. "To me, it's nothing whatsoever. To Kurt, who called to report a break-in and possible assault, it's a lot."

Fucking. Kurt.

"Possible assault?" Maggie scoffed, crossing her legs as she sat up straighter on the freezer. "Where the hell did they get that idea?"

The sheriff cocked her head at an angle of birdlike curiosity. "According to dispatch, the caller heard what they thought was a woman scream and thought whoever broke in might have assaulted someone who surprised the intruder in the act."

Maggie felt her face blanch, and her insides turned to rocky ice. A scream? She hadn't screamed. Had she? No, no. It had been more of a whimper, really. Or maybe a moan, but definitely not a scream. And surely it hadn't been that...loud?

Or had it?

If her vocalizations were in any way proportionate to the intensity of the pleasure McGarvey had coaxed from her, she'd have shattered every single one of the small rectangular windows at street level.

The sheriff's knowing gaze met hers, and Maggie swallowed around what felt like a wad of cotton jammed down her throat. "As part of my investigation, I reviewed historical renderings for the original structure and found an inconsistency with the blue-prints provided with the renovation permission from the Townsend Harbor Historical Society."

"You're investigating Madame Katz." The sheriff pronounced this like a declarative sentence rather than a question.

And for reasons Maggie didn't understand, she found herself confirming it.

"Yes."

The sheriff's lips tightened into a line. "No wonder the mayor has his Jockeys in a knot."

Curiosity gnawed Maggie's stomach hollow. She wanted nothing more than to press Kiki about what she knew but knew this was neither the time nor place.

"Which is why I secured permission from the historical society to show Miss Michaels the property," McGarvey offered. "When we discovered another mermaid carving in the passage, we elected to follow where it led, which is where we found this," he said, holding up the brothel menu.

The sheriff took it, her eyes widening as they flicked over the contents.

"It's the last one that has us stumped," McGarvey said. "Any theories?"

As ridiculous as it was, Maggie felt a prickle of irritation creep up her spine. The menu had felt like a secret between the two of them, and by consulting his ranking officer, he'd all but invited her into their investigation.

"Anyway," McGarvey continued, "after we found that, we followed the passage here, then Miss Michaels noticed what she thought was part of one of those mermaid carvings behind the deep freezer here, and—"

"You unbuckled your belt in case you needed to create an emergency tourniquet should she accidentally lose a finger reaching behind the freezer as she bent over it to get a picture?" The sheriff looked up from the menu, one expertly tweezed brow lifting.

McGarvey's Adam's apple bobbed beneath the clean-shaven skin of his throat. "Something like that."

They locked eyes as the sheriff handed the menu back, and Maggie felt the cool, damp air shift. Tension crackled between them like a downed power line.

And all at once, the realization hit her like a freight train.

McGarvey's twitchy nerves, his reluctance to look her in eye, the blurted admissions.

Sheriff Smoke Show and Deputy Trent McGarvey had *totally* fucked.

Maggie's lungs felt heavy and tight, her stomach a cold ball in her ribcage.

It wasn't the first time Maggie had felt like an outsider in this small town steeped in secrets and fueled by gossip, but this revelation stirred up something deeper, more personal. A something that delivered the ruthless knowledge that if the sheriff was McGarvey's type, then Maggie most definitely was not.

The radio clipped to the sheriff's belt squawked, and she thumbed a button to silence it.

"As much as I hate to interrupt your important work, I think it would be best that you two head back the way you came. Immediately, if not sooner."

McGarvey nodded, giving Maggie a *please cooperate* glance.

Though she knew the sheriff was doing them a favor by allowing them to leave covertly, being shooed away like a scolded teenager sincerely chapped her ass.

Either way, Maggie needed to be where the sheriff was not while at least a couple shreds of her self-esteem remained intact. Scooting down from the freezer, she plucked the folded parchment from McGarvey's hands and made a beeline for the door to the passage.

"If it were me, I'd talk to Vivian Prescott," the sheriff called right as Maggie closed her hand over the door handle. "Before she met Myrtle Le Grande and decided to scandalize a small Pacific Northwest town, she earned a Ph.D. in sexual anthropology."

Beautiful, athletic, powerful, *and* helpful.

Yep, it was official.

Maggie hated her guts.

Muttering a barely audible "thanks," she yanked open the door and barreled down the passageway. She didn't bother to look back to see if McGarvey followed, her steps quickening as her eyes began to sting.

"Hey," he called, his footsteps echoing on the stone as he loped to catch up with her. "Hold up."

"When?" Maggie asked.

"When *what*?" McGarvey asked, falling into step beside her.

"When did you and the sheriff screw each other's brains out?"

Maggie pulled ahead again as McGarvey stopped in his tracks. When he saw that she had no intention of waiting for him, he closed the distance, his hand landing on her shoulder to arrest her momentum.

Maggie whirled on him, shrugging away his sanity-stealing touch.

"Hey," he said, his eyes soft and his voice a calming rumble. "What's going on?"

Maggie stepped closer, searching his face. His jaw was tight, eyebrows knitted ever so slightly.

"Tell me I'm wrong."

He hesitated, shoulders slumping as he exhaled in resignation. "It was one time. Before she was the sheriff and after the department Christmas party. Someone came up with the brilliant idea of a drinking game where we had to take a shot every time Ethan tried to steer the conversation to something work-related."

"And this was a lot, I'm guessing?" Maggie asked, folding her arms beneath the shelf of her breasts.

"Judy in dispatch ended up horking about a pound of fudge into the Galatea fountain. Deputy Baker got alcohol poisoning and fell down the uptown stairs. Motherfucker is *still* on administrative leave."

The blindingly beautiful smile slowly wilted from his face as

McGarvey realized his attempt at levity had gone over as well as a turd in the punch bowl.

"We both regretted it nearly the second it was over, and we've only ever been colleagues since." Trent reached for her hand, but she pulled away, the image of him tangled in bedsheets with Kiki Forrester searing itself into her brain. Probably her thighs didn't even get tired when she rode reverse cowgirl.

"Look, it's none of my business, okay?" Maggie said. "But next time, at least do me the favor of asking before you decide to dump the details into the lap of one your one-night stands."

"I was only trying to—"

"I don't need your help," Maggie snapped. "And I certainly don't need your pity."

"Pity?" McGarvey's brows rose in surprise. "No. It's not—"

"And it never will be," she finished for him. "I need to get going. Thanks a metric fuck-ton for your help."

Without another word, she turned and headed for the exit.

She'd be damned if she let them see her cry.

THE BELL ABOVE THE DOOR ANNOUNCED MAGGIE'S arrival at the Lady Garden, her pocketbook slung over one shoulder and a chip the size of Fenway Park on the other.

"And if you use the oscillate setting, its little ears vibrate like this." A tiny, gray-haired, granny-aged woman jiggled a hot-pink schlong-shaped vibrator in size donkey at a pair of wide-eyed, middle-aged women whose expensive but pristine gorpcore screamed Midwestern ladies' trip.

Moving past a display of nipple clamps, Maggie paused in front a delicate confection of floor-length peachy silk and lace.

"And what can I help my favorite bartender with?" a buttery, British-accented voice asked.

Maggie turned to see an elegant woman with silver-blonde hair smiling warmly at her.

"Hi, Vivian," Maggie said, feeling a rush of genuine affection. "I was actually hoping to engage your expertise on a topic of a historical nature."

"First of all, I insist that anyone who's engaged in illegal activity with my wife call me Vee," she said. "Second, that would be a most welcome change from lecturing hapless men on the mysteries of the G-spot."

Maggie glanced down at her Manolo Blahnik satin pumps. "I'm sorry about the illegal stuff part. But in my defense, Gabe didn't tell me he'd engaged her expertise."

"Oh, pshaw," Vee said. "It's a service you've done me, actually. If the opportunity for good trouble doesn't present itself to Myrtle, she'll most assuredly manufacture her own. And believe me when I say that her aptitude in this regard is truly remarkable."

"I believe you." Maggie laughed, her chest tightening at the obvious fondness in Vee's expression.

Vee's warm, silky hand found Maggie's forearm and squeezed. "Why don't you come on back to my office and I'll make us some tea."

"That would be delightful."

Maggie followed Vee through a parted velvet curtain and stepped into a space lifted straight out of an antique boudoir painting. The office walls, painted in a rich hue of burgundy, were lined with artfully curated shelves that carried a multitude of erotic sculptures from across the globe and time periods. Each artifact embodied the raw and alluring power of human sensuality in its own unique way.

The room was lit by a pair of opulent Art Nouveau lamps, their golden light warming the rich hues of the furniture. An imposing dark oak desk claimed the center stage, and meticulous piles of books and wholesale catalogs with artfully arranged displays of bondage cuffs and ball gags were stacked neatly on one corner.

Now there was a career path she'd never considered. Bondage buyer. That would look good on a business card, right?

Maybe she could do that if this latest stab at a life reboot went the same way as all the rest.

"Now then." Vee busied herself at a credenza turned bar cabinet, clicking on an electric teakettle and withdrawing two delicate rose chintz teacups from one of the drawers. "Tell me how I may be of service."

Settling onto the sofa, Maggie quickly summarized her findings, finishing by reaching into her pocketbook to produce the brothel menu.

"Let's see this, then." Vee set down the steaming cups as she lowered herself onto the couch next to Maggie and lifted a pair of reading glasses dangling from a probably real gold chain around her neck.

The resiny scent of bergamot floated upward, perfuming the air around them as Vee paged through the pamphlet.

A frown creased the older woman's brow. "Where did you say you found this again?"

Maggie shifted, suddenly uneasy. "We found it in an armoire in Madame Katz's room in the Palace Hotel."

Vee arched one penciled eyebrow. "We?"

Shit.

Maggie had been so careful to make this sound like a singular pursuit when she'd narrated it.

She sighed. No point trying to hide it now. "Yes. Deputy McGarvey and I found it."

Vee lifted her cup and sipped with effortless grace. "The same Deputy McGarvey who arrested you, Gabe, and my wife?"

Maggie sipped her tea, conscious that she was imitating—poorly—Vee's aristocratic bearing. "That's the guy."

"What a delightful twist."

Leaning back onto the couch, Vee crossed her legs, a thoughtful expression creasing a face that age hadn't managed to rob of its classic beauty.

"Ariadne's Anchor," she mused. "It's not a term that I encountered in any of my research, and Victorian brothels were somewhat of a specialty of mine. Which leads me to think it may be code for something. Perhaps a discreet service offered to only certain high-profile clients?"

Maggie nodded slowly. "That makes sense. But what kind of service would be that much more expensive than anything else on the menu?"

Vee tapped her chin thoughtfully with a pearly nail. "Perhaps we're going about this the wrong way. The names of all of the other items have at least some correlation with the service itself. Which was also the case with the other brothel menus I studied when doing my undergraduate work."

"Do you happen to remember any of them?" Maggie asked, finding that she wanted to draw this conversation out just to sit in the calming wake of Vee's voice.

"Oh yes," Vee said. "'The Gentleman's Delight'—that's just a fancy name for a hand job. And 'the Duchess'—why, that's nothing more than your standard sixty-nine. But my personal favorite would have to be the 'Quivering Quill.'"

"I don't know if I'm afraid or intrigued to hear what that entailed," Maggie said.

"Both are applicable in this case," Vee replied. "Basically, it included inserting a quill anally before using it to write erotic poetry."

"You're shitting me," Maggie said, her eyes flicking to the pen tucked behind Vee's ear.

"I shitteth thee not," Vee conceded with a knowing wink. "But as to this particular offering, perhaps the reference to Greek mythology is more important than we realized."

"Ariadne was the one who helped what's-his-dick when it came to the maze of the Minotaur, yes?"

"Exactly!" Vee said, her eyes lighting up. "Ariadne was the daughter of King Minos. She gave Theseus a ball of thread to help him find his way out of the labyrinth after defeating the Minotaur."

"Right," Maggie said, nodding, "but what does that have to

do with...you know, the sexual stuff?" She gestured vaguely at the brothel menu, feeling more out of her depth than ever.

Vee sipped her tea, considering the question. "Well," she began slowly, "Ariadne is associated with many different symbols and concepts, including passion, mazes, vegetation, snakes, forgiveness, paths, and labyrinths."

"Okay..." Maggie trailed off. Her brow furrowed as she tried to connect the dots between these seemingly disparate ideas. She wrapped her fingers around her teacup, enjoying the warmth it brought to her chest, even as her thoughts spun like a top.

"Think about it this way," Vee suggested, leaning forward conspiratorially. "What if 'Ariadne' is a metaphor for something else? Something hidden, perhaps, or something that requires guidance to unravel?"

"Like a secret society?" Maggie asked.

"Perhaps," Vee agreed, her eyes twinkling with intrigue. "Or maybe it's something simpler. A code word, a password... Only those who know its true meaning would be able to access whatever it represents."

"Interesting." Maggie chewed the inside of her cheek, her brain working overtime to process the new information.

"Speaking of Greek goddesses," Vee said, setting her teacup back on its saucer with practiced grace. "I noticed you admiring the backless Tamara Marjolaine peignoir set. Would you care to try one on?" She gestured toward the delicate silk garment that hung enticingly from a nearby display.

Maggie nearly choked on her tea. "Those kinds of gowns are designed for sexy giraffes like Sheriff Forrester."

The second the name left her lips, Maggie regretted it. The same scalding tide of irritation and, okay, jealousy came flooding back to her.

She hadn't heard from McGarvey since she'd made her dramatic exit earlier, and for some damn reason, this really fucking bothered her.

"Darling, are you mad?" Vee replied, waving her hand dismissively. "Do you have any idea how desirable your body type has been throughout history? Had you been born in the neolithic era, they would have built temples to your name and sought your favor with animal sacrifices."

"I don't know about that," Maggie said, "but I wouldn't mind a sacrifice of some baby-back ribs about now."

"I'm afraid I'm fresh out," Vee said, smoothing the hem of her tailored pencil skirt. "But I do happen to have an excellent bottle of champagne, if plying you with it might change your mind about at least trying the set on."

"Fine." Maggie sighed dramatically. "But I'm sending you the therapy bill if it further exacerbates the genetic betrayal that is my legacy."

Pushing herself up from the couch, Vee walked over to the curtain. "Carol, would you be so kind as to set up the Marjolaine peignoir set in a dressing room for Miss Michaels?"

"You betcha," Maggie heard Carol reply.

"Now then, let's see about this Brut." Vee made quick work of uncorking the champagne, somehow managing to both avoid the deafening *pop* or spill a single drop of the liquid gold while decanting it into slim flutes that were probably real crystal.

BEHIND THE CURTAIN OF ONE OF THE DRESSING ROOMS with the expensive suds in her hand, Maggie eyed the silky confection.

Her fingers trembled slightly as she slipped into the luxurious peignoir, the fabric feeling like a whisper against her skin. The gown cascaded over her body, hugging her curves and flaring from her hips. It was as if the delicate silk had been tailor-made just for her, transforming her from buxom Irish girl next door into a sultry siren.

"All right, let's see you," Vee called out.

"Only if you promise not to laugh," Maggie warned, taking a deep breath before opening the door. "Or vomit."

Vee's eyes widened as she sucked in a quick little gasp. "Darling, you *must* know how absolutely divine you look."

Maggie's cheeks flushed. "Look, you don't have to sell me on it. It's obviously beautifully made. But I'm still not sure it's...me."

Because unlike everything else you own, this probably didn't fall off a truck.

"I wouldn't insult you by trying to sell you," Vee said, sipping her own champagne. "But one thing's for certain—if Deputy McGarvey sees you in that, he'll likely need a new pair of trousers."

"Vee!" Maggie protested, feeling the blush spread to her chest. But she couldn't deny the thrill that coursed through her veins at the thought of his reaction.

"Come on now, don't pretend like you haven't thought about it," Vee teased, a knowing smile playing on her lips.

Oh, she had.

Frequently.

Feverishly.

"Really, darling," Vee continued, her voice warm and rich. "This was made for you, and I insist that you have it. In fact, it's a gift."

Maggie's mouth dropped open. Though she wasn't able to remember the exact price, there had been lots of sevens and fours.

"Vee, I couldn't—"

"Shh," Vee hushed her. "Now, let me tell you something about our dear Deputy McGarvey." She leaned in conspiratorially, her eyes sparkling with mischief. "That man has an eye for beauty and a taste for the finer things in life. And you, my dear, are both." Maggie began to open her mouth, but Vee held up a finger. "A fact that this gown attests to most deliciously, and the reason you must have it. I ask only one thing of you in return."

Maggie's antennae began to twitch. "Which is?"

"A piece this lovely deserves a proper seduction. Invite our officer over this evening and practice the temptresses' art. Who knows," Vee said, her lips curving in a smile. "It might even bring you closer to answering Ariadne's riddle."

Turning back to the three-panel mirror, Maggie met her own eyes. "All right. I'll take it."

"Splendid," Vee said. "Just hand it out and I'll get it all wrapped up for you."

Maggie returned to the dressing room, fishing her phone from her purse so she could text McGarvey before she changed her mind.

Or her outfit.

She stared at the screen, tapping out several phrases and deleting them just as quickly.

Want to continue our hunt at my place tonight?

In the mood to help me solve a mystery?

Care to help me break in some more appliances?

Heaving a disgusted sigh, she settled on a simple but practical *My place. 8pm tonight.*

She hesitated for a moment before hitting send, her stomach doing a rollercoaster lift when it was too late to take it back.

"Well?" Vee asked from beyond the curtain.

"Invitation sent," Maggie said, carefully lifting off the decadent silk and handing it out. "I just hope I don't regret it."

"Relax, darling," Vee said. "And remember, he's just a man. A very handsome, charming man, but still just a man."

"Uh huh," Maggie said, stepping back into her own clothes. She hadn't even gotten her bra hooked when her phone buzzed.

I'll be there.

Maggie exhaled a breath.

Like the decadent negligee, her invitation revealed parts of her she wasn't used to offering casually.

She had never felt more naked.

Or more alive.

NINE

Probable Cause

A REASONABLE GROUND TO SUPPOSE THAT A CHARGE OF CRIMINAL CONDUCT IS WELL-FOUNDED

Trent's phone buzzed on the mahogany coffee table, disturbing the fortress of solitude he'd built with his case files and paperwork. The screen lit up with Maggie's name.

"Talk about a thirst trap," he muttered, tossing aside a crime scene photo that was as cold and lifeless as a bad dinner date. He eyed the paperwork, the words blurring into a bureaucratic soup that no longer held his interest. Maggie wanted to discuss their latest investigative foray into the Palace Hotel's cobwebbed corners, but Trent harbored the hope it could be something more...personal.

After he tapped back his reply, his thumb hovered over the send button, cautioning him with all the rational reasons this could wait until tomorrow.

Until daylight.

Until he wasn't so hungry.

Fuck it.

Trent rose, stretching out the kinks that had formed from hours of poring over documents. His heart did a little shuffle at the thought of seeing her. With a self-deprecating chuckle, he grabbed an expensive bottle of wine off the rack—an indulgence he justified as "politeness" rather than an excuse to impress.

Trent's fingers brushed over the tailored seams of his jacket as he slipped it on, checking his reflection briefly.

He looked too...something.

Thirsty, his conscience whispered.

"Fuck off," he told his reflection before grabbing his wallet and keys. "And behave."

The night air wrapped around him like a cool whisper as he locked his front door and made his way to Maggie's place. Townsend Harbor hummed quietly around him, tucked in by eight thirty p.m. on a school night. It was the kind of town where secrets were currency, and Maggie was hellbent on mining every last one.

What was he worried about... He didn't even have secrets to uncover.

It wasn't a date; it was business. Sort of. But as he climbed the steps, Trent did his best to ignore the electric current of anticipation that danced along his spine. Maggie had that effect—like a live wire hidden in velvet.

He knocked, practicing his most professional smile. But who was he kidding? Every time he saw her, with those fiery curls and curves that could make a preacher curse, he discovered himself wading chest-deep in lust. He was a man of carefully curated control, of finely tuned desires neatly kept in check and applied with practice and skill, yet Maggie Michaels had a way of making him *wish* for chaos.

Appreciate it, even.

A riot of color, heat, and stimuli assaulted him as the rush of her apartment door opening caressed him with the fragrance of something savory mixed with her own alluring scent.

The mystery herself was wrapped in a bespoke trench coat that hugged her like a second skin. Her grin was Cheshire cat-worthy as she beckoned Trent inside with a flick of her wrist.

"Oh good, you came," she said, the mischievous sparkle in her eyes doing funny things to his insides.

Not yet. Trent stepped over the threshold, his gaze drawn inexorably to the sinfully red soles of her three-inch-heels. "You're dressed for going out in that coat and Louboutins," he said, nodding at her feet.

"Or am I dressed for you coming inside?" She tossed back her curls and sashayed to the kitchen, the click-clack of her steps an extravagant melody.

Fuck. He loved shapely calves in heels.

Trent swallowed a rush of moisture as the smorgasbord of sights, scents, and sounds overwhelmed him with their delightful racket.

"Make yourself at home," she called over her shoulder, already busy clinking glasses and bottles together. "Throw your jacket wherever."

As he looked around, his eyes landed on the spotless surfaces and polished floors. There was a faint smell of lemon in the air, and he couldn't help but notice that everything had been meticulously cleaned and organized. He felt a pang of guilt, knowing she had gone through all this effort for him.

"Thanks, I'll just—" Trent moved to stow his jacket, but Maggie's voice cut through as his fingers grazed the coat closet handle.

"Wait, not that one!" There was a hint of panic in her tone that made immediate sense when an avalanche of fabric and fluff barreled out, burying his shoes in the domestic detritus of coats and linens.

"What the—?" He hopped out of the way of the leaning *towels* of Pisa as they toppled into a final pile of carnage at his feet.

"Oops." Her cheeks flamed a shade redder than her hair as she glanced from the pile to Trent's amused expression. "Guess I really need to do some spring cleaning."

"Didn't you *just* get here?" He laughed.

"Yeah, but my textile needs are vast and varied." She shrugged. "Shove all that back in there, will you? I'll make the drinks."

Trent chuckled. "Wouldn't it be better for everyone involved if *I* make the drinks?" he suggested hopefully. "Then maybe you can find space in the closet for the coat you're wearing."

"Ha-ha, very funny, McGarvey." The flush on her cheeks deepened to ruby, but her laughter rang genuine. "It's—uh—fashion, not function."

"Sure, sure," he drawled, stepping closer. "You look like you're about to spontaneously combust, though. It's warm as the oven in here. How 'bout you take it off?"

Maggie fanned herself theatrically with one hand while the other jerked a shaker with all the pornographic suggestion of those homoerotic Shake Weight adds from back in the day. "Listen, I've been practicing, and you can watch me dominate this martini and eat your words."

I'd rather eat yours.

Memories of her flavor, of the slick, hot, wet, delicious feast that was the confection of her body threatened to knock the starch out of his knees.

"Hit me with your best shot, Lady Mix-a-Lot," he said, unable to keep himself from folding the towels in a more stackable manner and finding them a secure place on the top shelf of the linen closet.

"Did you just dad-joke?" She snorted.

"No." Looking down, he grimaced. *Of course* she didn't fold her fitted sheets. She didn't even attempt to do anything but wad them up in a wrinkle pile. How did she even function? "What's in this recipe?" he asked, hoping to keep the conversation light and uncomplicated.

With a flourish, she recited the concoction she was crafting. "A splash of aged bourbon, a twist of lemon, a dollop of imported black forest honey, and a dash of bitters, the sweetness muddled by some brine from the olives—shaken, not stirred, to perfection, and whispered with my secret ingredient."

"Sounds both sweet and dangerous," Trent observed, watching her hands move with precision and confidence as she measured out the top-shelf vodka. "You know I have a taste for the finer things."

"That's why I picked this one," she replied, meeting his eye with a challenge as she handed him the glass. "Thought it might be up to par for our resident alcohol aficionado."

"Don't go telling people that—it sounds like a fancy word for an alcoholic."

She laughed as if he'd invented the idea of a joke and then held her glass rim to his for a toast. "Let's see if it passes muster."

The scent of citrus and spirits flirted with his senses. The first sip was bold, complex, and hit just the right notes, much like the woman who made it.

"Damn, Maggie, this is fire."

"Do I get a good student gold star?" she said with a wink, leaning closer into his space, heat radiating between them like the promise of a summer desert monsoon. "I was kinda hot for teacher."

Nearly choking on his next sip, he felt some of his chill slipping as he let her fire that flirt across his bow without an answer. "What smells so delicious?" he asked, glancing at the oven to avoid the lift of her sly smile.

"It's a surprise," she teased, her voice low and playful. "And slow down there, deputy, this isn't just any drink—it's got enough kick to make a mule jealous."

"Good thing I'm not a mule, then," Trent shot back, raising his glass in a mock salute before taking another sip. The liquid courage was smooth but packed a punch, warming him from the inside out.

"All right, spill it," he urged, setting down his empty glass on the coffee table. The flirtatious tension between them was palpable, an electric current that charged the air with expectation. "What did Vee have to say about our town's risqué history?"

Maggie rested a hip on the counter, the pose doing something rude to his loins. "Weeeell," she began, "Vee is a font of information and advice, I'll tell you that much. And somehow the accent makes the dirt sound even dirtier."

"Yeah, no, British people suck. They're always naming things after their lady parts. Like Fanny. And Regina, which is not pronounced how you would hope it would be..."

They shared a laugh made slick with social lubricant.

Maggie arched an eyebrow, leaning in closer. "And here I thought Townsend Harbor was all apple pies and church picnics."

"Oh, it is," Trent replied. "But those apple pies are laced with hallucinogens, and those church picnics get real *weird*."

"Apparently, there were a few more—ahem—'pies' being shared than we knew about." Her laughter was infectious, and he found himself grinning like an idiot.

"It's so impossible to turn down good pie," he quipped, enjoying the way her lips curled into a smile at his pun. "I've never been good at it, as you know."

"Deputy Trent McGarvey. Are you being bad right now?" she replied, her gaze lingering on him a moment too long. "Because what would happen if these walls could talk?"

"I'd just hope they're discreet," Trent said, chuckling. "Can't have the town scandal overshadowing your podcast debut."

"True," she conceded, tucking a strand of red hair behind her ear. "Though, I must admit, learning about everyone's...appetites has been rather enlightening."

"Enlightening?" he echoed, the word hanging in the air like a challenge. "Do tell."

"Let's just say"—she leaned in, her breath warm against his ear—"that some appetites are best explored without restraint."

"Sounds like a recipe for trouble," he managed, his voice rougher than he intended. His heart raced as the heat of her closeness seeped into his skin.

"Or for an unforgettable night," she countered, her voice dropping to a sultry whisper.

Trent swallowed hard. Their banter was spiraling into uncharted territory that made every nerve in his body sing.

The complicated martini wasn't the only thing tonight with a hidden agenda.

"Townsend Harbor's got more secrets than a nun's knicker drawer," she said with a playful glint in her eye.

"Never pegged you for the religious type," Trent quipped, his attempt to ride the wave of innuendo feeling more like a dog paddling in the deep end.

"I don't get on my knees for just anyone," she replied, her voice dropping to a husky pitch that sent a jolt straight to Trent's core. "Though I do tend to call God's name at the most important parts."

He cleared his throat, trying to refocus.

Maggie tilted her head, the corners of her mouth twitching upward. She reached out, brushing her fingers against the fabric of Trent's shirt as if by accident, but the touch lingered, sending a ripple of electricity up his arm. She was casual, yet deliberate, like a cat pawing at a ball of yarn, unraveling him one thread at a time. She leaned forward, her eyes shining with unspoken promises as they locked on to his.

He detected a hint of mischief there, a silent dare for him to dive into the unknown waters she was charting. "You know, Trent, sometimes the best way to understand a subject," she murmured, her breath tickling his skin, "is to get up close and personal. To explore and understand it. Learn what makes it hum..."

Trent's breathing sped up as if he'd been caught in a foot chase, the kind that ended with hands on knees, gasping for air. Only this time, his racing pulse wasn't from running down a suspect—it was all her.

Maggie, with her wit sharp enough to slice through a man's defenses, had him teetering on the edge of a cliff called "What the Hell Are We Doing?"

"Michaels," he managed, the word half prayer, half curse as he willed his body not to betray the heady rush of desire.

"Call me Maggie," she said, her voice low and smooth like whiskey over ice. "Everyone else does." Her hand rested mere inches from his own—a distance that might as well have been a chasm and a hairsbreadth all at once.

He was about to close that gap, to bridge the space with a touch, when the mundane ding of the oven timer cut through the thickening air. Trent blinked, the spell momentarily broken, as Maggie sprang up to tend to her culinary surprise.

"Just wait until you get this in your mouth." She pulled out a tray of flaky pastries, their golden crusts promising a taste of the divine. "Pork rolls," she announced with a flourish, setting the tray on the counter. "It's from this little Polish/Puerto Rican bakery on Long Island—you wouldn't believe it. They were featured on that show... What's it called? *Shitty Snack Shacks*? *Fucky Food*?"

"I don't watch food on TV I can't immediately eat." Trent's lips quirked into a reluctant smile despite the simmering tension.

He watched as she fussed over the rolls, her movements deft yet unnecessarily dramatic, as if she were presenting a treasure unearthed from a culinary crypt.

"The place looks like a front for a Mafia burial ground, but those pork rolls are divine. They could start wars, end feuds, or, you know..." She trailed off, shooting a coy glance his way.

"Or make a man lose his damn mind?" he suggested, his words threading the needle between jest and earnest.

"Something like that," Maggie replied, her laugh ringing clear and bright. "Careful, though. They're hot."

Trent watched as she plated the pork rolls, her movements disjointed, betraying inner turmoil. The flush on her cheeks wasn't just from the heat of the kitchen; it was a bloom of embarrassment or excitement—he couldn't tell which. A fine sheen of perspiration had begun to glisten on her forehead, and she shot furtive glances at the crackling fireplace like an Old West gunslinger ready to draw.

"It's heating up in here," he said. "Why don't you take off your coat?"

Her response was immediate and over-the-top—a swift clasp of the belted jacket as if it were a life vest on the *Titanic*. "No!"

"Okaaaay..." Trent replied, eyebrows raised. "You sure? Because you look about two seconds away from spontaneously combusting. And if Vee had a lot to say, and the oven stays on, you'll probably just dehydrate."

She let out a breath that could've powered wind turbines, and her shoulders slumped in defeat, hair framing her face like flames licking the edges of paper. With a sheepish yet rueful grin, she admitted, "I invited you over to seduce you. I thought you were clever enough to pick up on that."

Trent stood frozen, arousal mingling with confusion. "Seduce me?" He was as dumbfounded as a rooster finding a peacock feather in its coop. Did that make him the cock? "I'm sorry, Maggie, but I read this all wrong."

"Didn't you hear what I said about the pork rolls?" Maggie retorted, gesturing wildly as if directing airport traffic. "They're basically a love letter stretching from New England to the Atlantic City boardwalk. Plus, 'pork' is practically a euphemism for what I was hoping we'd—"

"Listen, Michaels," Trent said, scratching the back of his neck and clutching her surname like the flimsy intimacy barrier it was, "I don't know if—"

"I mean, if we were diving into unsexy food, I would have made my famous Boston baked beans, because *nobody* wants to deal with those repercussions in bed."

She was adorably earnest, but her attempts at seduction were about as subtle as a foghorn in a library. It was clear she was out of her depth, floundering in a sea of awkward innuendo.

"Okay, I get it," he said softly, stepping closer. "Pork rolls equal matrimony. Got it. But let's put a pin in the culinary fore-play, shall we?"

"Foreplay?" Her eyes twinkled, though her cheeks burned scarlet.

"Metaphorically speaking," he clarified. His gaze now locked on to hers, he noticed the flicker of desire dancing in their depths.

"If you wanted foreplay, I'd have done something with bacon and probably some kind of glaze with—"

Trent couldn't let her finish the sentence, so he did the only thing he could think of by crowding her back toward the counter with his big body. Reaching down and lifting her onto the gran-ite, he placed his hand at the nape of her throat, testing the pulse fluttering like a caged bird.

"Maggie?" he growled, scowling at her as all the levity drained from his body.

"Yeah?" She blinked her owlish eyes at him.

"Shut up."

He robbed her of her chance to disobey by capturing her mouth with his own.

MAGGIE GASPED AS MCGARVEY'S LIPS TRAILED A HOT, wet path down her neck. The ache between her thighs intensified with every nip of his teeth, every swipe of his tongue.

If only she'd read *Cosmo* like the other girls, they might have gotten to this part sooner.

Yeah, a familiar, tobacco-roughened voice belched in her ear. *We both know you wasn't like the other girls.*

Fucking Charlie.

It was bad enough his name was still plastered all over the legal documentation proving her right to exist. Now she had to put up with that ferret-faced asswad's voice tearing around her head.

Damn him.

A sharp tug on her earlobe shattered the fantasy, jerking her back to the present.

With a growl, Maggie sank her nails into McGarvey's shoulders and pulled him closer, mentally squeezing Charlie out.

Hunh. Wouldn't have figured you for the type to spread them for a guy who's so...fancy.

Anger flared, hot and bright.

As if Charlie had anything to say when it came to seduction. He was the kind of guy who considered her bending over to load the dishwasher a sexual proposition.

McGarvey pulled back, eyes narrowing as he studied her face. "Hey," he said, his passion-laced voice low and rough. "What's going on up there?"

Maggie forced a smile and trailed her fingers down his chest. "Nothing. Nothing at all. Why don't you come back here and remind me what we were doing?"

He caught her wrist, stilling her movements. "Nice try. But I can tell you're distracted. And for what I'm planning, I need your *full* attention."

Maggie swallowed against the lump in her throat. *Goddamn detail-noticing motherfucker.* His gaze was too perceptive, his mind too sharp.

With a sigh, Maggie dropped her hands to her sides. "It's... Charlie."

"Your almost-ex?" he asked, raising an eyebrow.

"The same," she admitted, feeling her cheeks grow warm. "He has this annoying habit of popping into my head at the worst times."

"Like right now?" he asked, a hint of humor lacing his words.

"Exactly," she said, looking down at her hands.

She waited a beat, anticipating the subtle shift in his features that would telegraph jealousy. Disappointment. Uninterest.

When these failed to materialize, she continued. "It's kind of like he's got a timeshare in the part of my brain that's determined not to let me enjoy any damn thing."

McGarvey studied her for a long moment, expression calm and thoughtful. "If this is too soon—"

"I... No. I mean, it's not. Like, at all." She made a vague gesture between them. "I just can't seem to turn my brain off, you know?"

"I know."

"I'm sorry," she said. "I'm basically ruining the entire mood."

"Don't apologize." He cupped her face in his hands, tilting her chin up to meet his gaze. "Talk to me. Tell me what sort of bullshit the bastard's saying."

"You know what?" Maggie said, fixing what she hoped was a seductive smile on her face. "I'd much rather you drown him out."

Hooking her ankles behind him, she pulled him closer.

Once again, Maggie felt herself melting, lost in the sweet press of his lips. She sighed into the kiss, warmth pooling low in her belly.

McGarvey's hands skimmed up her sides, clever fingers finding the underside of her breasts. She arched into his touch with a gasp, desire flickering to life inside her.

You didn't use to like it when I tried to tongue ya. Always bitching that you could still taste the pastrami I had for lunch, like you wasn't the one who packed it for me.

"Fuck's sake!" Maggie growled. Drawing back, she exhaled a hot, impatient sigh.

"Ready to talk *now*?" McGarvey asked, the self-destruction-worthy dimple flashing in his left cheek as he studied her face.

"I'm sorry," she said again, then, remembering he'd already told her not to apologize, blundered ahead full speed. "You've been so patient with me, and I—"

"We have all the time in the world," he said. "We can take it as slow as we need to."

He ducked his head, demonstrating by trailing kisses along her neck at a deliciously maddening pace. Maggie tipped her head back, eyes fluttering shut.

He dragged his lips to the sensitive spot just below her earlobe, flicking his tongue out to taste the hollow there. Shivers cascaded down her spine, and she grabbed his shoulders to steady herself, her breath hitching. He traced the curve of her hip before gently gripping the soft flesh.

Hips like that, at least a man will know you can cook.

The sound of her father's voice drifted through her mind, as familiar as the cadence of her own heartbeat.

"Okay," Maggie announced, sitting bolt upright, her eyes flying open. "Timeout."

McGarvey paused, brows drawing together in concern. "What is it? Am I moving too fast?"

"No, not at all. I just..." She shook her head, fully aware of how batshit crazy she must look right now. "For the record, I was really hoping we could skip this whole part and start fresh tonight, but since I've got an entire choir of misogynistic assholes chirping like cracked-out crickets in my ear, I guess we've gotta go there."

Hugging her trench tighter around her, Maggie crossed her ankles and took a deep breath.

"About you and Sheriff Forrester—"

McGarvey nodded knowingly. "I thought it might have something to do with that."

And a very particular something at that.

"Would you say she's more your usual type?"

He blinked at her, a furrow creasing his smooth brow as he looked down at her, surprise flickering in his eyes. "My usual type?" he repeated.

Maggie held her breath, silently cursing herself for bringing it up. But it was too late to take it back now. Instead, she tried to lighten the mood with a playful smile. "You know, tall, tawny, leggy, athletic raven-haired beauty in law enforcement. Um, basically the complete opposite of me?"

"Ah." Understanding dawned on his face, and he leaned back

against the counter. "Maggie, Sheriff Forrester is my boss. Don't you—"

"I mean if she *weren't* your boss," she interrupted.

"Let me finish." And why the gravel in his tone made her feel like she'd swallowed a brick, Maggie wasn't exactly certain. "Sheriff Forrester is my boss. We're around each other constantly. Late nights. Early mornings. Empty parking lots. If I wanted to still be fucking her, I'd still be fucking her. Make sense?"

Well, it did right up until the not-at-all unpleasant highlight reel of two such attractive people sport-fucking all over this Hallmark postcard of a town began unfurling in her mind.

Still, a welcome change from Charlie in his pit-stained tank top, his straight, crisp armpit hair like a full set of bangs as he plucked at an orange spot above the left nipple and issued the invitation for her to smell it and tell him if it was from the chicken parm or steak pizzaiola so he would know how long he'd been wearing it.

"I suppose," she said, fighting the urge to gnaw the inside of her lip.

"Then why don't you look like you believe me?"

His words were meant to reassure her, but Maggie felt the twist of insecurity in her gut all the same. "An overabundance of investigative skepticism?"

From the way his eyes softened, McGarvey obviously knew it was a blatant ploy on her part but seemed to be willing to assist her in perpetuating it.

"Oh, yeah baby," he said, positioning himself in front of her once more. "Hit me with that sexy journalist jargon."

Maggie narrowed her eyes at him in mock censure. "Are you making fun of me, deputy?"

"Wouldn't dream of it," he replied, the traces of amusement lingering in his eyes as his gaze moved down to her mouth. "Not when I could dream about this instead."

He traced a line down the side of her face before his knuckles brushed against her mouth. The touch was a mere flutter of contact, but it sent sparks darting up and down her spine.

His lips met hers in a gentle kiss that was all the more electrifying for its softness. He moved his hands to her waist, scooting her toward the counter's edge before cupping her knees.

"Open them," he ordered her. "Open your legs for me, Maggie Michaels."

And her body complied even though her brain did not.

I'll bet him and that tasty piece of a sheriff did it just like this after the Christmas party. On her desk. Or a file cabinet. Maybe the copier. I seen that in a movie once—

"But if you *had* to choose a type..." Maggie found herself mumbling against his lush lips.

McGarvey stilled, his next breath deep and slow.

They stayed silent for several heartbeats, a charged moment full of potential. Then he stepped closer to her, so close that the heat from his body brushed against hers.

"I know," she said. "I know I don't have any claim on your history, and it's not really any of my business, but—"

He captured her chin in a gentle grip and tipped it up until she was looking into his eyes. "My type is a woman who isn't afraid to call me on my bullshit. My type is the kind of woman who can turn wordplay into foreplay. My type, Maggie Michaels, is *you*."

How was it possible for one man to undo decades of damage with a few simple words? She didn't know, but gods, she was grateful for it.

"Thank you," she whispered, realizing he probably had no idea what she was actually thanking him for.

McGarvey smiled, brushing his thumb over her lower lip. "This is all the thanks I'll ever need."

Their mouths were a hairsbreadth from meeting when *more words* came tumbling out of hers.

"So you're saying you *haven't* been with anyone my size?"

McGarvey paused mid-lean, the dimple returning for an encore as he shook his head.

"I'm sorry," she sputtered, lifting her hands to her face. "I don't know why I asked that. That's a lie. I do. The way you were around the sheriff, how you were tripping all over yourself..." Her throat tightened, cutting off the remainder of her words.

In an instant, his face shifted from earnest to angry. His jaw clenched, and his eyes narrowed as he looked at her. "Fuck me. You didn't think I was embarrassed about being caught by my boss. You thought I was embarrassed about being caught with *you*."

The truth of it hit Maggie like a slap across the face. To her horror, she felt tears welling up in her eyes, and she tried desperately to blink them away.

"Hey," McGarvey murmured, his anger evaporating as quickly as it had appeared. He reached out to touch her arm, but Maggie pushed him away and covered her face with her hands.

Her vision began to blur as her lower lip twitched into a wobble.

God. Fucking. Damn it.

As tears spilled down her cheeks, she felt the solid warmth of McGarvey's hands on her knees.

"Even if you're not embarrassed by me," she said, her voice shaky, "I need you to know that I know I'll never be 'that girl.'"

McGarvey furrowed his brow, puzzled. "What girl?"

"You know," Maggie continued. "*That girl*. The one who sits alone at a coffee shop, and people walking by fall in love by accident. The girl that's pretty enough to pretend to be surprised when people tell her she is. The one whose hair looks effortlessly sexy in a messy bun, and having a sense of humor is a bonus feature instead of a requirement that justifies her presence. The one whose messes get to be endearing because it's a relief to know she's not as perfect as she looks."

McGarvey shook his head in disbelief. "No, *you* look, Michaels," he began, leaning in so close that she could feel the warmth of his breath on her face. His eyes were fierce, a storm brewing just off the coast. "I don't know what kind of asshole your ex was or what he said to you to make you think you're anything but a fucking feast for every single one of my senses, but I can assure you that by the time the sun drags its ass up over the horizon in the morning, you will know exactly how I feel about every part of your body."

The intensity of his words sent a shiver down Maggie's spine, making her heart race and her palms sweat. She searched his face for any sign of insincerity but found none. The truth was there, burning in his eyes like twin beacons, guiding her out of the fog of self-doubt.

So why did his declaration piss her right the hell off?

"I don't need your reassurance, okay?" she said, her voice trembling slightly. "I know that I'm allowed to love my body, and dress however the fuck I want. I know I'll never lack for men who want to fuck me. But before I'll ever get to know whether they like me, I have to make sure they like my body type first because I'm never not aware that I repulse certain men just by existing. I'm never not aware that for those men, any other weird, or annoying, or undesirable quality I have will always be multiplied by my size."

McGarvey's face remained impassive, but his gaze held a softness that made her pulse surge. He seemed to be searching for the right words to say, but they were lost somewhere between his brain and his tongue. Instead, he simply looked at her—*really* looked at her—and she could feel his gaze peeling back the layers of her soul.

Just then, Roxie trotted over, her tail wagging as she ran into the legs of all three barstools before gently nuzzling Maggie's ankle. As her hands fell from her face, she caught sight of her mascara-streaked fingers and felt a jolt of mortification.

"Shit," she muttered, staring down at her ruined makeup. "This is just great."

McGarvey took a step back, and, for a heartbeat, she thought he intended to turn around to leave.

She probably wouldn't have even blamed him.

But instead, he walked over to the counter, dampened a paper towel, and brought it back to her. Maggie stared at it, expecting him to hand it to her. Instead, he guided her hand back to her side and began to gently dab her tear-stained face himself.

"Here," he said, his voice gentle as he wiped the tear tracks from her cheeks. "Hold still."

"I'm okay," she said, attempting to swat him away.

"You've been crying, and you wear contacts," he said, his voice soft but laced with the faintest hint of humor. "One slip with those nails, and your vitreous humor will be part of your skin care routine."

She couldn't help the small, surprised laugh that bubbled up from her chest, even as she fought to keep her eyes from filling with fresh tears. His touch was featherlight, soothing away the sting of her earlier humiliation as easily as he blotted the mascara-smudged tracks on her cheeks.

"Thanks," Maggie whispered, feeling an odd sense of vulnerability as she sat still. The warmth of his hands on her skin sent shivers down her spine, while the intoxicating scent of him filled her senses.

"Better," he said, stepping back to survey his work. She nodded, touched by his concern.

"Well, this is officially the worst seduction ever, yeah? I went to all this trouble and couldn't even leverage the one tool in my arsenal that has anything to do with sex on purpose."

McGarvey raised an eyebrow, a hint of amusement dancing in his eyes. "And what tool would that be?"

"Vee talked me into this ridiculously lush silk slip," she explained, rolling her eyes.

"Go put it on," he said.

Maggie hesitated, suddenly unsure if that was the right move.

"Maybe I'd better just take a rain check for now." She slid off the counter, her feet barely touching the ground before McGarvey's hand seized her arm. He yanked her back, and she found herself flush against his body, feeling the hard planes of his chest pressed against her curves. As she gazed up into his eyes, a full-body chill shivered through her. The hunger in his leonine gaze was raw, almost feral.

"Go put on that silk slip," he growled, his voice low and commanding.

"McGarvey, I—" she began, but he silenced her with a firm but gentle hand at her throat.

"That wasn't a fucking request."

Maggie swallowed beneath his grip. "That's the thing. It's already on. Beneath this coat."

She watched the recognition dawn in the depths of his eyes and ripple outward through his features.

"I have an idea," he said.

Taking her by the hand, he led her to the bedroom and pointed her toward her closet. "You're going to go in there, and you're going to come out in whatever you feel the sexiest in. I'm going to wait out here for as long as you need. Got it?"

Maggie nodded, stepping into the closet and closing the door behind her.

Running her fingers over the velvet hangers, she experienced the jolt of unwelcome revelation.

They all belonged to her life with Charlie.

The only item she owned that her bloviating gasbag of a husband had neither acquired nor touched was the one clinging to her skin beneath this coat.

Maggie drew in a deep breath, unbelted the trench, and let it puddle to the floor. When she opened them again, she made herself meet her eyes in the full-length mirror affixed to the back of the closet door.

Now or never.

She found McGarvey lounging against the headboard, shirtless, watching her with hooded eyes. Maggie paused in the threshold, suddenly shy under the intensity of his stare.

"Come here," he rasped.

Heart in her throat, she crossed the room. McGarvey's hands settled on her hips, fingers tracing the curve through the silk.

"You're exquisite," he murmured, dragging his eyes down the length of her body. Maggie flushed, torn between embarrassment and pleasure at the blatant appreciation in his eyes. "And all mine," McGarvey added, meeting her eyes again. His smile turned predatory, sending a thrill of anticipation down her spine.

She smiled, desire melting her lingering shyness, and leaned down to capture his mouth in a searing kiss.

His hands roamed over her body, leaving trails of fire in their wake. By the time he eased her onto the bed beneath him, need pulsed through her veins like liquid flame.

"Please," she breathed against his mouth.

His lips curved into a knowing smile. "Patience," he murmured. Maggie whimpered in protest, arching into his touch as his fingers skimmed along the edge of her slip. McGarvey's breath hitched, his restraint visibly fraying. "You're going to be the death of me," he said, fisting a hand in her hair to angle her mouth up to his. She pushed at the waistband of his jeans, shoving the offending fabric down and freeing him.

He hissed in pleasure as she wrapped her fingers around his length, stroking in a slow, deliberate rhythm. His hips bucked into her grip, and Maggie grinned against his mouth, relishing the effect she had on him.

"Enough." Catching her wrist, McGarvey dragged it away from him and pinned it above her head, slipping his other hand beneath the fabric to find the source of her need.

Maggie arched with a gasp, writhing under the skillful strokes of his fingers. "Trent," she whimpered, beyond caring how desperate she sounded. His eyes gleamed, his breath coming fast.

"Not yet," he said hoarsely. She moaned in protest, but McGarvey refused to be moved. Not until she was trembling on the edge of release did he finally relent, settling between her thighs.

She cried out as he filled her, the slip bunching around her waist. He stilled for a breathless moment, gazing down at her with a mix of awe and tenderness that made her heart ache.

Then he began to move, and Maggie lost herself in the slow, relentless rhythm of their joined bodies. The rest of the world faded away, leaving only McGarvey and the exquisite pleasure spiraling through her once more.

Tonight, there were no doubts or fears. Only this—only them. And it was enough.

With a slow smirk, he reached out, pushing the top of her negligee aside, revealing the fullness of her breasts. A low growl rumbled from his throat as he palmed them, pushing them together. His thumbs brushed against her nipples, the contact sending a jolt of pleasure straight to her core.

Taking one nipple between his thumb and forefinger, McGarvey gently rolled it, sending electricity sparking through Maggie's body. Her back arched in response; a breathy moan escaped her lips. He continued the sweet torment on the other nipple, alternating between pinching and pulling gently, then curled his hips into her, filling her slow and deep.

She gasped, digging her fingers into his shoulders as he began to move. Each stroke brought her higher, closer to the edge, the pleasure building into a cresting wave.

"Trent..." she said again, her voice shaky with need. He silenced her with a kiss, his lips devouring hers as he continued his relentless rhythm, then slid his hand down between them, finding her sensitive nub and rubbing slow circles around it.

"That's it, baby," he urged.

A surge of pleasure rushed through Maggie, coiling tighter and tighter within her. She keened against his mouth, writhing beneath him as he drove her over the brink.

His breath hitched as she tightened around him, her walls convulsing in pleasure.

"*Fuck*," McGarvey roared, losing himself inside her in hot pulses.

Maggie came back to herself slowly, her cheek pressed against the warmth of his chest. His heart thudded steadily under her ear, his breathing deep and even. The slip had pooled down around her waist at some point, but McGarvey made no move to adjust it.

"You okay?"

Maggie smiled, nuzzling closer. "Mmm. Very okay."

McGarvey huffed a quiet laugh, squeezing her gently. "Good. Just wanted to make sure I didn't break you."

"Not a chance," she said dryly. She tilted her head back to meet his eyes, tracing the familiar lines of his face. "You know, for someone so particular about everything else in your life..."

He arched a brow. "Yes?"

"Nothing."

His eyes softened, crinkling at the corners. "Hey." He nudged her chin up with a knuckle. "Where'd you go?"

Maggie shook her head, smiling through the sting of tears. "Nowhere. I'm right here."

She leaned up and kissed him, slow and sweet. McGarvey made a low sound of contentment, tightening his arms around her.

"You are fucking irresistible, you know that?" He ran his hands down her sides, flexing when they came to the curve of her ass. "Every inch of you."

He deepened the kiss as his hands roamed over her body. By the time they broke apart, Maggie was breathless and trembling against him.

"I want this," she whispered, meeting his eyes. "I want you."

A slow, wicked smile spread across McGarvey's face. He gripped her hips and lifted, settling her more firmly against him.

"Well then, Miss Michaels," he purred, voice like gravel, "I believe you have my full attention."

She swallowed hard, anticipation and nerves swirling in her stomach.

He tilted her chin up, staring into her eyes. "You still with me?"

She nodded, unable to speak. His hands were warm against her skin, grounding and reassuring.

"Good." McGarvey leaned in, breath ghosting over her lips. "Because I'm nowhere near done with you yet."

He kissed her again, igniting a fire in Maggie's veins. By the time he pulled back, she was panting, desire clouding her thoughts. She whimpered, arching into his touch.

"Shh." He nipped at her jaw, then soothed the sting with his tongue. "I've got you."

One hand slid under her gown, teasing along the edge of her bra. Maggie gasped, clutching at his shoulders.

"Off," he commanded, grasping the hem of the slip.

She hurried to comply, tossing the silken sheath aside. His gaze raked over her, hot and appreciative, before he swooped in to capture one nipple in his mouth.

"Please," she gasped, desire burning white-hot in her veins. She needed more, needed all of him. "I need you again."

McGarvey chuckled. "Patience."

Dizziness swept over Maggie, and she clutched at him for support. He wrapped an arm around her waist, pulling her in close.

"We're doing it my way. Understand?"

Only when he guided her up to her knees on the bed facing the mirror affixed to the back of her bedroom door did she understand what he had in mind.

Maggie swallowed, heart pounding, and met his gaze in the mirror. His eyes were dark with desire, but there was a question in their depths. She knew, then, that he would stop if she asked. But she didn't want to stop. She wanted everything he was willing to give her.

And more besides.

"Now, look at yourself," he added, positioning himself behind her, his hands resting gently on her hips. "And see what I see."

Maggie's reflection stared back at her, flushed and bright-eyed. Her tousled red hair framed her face like a corona of flame, making her eyes look greener in the dim light. But it was the array of freckles scattered across her skin that caught McGarvey's attention next.

"See this?" he murmured, tracing one finger over the constellation, starting from her neck down to her shoulder and further down across her bare torso.

Maggie shivered under his touch, goosebumps blooming over every inch of her skin. "Yes."

"This is mystery," he whispered. "Even if it took me a hundred years, I'd want to map every single one. And this?" He traced the curve of her shoulder down to the swell of her breast, cupping it to relieve her of its weight. "This is beauty."

He kissed the spot he'd traced, his lips hot against her fevered skin. Maggie arched toward him instinctively.

"And this," he murmured, trailing his hands down to cup her ample hips. "This is desire."

She met her own eyes in the mirror—flushed and wanton, lips parted and eyes heavy-lidded with need. She looked...like sex.

Like passion.

Like need.

Like a woman.

He moved his fingers lower to circle her navel. "And this?" he asked. "Curvature that invites my touch." Maggie felt a shiver run down her spine at his words, her entire body humming with anticipation. "This," he continued, sliding one of his hands down to trace the outside of her thigh, "is strength."

And then he was moving her, guiding her onto the bed until she was on her back and he was above her, his body a delicious weight pressing against hers. His mouth found hers again, his hands wandering over her with a possessive touch that left her gasping.

"Tell me you want this. Tell me you want me."

"I want you," she breathed.

McGarvey's smile was slow and predatory. "Good girl." He

kissed her again, deep and claiming, and Maggie surrendered to the flames.

TEN

Hook and book

TO ARREST SOMEONE

THE NEXT MORNING, TRENT'S PERMA-SMILE FALTERED when he eased his cruiser into the chaos at Water Street and Townsend Boulevard. Someone had roused the rabble, and the citizens of Townsend Harbor had split like a bad romance over the city's proposal to replace the one working stoplight downtown with a roundabout. In lieu of torches and pitchforks, the local mob brandished signs that wobbled in the air like a flock of confused pigeons, each scrawled with bold proclamations either damning or praising the traffic circle that had yet to exist.

Intersections give me erections! one sign declared, while another retorted, *Don't be square—put a circle there!*

He let out a chuckle, shaking his head at the small-town fervor. The scene was a living, breathing embodiment of "quirky" —the kind of thing you'd expect to see in a feel-good flick where the biggest scandal involved Grandma's famous pie recipes.

A late-winter mist had given way to a vibrant blue canvas with fluffy clouds scattered about like cotton balls. The sunshine was golden and warm against the cool, crisp air. The charming Victorian buildings lined the streets, their colorful façades and ornate details a perfect backdrop to the adorable drama.

Damn, this was better than a No Point Shakespeare Company's production of *A Comedy of Errors*.

With a heavy sigh, Trent leaned back in his seat and closed his eyes for the space of a centering breath, realizing some of the ever-present tension in his shoulders was absent. Damn, but last night had been something else. His lips curled at the memory of Maggie's soft moans, the taste of her skin, the way she'd clung to him like ivy. He'd had to use every bit of his willpower to peel himself from bed and show up for his shift.

Days like this, he almost looked forward to. Nothing this hilarious ever happened in Albuquerque.

For a small town, they sure did have strong opinions about changes in infrastructure. The retirees who showed up to these kinds of protests had little else to do on a Sunday morning.

Trent parked amid the chaos and climbed out of his cruiser, scanning the crowd for any signs of violence. Thankfully, other than a few heated arguments and insults being hurled, nothing seemed out of control.

His ears were bombarded with the cacophony of discord as he wedged his way through the throngs of agitated townsfolk. Other officers had parked in the bank parking lot down the way to keep a distant eye on what had been a peaceful protest until Myrtle Le Grande showed up with a one-ton truck full of her stock in trade.

On this, day two of the protest, the seventy-something local queer icon and manure maven had backed her truck up to the side of the anti-traffic-circle warriors and jettisoned a large pile of excrement onto the walkway. As the deputy in charge on shift, it was his responsibility to de-escalate the situation.

Myrtle leaned on a big shovel next to a knee-high—well, thigh high for her—pile of dung that smelled so ripe his eyes began to water.

"Well, if it isn't Deputy Delish in the flesh," she greeted him with a knowing smile.

"Keep it in your pants, Myrtle," Trent quipped before turning to address several red-faced elderly with their bloomers in a bunch.

At their helm was the mighty Miss Janet, one of the local Christian soldiers who always seemed to be in charge of these debacles.

"We told her to keep her BS out of here, and look what she did!" Janet screeched.

"Hey, screw you, Janet, this is not your basic bitch bullshit. It's mostly llama dung, compost, and some horse urine to balance the pH!"

Trent put a staying hand on Myrtle's painfully thin shoulder. "This is now a contaminated area," he announced loud enough for the few dozen pink-cheeked stoplight enthusiasts. "You'll all need to get back while we contain the mess and get it cleaned up."

Myrtle made an obscene gesture of triumph. "That's what I'm talking about, McGarvey—you clear out these holy rollers and their boring signs! Shoo!" To his chagrin, she lifted her metal shovel and waved it at the encroaching conservative coven.

Trent whirled on her, doing his best not to loom over an old woman who came up to his nipples. "Myrtle...this is a serious offense. Rest that shovel on the ground or I'll be forced to take it."

"Your face says you're pissed, but those dreamy eyes are all afterglow," she teased, nudging him with her elbow, though she put the shovel's metal head back on the concrete. "Finally pulled our Maggie, eh? You sly fox."

"Mind out of the gutter, would you? I'm on duty." But the smirk tugging at the corner of his mouth betrayed him. It was true: he felt lighter than usual, despite the weight of his uniform and the morning's coffee yet to kick in.

"Sure, sure." She winked, lowering her voice to a conspiratorial whisper. "Heard she's quite the handful."

"More than a handful," he muttered, scanning past another cluster of residents, "and nowhere to be seen."

The truth was, Trent was begrudgingly fond of the chaos

Maggie brought with her—it stirred something deep within him, something he thought he had packed away when he left Albuquerque behind. But damn if it didn't make his job harder, especially when he found himself tiptoeing to the line of his own ethical no man's land.

Shaking his head, he realized something devastating in real time.

He was a goner.

Like, this was cause for some concern.

"Hiya, Myrtle." Local mechanic and ex-con Gabe Kelly sauntered over with his fiancée, Gemma, a stunning brunette with a sleek ponytail and a bangin' power suit.

"Gabe, Lyra, tell these Jesus freaks what you think of the church at large!" Myrtle yelled, pointing the fully automatic kill clip that was the ex-Catholic Bostonian's vocabulary. He'd spray these old folks with four-letter bullets, shrug his shoulders, and eat a giant sandwich while watching the carnage play out.

Lyra McKendrick, Gemma's twin and Gabe's future sister-in-law, had turned up for the protest, and if anyone had Myrtle's back, and vice versa, it was these two. Gemma, Trent remembered, had a pathological avoidance of all forms of conflict, while Lyra prided herself on wading into the middle with her righteous indignation and a mean case of ASD savant syndrome. Think what you want about Lyra—she was usually just as correct as she was abrasive.

"Don't you dare," Trent warned, though whether it was to Myrtle, Lyra, or Gabe, he wasn't sure.

Probably all of them.

"Roundabouts are a menace!" barked an astonishingly blond man with a chin wattle that would make a turkey proud. Trent recognized him as Bradley Osgaard, the local self-appointed Port Townsend online censor, ran and moderated Port Townsend pages on various social media apps, turning them into his pathetic online echo chamber. His color was as ridiculously high as the belt cinching his chinos up to his armpits, voice quivering with passion as he shook his fist. "They'll have us going 'round in circles, dizzy and more lost than a one-legged duck in a pond!"

Lyra snorted, pinning him with her unflinching, unsettling eye contact. "Statistically speaking, they reduce traffic accidents by thirty-nine percent!" The thick-framed glasses she wore told them she ate statistics for breakfast.

"Arrest Myrtle the turd-le, officer, we demand it!" Janet, her cheeks flushed with the kind of fervor usually reserved for discount sales at the local bakery, clutched her cardigan over a house dress and cast dirty looks at Lyra's designer drip.

"Oh please, Janet, you're complaining a lot for someone who smells like an old bowl of onions sat in the fridge too long," Myrtle groused.

The pungent smell of manure thickened the air, clinging to clothes and churning stomachs. Trent grimaced, watching as protesters scattered to escape the stench. The woman had gigantic titanium balls to call someone out on their aroma.

He had to give it to Myrtle... It was the most effective and least violent protest disbandment he'd ever seen.

"Who is responsible for this biohazard?" Every time Trent heard Mayor Stewart's voice, he had the spine-curling urge to cover his no-no squares.

"Don't worry about it—the perpetrator is being dealt with." Trent eyed Myrtle, who scraped her shovel across the concrete with more enthusiasm than necessary.

"Dealt with? She should be arrested!" The mayor stabbed a finger at Myrtle. "Disturbing the peace, illegal dumping—she's a menace!"

"I understand your concern." Trent kept his tone neutral, though inwardly he itched to elbow the guy into the pile, so the smell would match his personality. Myrtle might be eccentric, but she'd taken things too far this time. Still, he was in no great hurry to slap handcuffs on her itty-bitty wrists. "Rest assured, the situation will be handled appropriately."

The mayor sniffed, clearly unappeased. "See that it is. Or on your head be it."

Trent gave the man his best *what-the-fuck-ever* look before replying, "Yes, sir." As much as he loved his job, sometimes he hated it. "I will have to ticket and fine you, Myrtle. And if you don't clean this up immediately..." He let the threat of arrest remain unspoken.

"Oh, I know—I brought my checkbook!" Myrtle grinned. "Worth every penny, and make sure you spell my middle name right. Here's my license."

Pulling a face, Trent took the black latex gloves out of his utility belt and donned them before taking the stained, well-used identification.

Janet stamped her clogs in protest. "This town's gone to pot ever since that woman and her sort moved here."

Lyra took a step in Janet's direction, a dangerous gleam in her dark eyes. "What do you mean, her sort? Why don't you teetotalers get a life, or at least a fucking hobby. Gathering a posse to bully an elderly lesbian isn't a good look."

"Who you calling elderly?" Myrtle chirped.

Uh oh.

Trent placed himself between the mini conclave squaring off like the generals meeting over the battlefield, their deeply weird armies bracketing them, waiting for the charge.

"Ms. McKendrick, Myrtle is in zero danger of anything like that happening." He put up a hand against the local lawyer's famously barbed tongue.

"I know that," she replied. "How about someone WikiLeak that to the right hand of Jesus queer-hating Christ over there?"

"And while you're at it, take this shit sack of a mayor and this Igor-looking muthafuckah out with the rest of this garbage." Gabe threw every bit of his Southie accent into his tone.

"I will not stand here and be spoken to like this!" Mayor Stewart's hair ruffled in the wind, showing the liver-spotted scalp beneath.

"Promise?" Myrtle said. "Why don't you take your little secretary and split?"

"Secretary?" Gabe's eyebrow went up.

"Yeah. Mayor Spewart's wife won't let him have female secretaries anymore, so he's stuck with Bradley O, the keyboard warrior who wants to be like Michael Vick but with humans."

"I'll sue you for libel!" the pinkening Bradley O threatened.

"Good luck," Myrtle spat. "The only lawyer in town is on my side."

"The devil is on your side!" Janet cried, making the sign of the cross.

Myrtle whirled on her. "I will jump-kick the ass fat out of your lip fillers, Janet, see if I don't!"

The corpulent Christian gestured to Trent, who was trying extra hard not to enjoy himself. "Did you hear that? She just threatened me with violence. I demand you press charges!"

Trent physically put himself between the two women over fifty, making sure no one threw what objectively promised to be the funniest punch in the world.

"I wasn't joking about clearing out of here, all of you." He pushed more authority into his tone. "For everyone's health and safety, you'll need to leave until this is clean. Everyone. No exceptions."

Janet and her clan balked. "But our First Amendment rights—"

"May be exercised on any other part of any other street but this one." He opened his arms to herd the crowd further away so another deputy could tape off the area.

Myrtle cheerfully took up her shovel and began to transfer her precious poop from the ground back to her truck. "Like I'd waste this grade-A...waste," she mumbled to herself.

"You're a waste of space," Bradley told her, tapping his pen on his clipboard. "This isn't over, Myrtle."

"Eat shit, Brad."

Trent realized too late that Myrtle wasn't giving the smug

secretary a suggestion, but a warning. And before he could stop her, she'd used the wood handle of her shovel to poke the man in the back of his knee, buckling it.

Before anyone could react, he was sprawled face-first in Myrtle's manure.

Brad flailed hilariously and finally made his way to his feet when he realized no one was going to help him up.

To be fair, most people were laughing too hard.

"Gather your henchman, mayor," Myrtle said, raising a gnarled middle finger.

"Arrest this...woman!" Mayor Stewart demanded. "She just assaulted my—employee!"

Gabe scoffed, wiping tears of mirth from his baby blues before folding his tattooed arms over a chest built in a prison weight room. "Oh, c'mon, Spewart, it can't taste any worse than your fumunda-laden dick, and he seems to gobble that just fine on the daily."

He and Lyra touched knuckles as Myrtle laughed so hard she dropped her shovel with a clang.

Janet, apparently having had her fill of profanity for the day, lashed out at Myrtle in the way only a Karen of the highest order could do. "Where's your abomination of a wife, Myrtle? Trouble in paradise? Living in sin not working out for you?"

"You keep my woman's name out of your whore mouth!" Myrtle pushed her sleeves up her little arms like post-spinach Popeye ready to open a can of whoop-ass.

Trent turned on Janet, the last of his good humor a martyr to her bigotry. "Ma'am, you'll take that hate speech somewhere else right now."

"Or what?" Janet's eyes turned ugly(er), lip lifting in a vampiric snarl. "Better to smell like onions than shit and *tuna*..."

"Oh, I'm about to lay down some dolphin-safe whoop-ass on this bi—"

Trent caught Myrtle as she advanced on the woman twice her

size and half again her height, before she could go all Will Smith on Janet's obviously fraudulent cheekbones.

Somewhere from behind the ringing in his ears caused by his elevating blood pressure, Trent heard the mayor demand Myrtle's arrest, along with that of a few others.

"You saw what she did! All of you!" The mayor pointed as if Myrtle wasn't dangling like a recalcitrant toddler from Trent's careful grip. "She's finally going to answer for her shenanigans!"

"Shenanigans? That was barely even hijinks!" Her eyes were bright and owlish with innocence. "How is it my fault his knee ran into my shovel?"

"I saw nothin'." Gabe shrugged, winking at Myrtle before casting Trent a stony look.

"I might have seen Bradley lunge first," Lyra added before turning to Trent with her unsettlingly frank assessment.

He wondered what she saw.

"You ask my client nothing until I meet you at the jail, you understand? And if this shit-covered motherfucker presses charges, I'll make sure every press outlet in town knows he was beaten up by a seventy-year-old woman who weighs all of seventy pounds."

"Hundred and six!" Myrtle insisted. "I'm back on carbs, and Gabe's been pumping iron with me."

"Shut your mouth, Myrtle!" Mayor Stewart ordered her.

"You first!" And damned if the crepey-skinned, bird-boned biddy didn't wrench out of Trent's gentle grip, drop to gather a handful of her product, and hurl it right into the mayor's face with the precision of post-roids A-Rod.

"This stops *now*," Trent growled.

For a moment, everyone (finally) hesitated, having caught the glint in his eye his father had once called his "fuck around and found out" look.

"Myrtle, drop those gloves to the pavement."

She complied.

"I'm sorry, but I'm placing you under arrest, for assault, but I won't cuff you unless I see you reach for that pile again, you hear me?"

When he expected her to be chastened, she turned around and secured her own wrists behind her back. "I can't be trusted around these ass-waffles. If Vee weren't with your lover at the Palace, she'd be here putting every single one of you to *shame*. To fucking shame!"

Reaching for his cuffs, Trent warmed them with his fingers before securing them loosely on her tiny wrists. "You have—"

"I know, I know... I have the right to remain silent, anything I say can and will be, blah blah blah... I've been getting arrested at protests since before you were born, kid."

After Mirandizing her properly, Trent allowed his crew to disperse the rest of the passionate protesters as he buckled the pungent lady into his back seat.

Ugh. He would never get the smell out, unless he could—

A thought hit him upside the head with all the force of the flat side of Myrtle's shovel.

"Wait just a second... Did you say that Maggie and Vee were at the Palace Hotel?" he asked his rearview mirror.

The little white lady turned impossibly paler, her eyes shifting in a way that told him her next words were an absolute lie.

"Nope? I said... Erm... Alice's... My pal, Alice. She wanted to meet Maggie, so Vee took her over there. She'll come and bail me out before I can squat and cough, and we'll go have victory drinks at Sirens. Maggie isn't working, so the drinks will be better."

Trent's temper spiked so incredibly hot he bit down on his lips so as not to say something the old woman didn't deserve.

She was the woman betraying him at the moment.

Goddamn.

The morning had been so perfect. Waking to Maggie's warm body beside him. Sinking into her as he pulled her to his chest. Burying his face into the fragrance of her hair.

Had she been planning to lie to him all day?

He had a perp in his back seat. His day crew at the crossroads. His boss had the day off.

And somehow...he couldn't bring himself to reach for his radio and send the town police to catch her in the act.

She'd be arrested for trespassing, and this time, Mayor Stewart wouldn't hesitate to throw the book at her.

He should have listened to Maggie in the first place when she asked if he'd stay with her.

And tied her to the fucking bed.

ELEVEN

Flame

SETTING A DRINK ON FIRE BEFORE SERVING. USUALLY SEEN IN SHOTS

"LET ME TELL YOU, UNTIL YOU'VE HAD TO EMPTY THREE gallons of urine out of a shop vac at the end of the Lieutenant John J. McCorkle fishing pier at three a.m. on a Sunday morning, you just haven't *lived*." Darby shot the rest of her whiskey and set her glass down with a satisfying thunk that punctuated the end of yet another killer story, this one about stage-managing Boston's annual Bondage Ball.

Maggie held a hand to her aching stomach with one hand, dabbing her eyes with the corner of her apron with the other. "How on earth did we never run into each other in Boston?"

"You know those Kelly boys," Darby said, swiping a knuckle at the corners of her thick lashes. "Notoriously territorial. They don't like to share, even with each other."

A smile tugged at the corner of Maggie's lips. "Especially with each other."

At the bail bonds office where they'd met, a friendship with the notoriously OCD and frequently demanding Mark Kelly would have been the last thing she have predicted. Especially since he'd tried to get her fired so frequently.

But that had been before they'd bonded over a shared love of *Love Island*.

"Another?" Maggie asked, lifting the bottle of bourbon.

"Why not?" Darby asked, her dark eyebrow lifting toward her crown of cotton-candy-pink hair. "I'm not driving."

"That's a relief," Kurt, who'd been oh-so-inconspicuously hovering near the garnish tray, muttered.

"Someone tie a tire iron to your testicles, or just being extra salty today for fun?" Darby asked, shooting him a pointed look.

"As delighted as I am that you've found someone who seems to share your penchant for stories involving mafiosi and bodily fluids, do you think you might be able to take a break from the *hot goss* to make the drink order I put in about a fucking year ago?"

Under normal circumstances, this would be about the time when Maggie considered the merits of braining Kurt with a swizzle stick.

But for some reason she didn't quite understand, she felt... calm? Relaxed? No. Serene.

Hell, even the eardrum-bloodying cacophony of voices, silverware scraping on ceramic, and the goddamn accordion player who'd set up shop on the beach below the restaurant's third-floor balcony and begun working his way through Weird Al's catalog hadn't managed to ruin her mood.

And that was even *after* a seagull had mayo-bombed the most perfect martini she'd made yet.

"And what are you thinking about that's got you smiling like the cat who deep-throated the canary?" Darby asked, a sly grin twisting her hot-pink pout.

"Oh my God," Kurt sighed, pinching the bridge of his nose. "I literally cannot with you two."

"Easy there," Maggie said. "Don't get your man-panties in a twist. I'll make your drinks now."

And to Maggie's great delight and Kurt's utter shock, she did just that. Quickly, and without even having to look up the recipes.

Kurt eyed them like they might sprout arms and pull a switchblade on him. "You've been practicing?" he asked.

"Something like that," she said.

And oh, how fucking delicious that something had been.

Flashes returned to her in lurid detail. Gasped breaths and hot words. Teeth, and tongues, and—

"So you and McGarvey, huh?" Darby waggled her eyebrows suggestively.

Maggie blinked at her, feeling heat bake the surface of her cheeks.

"And before you ask, Judy in dispatch is already putting the word out that you two are an item. And by item, I mean informing anyone who happens to call in to the station that Sherriff Forrester busted you two doing it in the basement of this very building."

"How did she— I mean... Where the hell would she get that idea?" Maggie sputtered, turning to the bar under the guise of returning the bourbon to its rightful slot.

Darby waited her out, her expression patient and amused when Maggie turned back around.

"Listen," she said, stretching a hand across the bar's scarred surface. "As a fairly recent transplant who's also been on the receiving end of Townsend Harbor's rumor mill where a certain former sheriff is concerned, there's a couple things you really ought to know." Lifting the glass, Darby let the amber liquid kiss her lips.

"Such as?" Maggie asked, picking up a damp bar mop and swiping away a small flurry of margarita salt.

Darby thumbed a salt flake she'd missed and flicked it over her shoulder. "Such as, being seen talking in public for more than ten seconds is tantamount to foreplay."

"Uh huh," Maggie said, mentally reviewing every run-in she and McGarvey had had since she arrived.

"Also, if you're seen entering a building together, someone is definitely going to assume it's to fuck."

Had Darby delivered her second pronouncement a moment sooner, she'd be wearing the watery Sprite Maggie had been nursing. "I see," she said.

"And if you ever want to keep something a secret, under no circumstances are you to involve Myrtle Le Grande. I love the woman, but freight trains are subtler."

Fucking *now* she told her. Because if everything had gone according to the plan they'd worked out, Myrtle would have been a significant part of McGarvey's afternoon.

Maggie cleared her throat. "Gabe certainly seemed to think she was capable of keeping a secret."

"Please." Darby snorted. "Gabe's idea of a secret is something that you have to threaten people with bodily violence not to disclose."

Maggie's shoulders suddenly felt heavy, the heart beneath them equally leaden. At least she'd elected to make her earlier sojourn back to the Palace Hotel with Vee instead of Myrtle.

"Speaking of secrets, please thank Ethan for me," she said, eager to change the subject. "Those letters he had you bring me from the Townsend family's personal archive were more helpful than you know."

Darby's eyes brightened. "So the note he sent with them made sense to you?"

"No, his note was fucking vague and obtuse." Maggie laughed. "But I was able to do a lot of interpreting based on context."

"He's a subtle bastard," Darby said dreamily, staring into her glass as if the ruggedly handsome sheriff's face may be haunting the bottom of it. "So...did you find anything?"

"Did I find anything?" Maggie echoed, giving Darby a sly grin. "I found *everything*."

Darby raised an eyebrow. "Oh? Do tell."

Maggie took a deep breath, her mind racing as she recalled the moment everything clicked into place. She remembered sitting at her kitchen table, the worn parchment spread out before her, the faint scent of aged ink filling her nostrils. Her body buzzing as her eyes moved over the looping, elaborate script.

She had read the letter, written in overblown Victorian

English by none other than Ethan's great-great-great-grandfather, Everett Townsend. The recipient? One Reginald Stewart.

The body...exceedingly odd.

At first.

My Most Esteemed Compatriot,

It is with heavy heart that I'm afraid I must write to you of a matter which I fear you might find upsetting. You will recall our previous arrangement, wherein I found myself in need of an agile and dedicated mouser to address the rat infestation which the Midnight Mariner was beset with. At such a time as I did confide in you, you were kind enough to give into my keeping a certain Scottish Fold you'd adopted from a shipyard in Glasgow. Well, I regret to inform you that, far from the agile and enterprising creature you presented her to be, she proved to be a significant nuisance to both the ship and its passengers. Not only was she utterly uninterested in reducing the number of rats onboard, but myself and several other members of the crew began to suspect that this willful creature was actually assisting the diseased rodents in their escape. It was for this reason that I found it necessary to bind the beast and fling it overboard in a burlap sack, where I could be assured she would not bedevil either of us any further. As our fortunes are so intimately linked in this respect, I know I may be assured of your gratitude for resolving so noisome an impediment to our combined venture. Pray, good sir, if I may be so bold, a financial contribution to our enterprise would be a most welcome demonstration of your continued faith in our shared endeavor. Though I doubt if any significant resources will be willingly allocated to recovering one missing pussy, all things considered.

Sincerely and entirely yours,
Timmothy Scott Stewart

P.S. Should you be searching for the means by which your late pussy so stealthily provided her intended prey a means of escape, I'd recommend you conduct a thorough search of her typical haunts. It seems she was somewhat more resourceful than either of us realized.

Darby nodded, listening intently.

"I mean, subtle, Great-Grandaddy Townsend was not," Maggie said, coming to the end of her summary.

"Fucking right?" Darby asked, shaking her head. "So you think it was really the old Mayor Stewart and Grandaddy Townsend who were into the human trafficking?"

"Certainly seems that way to me. And if Madame Katz somehow found out and was using the tunnels to the Palace Hotel to help them escape, that would be more than enough motive for those two to want to make her disappear."

Darby heaved a disgusted sigh. "Fucking men."

"Tell me about it," Maggie agreed. "This town has more drama than a telenovela."

And now she was part of it. Really, she had tried to resist becoming involved.

Sort of.

A little.

But if McGarvey somehow found out about her involvement in today's little stunt... Well, things were going to get significantly more complicated.

Complicated. Like the man whose voice lived in her brain. The man whose touch lingered on her skin. The man who—

—was standing in the doorway of Sirens looking like he was about to take away someone's birthday.

And maybe beat them with it.

Which shouldn't even be a thing, but with the way his—well, everything—was flexing, he probably could.

It was in the process of noticing the *everything* that additional concerning details began to reveal themselves to Maggie's keen investigative eye.

His clothing, for one. The tight black t-shirt and jeans fit him just as well as every exquisitely assembled ensemble she'd ever seen him wear, but it was somehow...wrong.

"Jeans!" she said, not realizing she'd spoken aloud until Darby raised an eyebrow at her.

"What was that?"

Past the pink crown of Darby's head, Maggie saw McGarvey's narrow-eyed gaze begin its eventual swivel in her direction, and she dropped it like it was hot down below the bar faster than fucking Frodo at the Black Gate.

"Nothing," Maggie said, pretending to be engrossed in examining the glassware dishwasher racks. "Just... Um, remembering I left my...jeans at home. And they're my favorite pair!"

"Ooookay," Darby drawled, head cocked at a curious angle as she peered past the collection of mermaid-shaped draft beer tap levers.

Meanwhile, Maggie's mind was Tokyo-drifting straight into some very unwelcome realizations. If McGarvey was here, wearing non-work attire, and appeared to be freshly showered, then...

Oh.

Sweet.

Mother.

Of.

Fuck.

What had Myrtle *done*?

Scrunching down over her shoes, Maggie crouch-walked toward the bar's waist-swinging door that allowed a narrow slice of vantage through which she could track McGarvey's movements without being seen. Perhaps the one time in her life that being vertically challenged proved to be an asset.

Only, just as she had the absolute mouth-watering perfection of McGarvey's body perfectly lined up in the gap, a black-apron-veiled crotch shoved itself into view.

"Ugh, where is she *now*?" Kurt huffed dramatically, setting his tray on the bar's hinged fold-open segment above her head with a hollow slap.

"She's right here, you dick!" Maggie whispered and poked the exposed knob of his hairy ankle with the tip of her nail, feeling a vicious stab of satisfaction when Kurt nearly leapt back a full foot.

"Mag— Ow! Jesus." The tips of his manicured fingers brushed into view as he bent at the waist to massage the part of his shin Maggie had shoved the swinging door into.

"You want to kindly get the fuck out of the way?"

"But what are you—"

"I think she wants you to move," Darby helpfully translated. "Shove off. Make like a tree and get outta here. Take a flying fuck at a rolling donut. Got it?"

"But what about my drin— Oof! Hey!"

Maggie watched as Kurt's annoyingly pristine, sockless loafers —which, ew—executed an impressively graceful spin of the kind used to recalibrate body weight after it'd been abruptly and/or violently shoved off its axis.

"I think that table over there needed some water *really bad*," she heard Darby say, followed by an overly bright "Trent! Hey!"

The golf ball that had lodged itself in Maggie's throat morphed into a hedgehog.

Made of lava.

"Darby."

Maggie wasn't sure what annoyed her more. That the deep, throaty rumble of McGarvey's voice had the power to make her panties wet even when she was actively hiding from him, or that her gnome-like waddle had wedged said—now-damp—panties firmly against Maggie's crotch in a way that made her equal parts irritated and aroused.

"I thought you were on duty this afternoon. You playing hooky?" Darby asked in a teasing purr meant to pre-offer collusion. Beneath the slice of door, the slim stems of her vintage, red stiletto peep-toe pumps lifted and pivoted toward the bar.

Darby had turned to face him, offering Maggie cover. Despite the strangeness of her circumstances, she felt a rush of gratitude. That was ride or die shit right there.

Hopefully the former, but—

"Where is she?" McGarvey's nearly growled question made gooseflesh rise on Maggie's forearms, rippling outward like the tide.

"Chris?" Darby asked. "She actually stepped out to go get more Swiss chard from the co-op because they're already almost sold out of the faux-fish tacos, if you can believe it."

"I don't."

"I know, right?" Darby's infectious laugh tolled out over the convivial din like a bell. "Why in God's name would you sell out of bitter leaves pretending to be chicken when battered fries exist? Speaking of, what are you doing for dinner? Ethan's just got a new smoker, and if I don't bring home something that used to ambulate, I'm liable to find him looking for the smoke ring on my last pack of part-skim mozzarella sticks. Come to think of it, that doesn't sound half bad. Five o'clock sound okay to you? I'll be damned. It's four forty-five right now. Can we take your car? I biked here and Ethan's likely to choke me if he has to replace the heels on these vintage Louboutins *again*."

"Darby." McGarvey's voice was low and tense, cutting through her avalanche of words like a hot knife through butter. "I'll ask again. Where is Maggie?"

Maggie's heart pounded at the mention of her name, a wild rhythm against the silence that followed. She pressed a hand over her chest, willing it to quiet down.

Darby let out an exaggerated sigh. "Did you not hear a word I just said?"

"Unfortunately," McGarvey said. "And you know damn well I'm not asking about Chris."

"Well, you are dead wrong there." Darby giggled. "I haven't the faintest idea who else you might have business with in this fine establishment."

"Margaret fucking Michaels-Wiggins." Each word was accompanied with a flat slap of a palm on the bar that made Maggie tingle in places that made no damn sense for someone crouched under a counter like a troll beneath a bridge.

And a troll who'd apparently earned back her married name.

"Haven't seen her." Maggie heard the shrug in Darby's voice and found herself holding her breath as she examined the odd patterns in the wood grain.

"I know she's here," McGarvey rumbled.

"How's that?" Darby said breezily.

"I can smell her."

A jolt of electricity shot straight from Maggie's toes to the crown of her head.

She quickly lowered her chin to sniff the armpit of her work shirt, but only smelled the earthy fug of the fried food that always clung to her hair and clothes after a shift. Underneath, she detected the faint trace of her own musk, a mix of vanilla-scented body lotion and sweat. Had he really picked up on that?

No sooner had she asked herself the question when it was answered by a deluge of sensory memory. His soft lips and rough stubble against her skin as he dragged his face along her every curve and hollow, breathing her in. His hot breath mingling with hers as he'd whispered filthy words to her in the dark...

"Um, okay, creeper," Darby drawled, the smokiness in her voice suggesting she'd taken a sip of her bourbon. "But I wouldn't go around announcing that to people. It's a little off-putting, if you catch my drift."

"On the topic of animals with heightened senses," McGarvey said, his voice dropping low as Maggie watched the soles of his court shoes inch closer to Darby's heels. "I know she's here, and you can either tell me *where*, or *I* can tell Ethan about the deposit a certain fuchsia-haired coffee proprietress put down on a certain pair of Irish wolfhound pups being fostered by a certain sheriff despite also being in possession of the knowledge that a certain brewery owner has expressly forbidden even the consideration of adoption of any canine companions before he's had chance to finish the dog run on a certain house."

Maggie's heart dropped into her guts at the sound of Darby's sharp inhale. Now that McGarvey tasted blood in the water, it was all over but the handcuffs.

"Wolfhounds?" Darby's voice broke in an octave that might have been amusing under different circumstances. "I mean, in this economy?"

Resigned, Maggie braced herself against the side of the cupboard to crawl out from under the counter, but paused when she noticed a raised knot in the wood that sank under the pressure of her palm. Leaning in closer, she examined the darker border of the cabinet's trim.

Running her fingertip over the wood, Maggie stopped at the knothole and lightly pressed it again. Though stiff, she felt the definite resistance of some sort of pneumatic mechanism behind it. When it reached the limit of whatever mechanism controlled it, she heard a discreet but distinct click.

Which was when she noticed that what she was seeing wasn't a decorative inlay at all.

It was a *door*.

A door that might, perhaps, connect with a crawlspace that in some way connected with a passage that led to Sirens' basement?

"For the last time," McGarvey began, the dark thrill of cornered prey honing his words to a fine edge. "Where. Is. She?"

With a heady rush of adrenaline, Maggie placed her full palm against the wooden door panel and gave a ginger push. To her amazement, it swung smoothly and silently inward, revealing a dust-laden tunnel crawlspace that extended at least the length of the bar before it snaked away into gloomy darkness.

"Is this new?" Darby asked, giving the bar's pass-through door the tiniest tap with the back of her heel.

That was her cue.

Quickly crossing herself before pushing the trapdoor inward with one hand, Maggie planted the other inside the passage and wriggled through. She eased the panel shut behind her just in time to hear Darby's startled squawk followed by the line cook's outraged exclamation as McGarvey apparently pushed his way behind the bar.

Fumbling in her pocket for her phone, Maggie switched on the flashlight app and aimed the beam down the tunnel. The light shone weakly, illuminating a faint trail in the thick layer of dust.

Once again, chills rose on her arms and climbed her neck.

Someone else had been in here.

Recently.

She gulped down a breath and began to crawl, her skirt catching on rough splinters of wood as she moved deeper into darkness. Grit crunched beneath her knees as the air grew cool and damp. She reached out her hands, touching the damp dirt walls of the passage until she came to a split in the tunnel.

Playing her phone's pale beam over the walls, she sucked in a little gasp.

There, on one side of the split, was a mermaid. On the other was an anchor.

Ariadne's Anchor.

Vee's words returned to echo in her head like a haunting invitation.

So if Ariadne's myth truly had been an apt metaphor for the most expensive item on Madame Katz's menu, then who had been the monster in the maze? Townsend? Stewart?

Maggie sat back on her heels and peered down each tunnel, contemplating which path to take.

Aiming her phone down at the passage's floor, she noticed the trail broke toward the anchor side.

So would she.

Adrenaline electrifying her veins, she'd braced against the base of the wall to get a picture of both motifs when her fingers brushed across something...warm.

And furry.

Maggie sucked in a gasp that came with a lungful of moldy air and dust that promptly sent her into a coughing/sneezing fit with exorcism-quality racking retches.

She yelped and jerked her hand back, dropping her phone in the process. The light flickered uncertainly for a moment before stabilizing, casting eerie shadows on the walls of the tunnel before the something *moved.*

And she shrieked. The echo of her terrified wail bounced off the dank tunnel walls, startling something overhead. With a flapping sound, a bat—or maybe several bats—took to panicked flight around the darkness.

"Oh my God, oh my God!" Maggie yelped, slapping at herself as the creatures whizzed by and shot out into the tunnel beyond her. Panting hard, she turned back to her phone and scrambled backward on all fours.

Her impact on the wall behind her wasn't as hard as she'd expected.

Partly because the wall seemed to fall away the second she hit it.

Her confusion was intense, but brief, as she tumbled blinking into daylight.

In the hallway outside Sirens.

Directly at McGarvey's feet.

TWELVE

Dirty

A "DIRTY" DRINK WILL HAVE A SLIGHT TWIST IN COLOR AND TASTE BY CHANGING A CORE INGREDIENT

"I KNOW WHAT THIS LOOKS LIKE, BUT WE'RE TOTALLY not going to fuck!"

Maggie waved to Cady Bloomquist by way of greeting as McGarvey marched her down the block across the street from Nevermore Bookstore.

The busty blonde bookseller and an alarming number of Water Street's other shop owners and assorted patrons had spilled out of their respective boutiques to gawk at the sight of Deputy McGarvey marching her down the street with a hand on the back of her neck.

His fingers flexed ever so slightly against her skin every time she got to the word *fuck* in the phrase she'd been tossing out to the gawkers like so many Mardi Gras beads. Served the fucker right for refusing to speak to her.

"Uh...okay?" Cady called back, lifting a hand whose index finger was still sandwiched between the pages of the book she'd been selling to the woman beside her, who looked confused, if not exactly upset, to have her purchase interrupted for this local spectacle.

"Hey, Maggie!" Parked on the sidewalk in front of Bazaar

Girls was Gemma, something with a lot of pink and red unspooling from her rapidly clicking knitting needles.

"Hey, Gemma," Maggie shouted back. "Just so you know, I'm very aware that since I'm being steered down the street toward Deputy Trent McGarvey's place of residence by Deputy Trent McGarvey, I'm technically subject to the local ordinance that states that it must be assumed that we're about to fuck—"

Flex.

"But I just wanted to clarify that I will not, in fact, be fucking Deputy Trent McGarvey, if that's something you'd like to incorporate into the city council's next meeting minutes."

"Duly noted!" the petite brunette called back, her thumb jutting up from fingerless gloves in the same shade of apple green as her plaid skirt.

So it continued for the remainder of the block, Maggie's recitation repeated in forms customized to the various Water Street business owners and their patrons, punctuated with the occasional tinkle of storefront bells as more onlookers emerged to gape.

And also to openly discuss Myrtle's crap-tastic coup and subsequent shituation with Mayor Stewart.

Both of which, Maggie gathered by his air of general cold-blooded contempt, McGarvey had the distinct displeasure of resolving.

"Really, you should be thanking me," Maggie muttered out the side of her mouth as they approached the entrance to his building. "I'm over preserving your sterling reputation while you march down the block like that menacing, mercury-looking motherfucker from *Terminator 2: Judgment Day.*"

McGarvey at last released his grip on her neck, the evening-chilled air cool where his fingers had been as he unlocked the building's main door and held it open for her.

Maggie hesitated, clutching the purse that Darby had rushed over to give her before McGarvey herded her toward the pub's exit.

"I could bolt right now, you know," she pointed out, parking a hand on her hip as she looked up at him. "So technically, the fact that I'm *not* bolting right now would make me a *good girl*, wouldn't it?"

McGarvey's gaze remained implacably calm and maddeningly neutral.

"Too soon?" she suggested, giving him a nudge with her elbow.

Apparently so.

With a sigh, Maggie began to climb the stairs, moving aside when she hit the landing so he could unlock his front door.

"You know it makes not one lick of sense for you to be gentlemanly about making me go first when you're being all assholey about not speaking to me," she said, hanging back on the threshold.

McGarvey only blinked at her.

"You really are a butthead, you know that?" she huffed, marching past him.

No sooner had she crested the top of the stairs and stepped out of her work shoes, McGarvey relieved her of her purse and began unbuttoning her coat with businesslike and brusque efficiency that for some damn reason made her nipples pucker within her bra.

"Okay, the butthead thing was uncalled for," she said as he shucked her coat from her shoulders and transferred it to a hanger with a flourish. "Especially considering the ample provocation you suffered. By the way, I definitely need you to know that I had no earthly fucking idea what Myrtle was planning."

She glanced at McGarvey, whose raised eyebrow managed to communicate an especially astonishingly large volume of *fuck you*.

"All right, yes, I did technically ask her to create a diversion so Vee and I could sneak back into the Palace Hotel, but I didn't steal anything, break anything, or even get caught this time!" Maggie reported, uncomfortably aware of the chirpy, cheerleader-esque edge her goth-lite high school self would have hissed at her in the hall for. "And *dude*. You won't even believe what I found."

McGarvey's fingers grazed her waist as he began to untuck her Sirens-issue t-shirt from the elastic waistband of her skirt, and, for some damn reason, she found her arms lifting. "Wait, rewind. First, you need to know about *the letter*," she said, dipping her voice into the salaciously sultry purr that always had her podcast listeners pumping eggplant pixels into the comments of her TikTok clips.

So McGarvey was, of course, totally fucking immune.

"Okay, TLDR version, Ethan Townsend's great-great-great-great-grandfather apparently had some sort of joint shipping venture going on with some distant relative of Mayor Stewart's, only it sounds like they may have actually been dealing in *human* cargo, if you get what I'm sayin'."

Feeling a draft, Maggie glanced down and was more than a little surprised to note that her corduroy skirt was puddled around her painted toes like the skirt of a Christmas tree. She stepped out of it and followed McGarvey down the hallway, talking as they walked.

"*Anyway*, Ethan was kind enough to dig through his family's correspondence archive—like, what family even has that? I mean, the closest thing my family has would be that one drawer in the kitchen with all the old phone chargers and Chinese takeout menus where my mom would stuff letters from bill collectors she didn't want my dad to find."

Maggie's spiky laugh had been meant to hook McGarvey with the relatability of the anecdote.

So why did she feel pierced?

"Whatever," she said, wiggling away from the pinprick of darkness in her chest threatening to spread. "So Darby brings me this letter from Ethan's great-great-great-great— Fuck it. Can we just call him Graddy? Or maybe Grandzaddy? I'm assuming he was probably also dashing in a non-verbal but meticulous

Montana farm boy meets Marlboro Man meets John Wick meets
Mad Max meets Mr. Rogers kind of— Holy *fuck*."

Her train of thought abruptly derailed, Maggie drifted
forward to pet the gleaming chrome masterpiece whose front-
facing porthole McGarvey had heaved her dust- and flying-
rodent-dropping-soiled clothing into.

"I'm pretty sure this thing has more tech than Fawkes."

McGarvey punched some buttons that made the machine
chirp to life with a merry ping, his fingers deft in their selection of
what she suspected was the *needs the Lord* cycle.

"Fawkes was my Fiat," Maggie said, deciding his hesitation
over the start button counted as curiosity. "As in the burning
Harry Potter bird. Not that fucker that tried to do the same damn
thing to the Houses of Parliament."

The ache widened, deepened as the image of the cherry-red,
snub-nosed sparkplug of a car sitting on the curb outside their
Boston row house on the morning of her twenty-fifth birthday
invaded her mind.

Oversized purple bow and all.

It had been such a *her* car that she'd burst into tears, even
ignored the joke about worker's comp claims Charlie had made
when she leapt into his arms.

Because, for just that split second, she'd believed that Charlie
knew.

Knew *her*.

Got *her*.

Loved *her*.

Of course, if she'd *known* that he and Fast Eddie had boosted it
from an eighteen-wheeler hauling repossessed vehicles from Jersey to
Ohio, she probably wouldn't have given him a thank-you blowie on
the New Jersey Turnpike on the way to Atlantic City that weekend.

The washer's cycle was so quiet, Maggie wasn't even aware it
had started filling until Trent moved to slide the closet doors
closed.

"Where was I?" she asked, tapping a nail against her lips. "Oh, right. The letter from Grandzaddy Townsend to Mayor Stewart's *incestor*."

If McGarvey picked up on the joke, he made no acknowledgment. Maggie padded after him as he made his way into the kitchen, where he bent to consult the cleaning supplies arranged on tiered shelves beneath the sink like an angelic choir.

"He used this super-weird cat metaphor, but basically, as far as I can tell, Grandzaddy Townsend somehow nabbed Madame Katz and yeeted her over the side of one of their Shanghai ships so she'd quit cockblocking their human capital. Oh! And he gave ol' Spewart Senior the shakedown."

The cool granite countertop felt delicious on Maggie's forearms as she leaned against it and watched McGarvey evaluate his options.

"Do you know what this means?" she asked. "Madame Katz might actually have been working *against* them. That because she owned buildings that were ideally situated between the docks, she might have been using a brothel to help people *escape*."

Goosebumps rose on Maggie's exposed skin, infecting her with the same sweet rush of adrenaline she'd felt when she first seized this possibility.

She stared at McGarvey's broad back through the fabric of his t-shirt, willing him to *feel* this. To understand not just what it meant, but what it meant *to her*.

Instead, he pulled out a neatly folded rag and a bottle of something so potent it could very well be the chemical cousin of napalm before walking back through the living room to the foyer. There, he began liberally spritzing the general area of her arrival in addition to just about every surface she'd touched.

Which was just...just...

"Fucking *rude*," she huffed, crossing her arms defensively over her chest.

Which was rapidly turning a blotchy pink as her Irish shot up faster than the unfortunately named urchin Charlie and his dead-beat Grandpa Joe in the also unfortunately named Wonkavator.

Way past give-a-shit, Maggie parked her hands on her hips and stepped out to block McGarvey's path.

Which was when she accidentally caught her reflection in the elegant mirror on the entryway wall.

And oh, how it did her dirty.

Shreds of cobweb still clung to her fiery curls like so much Silly String. Gray streaks of dust streaked her face, neck, arms, and knees. Something that looked suspiciously like motor oil—if she was lucky—streaked the forearm she'd rested on McGarvey's surgically clean countertops. And was that—*oh dear God*—fucking *guano* in her hair?

Not to mention the absolutely uncalled-for assault on her general person the cool overhead canned lighting was currently perpetrating.

Looking at her reflection in McGarvey's mirror, she was confronted with the same version of herself that had once caused her to skip meals when she found that she could live on compliments and control instead. Every pucker and fold, every silvery pink scar an indictment of what other people saw when they looked at her.

Someone whose body—whose life—they were quietly relieved not to have.

Somebody whose presence made them feel superior by comparison.

Never before had that comparison been starker that in this perfect man's perfect palace of solitude.

Maggie barked a laugh that hit her a shade too hard and too low in the chest. "I look like a trash gremlin chimney sweep," she said, quickly biting the inside of her cheek when her throat began to close. "An unemployed trash gremlin chimney sweep," she added. "Because whose chimney could I fit down? Right?"

Wonder of wonders, it was *this* sentence that finally extracted a growled word from McGarvey's throat.

"Shower."

She found she couldn't move until he did, almost like she needed to mirror his steps as she would if following footprints in the snow, disturbing as little as possible.

Stepping over the threshold into the spa-like expanse of marble tile, Maggie did her level best to keep her eyes averted from any reflective surface.

Which was *super* fucking easy, given how the man cleaned.

Standing there, vulnerable and half-naked, Maggie hugged her arms beneath her breasts as Trent turned knobs and flipped levers. Once he'd conjured a magical waterfall from the ceiling, he turned to her.

"Get in," he rumbled.

"Oh wow," Maggie muttered, releasing the econo-sized clasp of her bra and peeling it from her breasts. "Two whole words this time." Flinging it over the towel rack, she slipped her panties down her hips and kicked them toward the vanity. "I'll have to think of something really humiliating so you might manage a whole sentence."

His nostrils flared as she stepped into the cobalt-tiled glass stall, gingerly easing herself beneath the downpour.

Which felt...delicious.

Maggie closed her eyes and stepped fully into it, wishing the water could wash away the concentrated muck she felt lodged somewhere deep in her middle. A core of cheapness...of wrongness she couldn't shake.

So immersed was she in her thoughts, she jumped when a heated sluice began dumping down her back.

She glanced over her shoulder, surprised to find McGarvey there, disappointed to note that the even, dispassionate expression on his face hadn't shifted.

Nor had any other parts of his body, for that matter.

With the shower hose attachment, he began rinsing her off, his movements tender yet calculated.

She shivered as the warm water cascaded over her shoulders

and down her back, and she tried to focus on the comforting sensation instead of the storm brewing in the air between them.

"You know, this not-talking thing really doesn't help either of us," she pointed out.

Feeling a slight, cool pressure on her scalp, Maggie bunched her shoulders toward her ears before the weight of his hands followed, working through her locks, massaging her scalp with a firm yet gentle efficiency.

Wouldn't you fucking know it, her body began to respond to his ministrations, her skin tingling with pleasure that hummed through her like a live wire. She fought the urge to let out a contented sigh, not wanting to give him any more ammunition against her.

And the better her body felt, the more volatile her feelings became.

"Look, if you're going to insist on inflicting your fastidious, clean-freaky shit on me, you could at least tell me what the hell it's about."

His hands lifted from her scalp and were replaced with the handheld spray's tingling touch.

"If you won't tell me, I'll just have to guess," she said, glancing at him over her shoulder. "And if my instincts are correct, I'm going to say...daddy issues."

In her peripheral vision, Maggie noted the subtle flex of his jaw.

Bingo.

He picked up a loofah and began scrubbing her body. The rough texture tickled her skin, sending goosebumps up her arms and legs. She bit her lip to hold back a moan, determined not to let her body betray her.

Maggie studied the steam drifting lazily toward the ceiling, attempting to fill the silence between them. "You know, my Uncle Conny had a strange habit," she began, lathering her hands with soap, knowing he could see them slowly playing over her breasts. "Whenever the Celtics were playing, he'd count his jar of toenail clippings. Said if he didn't, they wouldn't win. I used to think it was ridiculous until they lost that one game when he forgot." She chuckled at the memory, making circles over her nipples in the frothy foam before turning around to face him.

Because fuck it. If he was going to keep up this emotionally stunted silent treatment, she could energy-match that shit in a heartbeat.

"People create those rituals for all kinds of reasons," she said, stepping back to let the water run in rivulets down her breast and belly. "But mostly, it comes down to control. When you're in an environment where you don't have much of it, you take it where you can. Sometimes, you take it where it earns you the most social currency. From a parent, say. From a father."

Noticing the furrow between his brows, Maggie continued.

"Say your father is an especially regimented guy. And nothing you do quite seems to measure up. *Except* when it comes to getting straight As. Or maybe...cleaning your room to military precision?"

"Don't." The tendons beneath the smooth brown skin of McGarvey's neck rose like bridge cables.

"You're always so composed, so in control of everything around you." She glanced sideways at him, allowing a playful smirk to grace her lips. "It's kind of...compulsive, almost."

His fingers flexed against the sloping muscle of his thigh.

"Maybe," Maggie mused, tracing a soapy finger along the curve of her collarbone, "you just need someone to show you how good it can feel to let go." She drew the tip of her finger down between her breasts and across her stomach, leaving a trail of suds behind. "Someone who's not afraid of getting a little dirty in order to make you come...undone."

Her words hung heavy in the humid air, and she could practically feel the weight of McGarvey's gaze as it flicked to her—a brief, heated moment before he looked away again. But she'd caught the spark of desire in his eyes, and that was enough.

"Have you ever really let go, Trent?" she asked, her voice low and sultry as the water continued to pour over them. "Or are you too afraid of what you might find when you do?"

The silence stretched on, the only sound the steady roar of the shower.

The moment hung in the air like an electric charge, anticipation building between them amidst the steamy shower. Maggie traced slow circles around her nipple with her fingers, teasing it into a hard peak. She locked eyes with McGarvey, challenging him to break his stoic silence. The rush of power she felt when she noticed the unmistakable bulge growing in his pants was intoxicating.

"Mmm," she purred, sliding one hand down her body to rest between her legs. Her fingertips danced over her sensitive folds, sending a shudder through her. "Imagine," she whispered, moving the shower attachment lower, directing the stream of water between her legs. The sensation made her gasp, and her hips bucked forward involuntarily. "Imagine how good it would feel to just take what you wanted right this second."

McGarvey's eyes were hooded and dark, his breath coming in short, ragged pants.

"Please, Trent," she urged softly, her own body trembling with need. "Let me see you."

The hot water cascaded over her body as the shower attachment pulsed against her most sensitive spots, the sensation becoming almost unbearable. Her breath hitched in her throat as she moaned Trent's name, her eyes never leaving his.

"I'm imagining you right now," she gasped, her voice thick with desire. "Your hands on me, your lips trailing down my neck, your teeth grazing my collarbone. The feel of your hard, throbbing cock pressing against my thigh. Then slipping between my legs."

She paused, holding still through another shudder.

"Picture yourself inside me, filling me completely. Your fingers digging into my hips as you give yourself to me as hard and fast as you want to. Because I *know* you want to."

As the pleasure built within her, Maggie felt her legs begin to tremble, her body teetering on the edge.

Opening her eyes, she met the angry animal need in his.

"I'm going to come, Trent," she whimpered. "Oh, God, I'm going to—"

McGarvey lunged forward, wrapping one hand around her throat and pinning her against the shower wall, fastening the other over her wrist and jerking the shower attachment away mere seconds before she lost herself.

"Enough, Maggie," he growled, his eyes dark and stormy with conflicting emotions.

Her pulse thundered in her ears, her chest heaving as she fought to catch her breath. The taste of power still lingered on her tongue, mingling with the bittersweet frustration of being denied release. She stared defiantly into McGarvey's eyes, a wicked grin spreading across her lips.

"Scared you might actually enjoy it?" she taunted him, her voice barely more than a whisper.

"Damn it, Maggie," he muttered, the struggle between desire and restraint playing out on his face like the world's most erotic tug-of-war.

His grip on her throat tightened ever so slightly, a silent warning that they were dancing dangerously close to a line neither of them had ever crossed before.

A bead of water raced down the curve of Maggie's breast, catching the light like a tiny diamond before disappearing into the depths of her flushed cleavage. The moment hung suspended in time, a precarious balance between past and present.

"Trust me," McGarvey said, his voice a low rasp filled with warning and frustration, "you don't want to see this side of me."

For a heartbeat, Maggie hesitated, staring into the turbulent sea of emotion swirling behind his eyes.

"You're right, Trent," she replied, her voice steady despite the heat coursing through her veins. "I don't just want to *see* this part of you. I want to taste it. Breathe it. I want to *feel* it."

His eyelids lowered as she lightly grazed his thickening cock before wrapping her hand around it and beginning to move.

"This...isn't a good part...of me," he panted in time with her ministrations.

"I don't just want part of you, Trent McGarvey," she said, brushing her slick palm over his swelling head. "I want the whole *fucking* thing."

"Fuuck," he groaned, his eyes darkening with desire.

"I want every last drop, Trent," she whispered, leaning in closer. "And I want it messy. And hot. And *hard*."

A primal growl reverberated through his chest as he yanked Maggie toward him, their lips, teeth, and tongues tangling together in a raw, hungry sweep. McGarvey wrenched his mouth away, gazing down at her with a heat that threatened to melt her knees.

"Don't say I didn't fucking warn you."

THIRTEEN

Person of interest

SOMEONE WITH KNOWLEDGE OR
INVOLVEMENT IN A CRIMINAL INVESTIGATION;
MAY BE A SUSPECT, WITNESS OR SOMEONE
WITH CRITICAL INFORMATION

TRENT'S JAW LOCKED, HIS NOSTRILS FLARING AT THE
air thick with the kind of tension and fury that could ignite wild-
fires. Maggie's last words, a brazen challenge that danced wickedly
across the lines of decorum, hung between them like a dare he
couldn't refuse. His pulse thrummed in his ears, a testament to
the internal battle raging within him—a clash of duty and raw
desire.

The air between them crackled for a moment, shifted from
one source of heat to another, the alchemy of anger and lust
bubbling beneath the surface like magma ready to erupt.

Now was the time to go. To walk away or to put her in cuffs
and take her in to where she'd be safe from this snarling need
that'd grown claws.

It was go or...

"Well? Are you just going to stand there looking like a deer
caught in headlights?" Maggie's voice was laced with impish
provocation, her bright red hair a fiery halo in the dim light of her
living room.

Fuck it. This was his damned apartment. He wasn't going anywhere.

In two decisive strides, Trent closed the distance between them. Any chance of more banter evaporated as he yanked her close and captured her lips with his.

It was a kiss that spoke of unchecked yearnings, a prelude to promises whispered in the dark. As their lips met, Maggie's scent —a tantalizing blend of vanilla, jojoba, and something uniquely her—filled his nostrils, stoking the temper that fueled his lust. His hands found her hips, and he pressed his fingers into the soft curves he'd learned only the night before with bruising strength.

Those eyes. Intelligent. Bright. Observant.

She couldn't see him like this.

Maggie's breath hitched as he turned her to face away from him before bending over the back of the black leather couch that had seen its share of lazy Sunday afternoons. Trent didn't hesitate. With a swift motion, his zipper was down, the sound cutting through the silence like a starting pistol. His mind was a haze of Maggie—her scent, her heat, the way her soft sex beckoned from beneath the globes of her round and ample ass.

"Yes."

It was the whisper he'd been waiting for.

As he entered her with a rough thrust, Trent was careful not to cause her any pain. He couldn't remember the last time he'd felt so frenzied with lust, his thoughts a whirlwind of sensory details and animalistic urges. Yet beneath it all, he was aware of a tenderness that caught him off guard.

"Fuck yes," he echoed, inwardly bemoaning that he hadn't been able to wait to undress. If he had, the chisel of his hip flexors would be tucked against her beautiful bare flesh.

He held still for as long as he could. Seconds. Minutes. He couldn't be sure. Incrementally, the teeth-clenching tightness of her core gave way for his intrusion, relaxing the grip from *this will be over too soon* to *fits like a glove.*

Each brutal thrust was a revelation, a liberation from the man who prized control above all else. Townsend Harbor's rain-soaked serenity had nothing on the storm that raged in the confines of this soulless living room with its hotel décor.

"God," Trent grunted, every stroke a testament to the pent-up longing that had simmered between them for far too long. Maggie's response was a moan that reverberated through his bones, a siren song urging him to abandon the shore for the tumultuous sea of their shared desire. His breath exploded out of him in rhythmic, ragged gasps, his movements becoming more frenetic as his thoughts became more garbled. Reason? Logic? His goddamned humanity?

Those had deserted him the second she bent over.

Maggie was no passive participant; she met him thrust for thrust, a provocative challenge sparkling in her voice.

"Yes. Harder. More," she said in rhythm to his relentless strokes, her words laced with a devil-may-care demand that set his blood on fire.

Her smoky voice hung in the air like an electric charge, igniting something raw and primal within him. It was as if she'd lit the fuse to a powder keg of emotion that Trent had kept buried under layers of sarcasm, good nature, and meticulous order.

He knew anger—anger at the world, at the job, at himself— but what roared through him now was different. It wasn't just temper or anger; it was a hurricane of passion, possession, and something even stronger. Something he couldn't begin to identify.

Something maybe no one had invented a language for yet.

"Damn you," he growled, the sound almost foreign to his own ears. She was peeling away the veneer he'd polished so carefully over the years, revealing the man who craved the wild, the unscripted—the real. This wasn't just about sex; it was a seismic shift, toppling the walls he'd built around himself.

"No, fuck me," she gasped.

He bent over her back to thread his large fingers in the silk of her wet hair, anchoring her neck back tight as he used the tension to truly follow her orders.

"You wanted dirty?" he snarled against the shell of her ear, a warning. A question. An urge building within him.

"Yes. More," she urged, her voice a blend of defiance and desire.

Fueled by her dare, Trent lifted his hand, hovering for a nanosecond to question whether or not they should cross this new boundary. Then, with a firmness that made them both gasp, he brought it down, spanking her round backside with a force more than gentle but less than punishing. The sound—a sharp, satisfying smack—ricocheted off the walls, mingling with Maggie's equally lethal cry of pleasure.

After one more pop with his palm, she shuddered and bucked, her moans and mewls crescendoing along with the muscles clamping rhythmically on his cock.

A scream erupted from her that was his undoing.

He couldn't hold back, even if he wanted to. Maggie's provocations were a red flag to the bull of his control, and he charged, driven by a need to claim, to conquer...

To connect.

This was their dance, one where humor and tension twirled around each other in a dizzying rhythm, culminating in decisions neither of them meant to make.

They were close, so close to the edge of reason, the brink of utter abandon. And as they teetered there, Trent realized that Maggie wasn't just some siren leading him to his downfall. She was the compass pointing him toward a truth he'd long denied— the intensity of living without masks, the vulnerability of genuine desire, and the terrifying thrill of letting go.

That realization sent him spiraling after her into the abyss.

His breath came in ragged gasps, his heart thundering like a drumline as he rode the crescendo of their shared frenzy. Maggie's back arched, a silhouette of pure feminine desire, her crimson locks cascading down like fiery waves.

She was a vision of voluptuous passion, a masterpiece sculpted by the hands of wanton need.

A goddess in exile.

The world narrowed to the electric connection between them, a circuit completed, energy flowing unchecked. He watched, mesmerized, as ripples of bliss shuddered through her—the way her shoulders trembled and spine arched, lips parted, and skin flushed with the rosy hue of satisfaction. He loved this—her unguarded moments, raw and beautiful.

As the last tremors of pleasure subsided, a wave of anger washed over Trent. Not at her, never at her. At himself. The realization hit him like a cold shower on a steamy summer's day—he hadn't turned her in for trespassing during her podcast sleuthing. His legacy, his very identity, was built on law and order, yet here he was, breaking both, all because he couldn't bear the thought of betraying Maggie.

So he'd betrayed himself instead.

He fought for breath, for sanity, for something to say as their panting hung like mist in the aftermath of their storm.

Finally, he allowed himself to straighten and ease out of her.

She sighed but made no effort to move.

A flush of panic creeped up his neck. "Did I— Are you okay?"

"No," she said gustily, turning to face him with an expression so pleasantly languorous, she might as well have been drugged. "I don't think I'll ever be okay after that," she admitted with a dopey half-grin. "What else makes you mad? I want to do it again."

Trent knew she was flirting, but he turned away, troubled. He went to get them both a washcloth before he could rush out an idiotic reply.

Here was a side of him he never showed to the women in his bed. In this country, he had to be extra careful of perceived sexual aggression. It was a word he avoided at all costs.

Culturally. Vocationally. Sexually.

She would never understand. As incredible pleasure still

thrummed through his every nerve ending, shame followed quickly as the victor's memento mori.

Instead of allowing him to brood, Maggie turned to face him, eyes alight with a hunger he recognized. Because it was the same insatiable one that lived inside of him.

"Come back from wherever you're going," she whispered, shaping her hand to his jaw. "It doesn't look like a happy place."

Slowly, deliberately, she reached for the hem of his damp shirt, her fingers dancing along the fabric before she peeled it away from his slick skin. Trent stood exposed, every defined muscle testament to his disciplined life, but in this moment, it was Maggie who held the power.

"Seems like I'm not the only one who's been hiding things," she teased, tracing the lines of his abs with a mix of wonder and ownership. Her touch ignited a different kind of heat within him, one that simmered with tenderness beneath the boiling surface.

"I'm an open book," Trent responded, a wry smile playing on his lips. But behind the humor lay an unspoken truth—a camaraderie that went deeper than flesh, a bond forged in the fires of vulnerability and trust.

Maggie's moan of appreciation was a siren call, and Trent felt himself irresistibly drawn into the depths of her oceanic eyes. With the confidence of a woman who knew the power she wielded, she guided his hands to the small of her back, pressing against him as if they were two pieces of a puzzle that the universe had finally decided to click together.

"Let me show you how it feels to really let go," she whispered, her breath a warm caress against his ear. She led him down onto the couch, her movements slow, deliberate, like honey dripping from a spoon. The frenzy of their previous encounter melted away, replaced by an exploration that was no less intense but far more profound.

Trent was lost in the sensation of Maggie's curves beneath his fingertips, the softness of her skin contrasting with the hard lines of his own body. She moved atop him with a rhythm that seemed to speak directly to his soul, a languid dance that was at once new yet achingly familiar.

The way she looked at him, with such trust and openness, made something inside Trent stir—something he'd kept shackled for far too long. Her eyes held not just passion but a playful challenge, as if daring him to dive into uncharted emotional waters.

She'd plunge first if he wasn't careful.

And that just didn't fucking sit right with him.

It was in the ebb and flow of their joined bodies that Trent found himself adrift in thoughts he'd never dared acknowledge before. The realization struck him like the first thunderclap of an oncoming storm: life without Maggie would be like a painting stripped of color, a book devoid of words.

Something...unimaginable.

He hesitated, almost blown over by the strength of his reaction of that inner revelation.

Did she know? Did she realize just what the fuck she *did* to him? Was she doing it on purpose? Seducing him within an inch of his sanity without giving him an easy pathway back to reason?

He marveled at the paradox of their connection, how the raw physicality of her gentle, curious exploration of his topography could unearth emotions so intricate and complicated.

So...fragile.

In Maggie's embrace, he discovered a safe harbor where he could anchor his most intimate fears and desires, a sanctuary where the masks he'd worn for so long dissolved into nothingness.

Danger alarms and red flags waved in his mind's eye as she pulled him down so he stretched out long above her, their tongues dancing and sparring as he settled into the cradle of her body, chest to breast, hips undulating together, until his thickening cock found her drenched clit. Their intimate flesh branded hotter than the caresses they passed over smooth skin with their fingertips. He circled the head of his sex over the pliant hood of hers, teasing the engorged little nub there, testing its sensitivity and making her gasp and writhe before he thrust home once again.

This time, he took his time with her, peeling back to watch her eyes as he inched inside of her slick heat. They shone with a moisture he couldn't identify, but no tears spilled as he stretched her legs wide, wider, reaching in between them to pay attention to the bundle of nerves now exposed by her open thighs.

She didn't blink, only breathed to whisper encouragements. Naughty little nothings he'd never remember. Or always would.

The soundtrack to the night he fell hard for the woman he shouldn't even glance sideways at.

His body didn't give him time to consider the pang in his chest, as it was followed by the gradual onset of a tide of pleasure he'd never known.

As the crest of their shared passion receded, leaving them in the gentle shallows of contentment, Trent breathed in the truth with newfound reverence. Here, entangled with Maggie in the quiet aftermath, he understood that love wasn't just a spark or a flame—it was a fire that could both consume and cleanse. And if the flame was always so warm, so well-tended...

He might just be ready to be consumed by it.

Trent's arm was a band of warmth around Maggie's waist, their legs a tangle of contentment beneath the soft throw blanket that had somehow survived their earlier tempest. He could feel the steady rise and fall of her chest against his side, each breath a whisper of serenity. The glow from the fireplace painted their skin in hues of gold and amber, cocooning them in its gentle radiance.

"Did we just... Was that even...?" Maggie's voice was a sleepy murmur, trailing off into the stillness as she sought the words to capture the indefinable.

"Earth-shattering? Mind-blowing? Clichéd as it sounds, I think we ticked all the boxes," Trent replied, the corner of his mouth quirking up in a post-bliss smirk. His fingers traced idle patterns on her arm, skimming over freckles that reminded him of constellations—each one a tiny point of light in the universe of her lovely skin.

The pink and gold of her Irish heritage and the dusky teak of his African one made for a visually stunning contrast as he charted her body like the old colonizing explorers had done to the world at large. Committed every curve to memory. Every valley, crevice, soft spot, every fine hair lifted in awareness and pleasure.

"More like galaxy-imploding," she said with a chuckle, tilting her head back to lock eyes with him. In the dim light, they sparkled with the remnants of raw desire and something softer, something treacherous to a heart that had thrived on solitude.

Beneath all that, his masculine ego purred with a feline sort of pride.

"Galaxy-imploding," he echoed, letting the term roll off his tongue as though he were tasting a fine wine. "I'll have to remember that for the next time I'm bragging at the bullpen."

"Ha, as if you'd kiss and tell," Maggie teased, poking his ribs playfully. The action sent a jolt of awareness through Trent's body, reminding him of how easily she navigated his defenses.

"You don't know me," he pretended to grouse, tossing a saucy look down at her before kissing the tip of her nose.

"Please," she said, wriggling somehow impossibly closer. "Tell me one time when you lied on purpose...and being undercover doesn't count."

Damn, he was going to use that one.

"I only lie about the fishing trips," he admitted, the truth laced with humor. "I think it's a chromosome thing, because I've never met a masculine-presenting person tell the truth about the size of the catch and it doesn't grow ten pounds with each retelling."

"Good thing I'm not a fish, then," Maggie said, her tone a mix of sass and sweetness that made Trent's heart do an odd little flip. "You caught me, deputy. What's the protocol now?"

"Protocol states that I should probably let you go," he confessed, his voice wavering slightly as the weight of his earlier revelation pressed down on him. "But damned if I'm not much good at following rules when it comes to you."

"Then don't," she whispered, the simple command wrapped in vulnerability. Her hand found his, fingers threading through his with a promise of more than just physical connection. "Break the rules with me."

Her words were a key turning in a lock, releasing parts of himself he hadn't even realized were shackled. "Maggie, I—" He paused, the enormity of what he wanted to say looming before him like a precipice. "I've never been this reckless with anyone before. Hell, we didn't even use a condom."

"That's okay." She shrugged. "I have an IUD."

His relief must have been apparent, because she giggled a little.

"Reckless is just another word for living, McGarvey." Her smile was a crescent moon in the night of his uncertainty. "And I've got a feeling we're going to do a little bit more of that with each other before we're through."

In the quiet aftermath of their confessions, the room seemed to hold its breath, the only sound their synchronized heartbeats writing a rhythm for a future uncertain but tempting as the dawn. Maggie's head rested against his shoulder, her red hair a fiery contrast to the subdued tones of his living room—a vibrant reminder that life was meant to be lived in Technicolor, and Trent was suddenly eager to paint outside the lines.

He bullied Maggie off the couch and into his bed, their legs tangled beneath the cotton throw as they let the fireplace warm their bare skin and cool their ardor.

Her breath was a soft cadence against his neck, stirring something tender within him—something that felt suspiciously like roots taking hold in unexplored soil.

A comfortable silence settled between them, the kind of hush that spoke volumes more than words ever could. They were two souls, stripped down to raw desire and now wrapped up in the quiet understanding that what they'd shared transcended physical release.

As Trent held her, the reality of their bond—an intricate tapestry woven from heated glances, whispered innuendos, and now this—settled over him like a blanket. It was warm, it was protective, and damn if it wasn't as scary as a chicken coop at a fox convention.

"Hey," Maggie began, tracing idle patterns on his chest. "I can hear you brooding. What's up?"

"Nothing much," he lied, because how did one explain that he was wrestling with the fear of losing something he never knew he wanted until now? Instead, he steered them back to safer waters. "Just thinking about how I'm going to get you out of here without my neighbors starting a betting pool on our...extracurricular activities."

She laughed, a sound that bubbled up between them like a clear spring. "Let 'em bet. I'll throw in twenty bucks on us lasting longer than the milk in your fridge."

"Bold move," he teased back, even as his heart performed an odd little flip at the thought of a timeline extending beyond the confines of tonight. "But you're on."

The laughter faded, leaving a poignant stillness that stretched out like the rolling fields and primeval forests surrounding the town. There was an undercurrent of uncertainty there—a silent acknowledgement that they were standing on the edge of something deeper than either had planned.

"Whatever happens..." Maggie whispered, "I'm glad we did this."

"Whatever happens," Trent echoed, his jaw cracking on a yawn.

The world outside faded, leaving only the soft sounds of the fireplace, the evening wail of the wind through the marina.

For once, Trent McGarvey wasn't thinking about appearances, about the meticulous order he so often clung to. All that mattered was Maggie—the woman who'd managed to unravel him with nothing more than a look and a challenge that he'd been powerless to resist.

FOURTEEN

Twist

A PIECE OF CITRUS ZEST (A THIN, CURLED SLICE
OF A CITRUS FRUIT PEEL) ADDED TO A DRINK
FOR FLAVOR OR DECORATION, EITHER IN THE
DRINK DIRECTLY OR HANGING ON THE SIDE OF
THE GLASS

THE FIRST THING MAGGIE NOTICED AS CONSCIOUSNESS crept back was the warmth radiating from the strong arm draped over her. The second: just how good the bazillion-thread-count sheets felt swathed around her naked body. The third: the faint scent of sandalwood. The fourth: the collection of classic novels lining the bookshelf across the room.

Oh, right.

McGarvey's place.

A tiny smirk played at the corners of her mouth as she shifted her gaze to the painfully, impossibly beautiful man lying beside her. His deep chest rose and fell in a steady rhythm, his handsome face completely slack in sleep.

She had matched his passion, toe to toe—among other parts. Rode him like he was the last Harley out of the mouth of hell. Snatched his soul and sucked it dry like a soup dumpling.

Fucking took. Him. Out.

And somehow, draining enough intensity from him to allow

him this kind of rest felt like doing something worthwhile. Something she could keep, even if she couldn't keep him.

And looking at him, at the raw vulnerability stripped bare by sleep, she realized something new. A small flutter in her stomach as delicate as a moth, but no less real for its subtlety.

She wanted to keep him.

Wanted to keep *this*. The feeling of his arm around her like something worth protecting.

But he can't protect you from dangers he doesn't know about.

Unease spread like an oil slick in her stomach.

She searched his face, asking in her mind a question she couldn't when those leonine eyes gazed intensely into hers.

If she told him everything, would he understand?

Would he even want to try?

McGarvey stirred in his sleep, making Maggie's heart stutter.

She couldn't afford to entertain these thoughts.

Lifting her head from the pillow, she squinted into the silent serenity of his room.

The clock on his dresser was out of her line of sight, but judging from the light, or lack thereof, she guessed the early winter evening was imminent. Not wanting to wake Trent just yet, she carefully disentangled herself from him and slipped out of bed. Her skin tingled as it met the cool air of the room, McGarvey's ministrations having left it hypersensitive.

She tiptoed across the room toward the hallway, breath held in anticipation of the creaking floorboards betraying her presence.

If they did, McGarvey was sleeping hard enough not to notice, thank God. After borrowing his deliciously plush bathrobe from the bathroom, Maggie slipped into it and approached the laundry closet.

Their frenzied, multi-location tangle hadn't included switching her laundry into the dryer.

Gingerly opening the washer's porthole, she drew out the damp wad of her clothing and lobbed it into the dryer, shushing the machine when it chirped to life.

After several moments, she managed to push a combination of buttons that made her sodden items begin to cartwheel in the drum.

Next, hydration.

Between sweat and various other bodily fluids, she wouldn't be surprised if she'd lost a good five pounds if she stepped on a scale.

But for once, she hadn't the faintest desire.

All she needed to know about her body, Trent McGarvey had bitten, sucked, licked, kissed, and thrust into her.

The thought curled the corners of her kiss-swollen lips as she uncapped the bottled water she swiped from the fridge and set off toward the foyer in search of her purse.

When she found her phone by feel, her stomach dropped when the screen lit up with a veritable scroll of notifications.

Eleven missed calls.

Ten voicemails.

The number that the first three were from made her heart leap into her throat.

Queensboro Correctional Facility.

Charlie.

Here in McGarvey's immaculate kitchen was the last place she wanted to hear *that* voice, but the idea of carrying their content in her purse like a bomb until her clothes were dry and she could get home to Roxie seemed infinitely worse.

Fingers trembling, she turned the volume down and pressed play on the first one.

"Hey, Shortcake..."

Ice water replaced her blood at the sound of that once-familiar voice, roughened by four years of a life lived in the roughest of places. Maggie clutched the counter for support, her palms already growing clammy.

"Got good news, baby doll. They're lettin' me out early. You can pick me up at Queensboro anytime after noon." An oily chuckle. "Wear that green dress I like, okay? The one with the lace over your tits. You won't be needin' no panties, if you know what I mean…" His voice trailed off into another repugnant chuckle.

The queasy feeling in her stomach intensified; her knuckles were white against the counter's edge. She swallowed around a desiccated throat, hesitating for a moment before pressing the next voicemail.

"Hey, doll face, me again," Charlie began, somehow managing to sound both ingratiating and menacing. "Didn't pick up, huh? You must be busy getting yourself all pretty for me." His voice dripped with sarcasm. Suddenly, he was serious again. "When you come pick me up, bring a twelve-pack of Bud and some of them pork rolls you used to make? My mouth is watering just thinkin' about them."

The memory was having quite the opposite effect on Maggie.

"Can't wait to see you, baby."

A single bead of sweat trickled down Maggie's ribs as she pressed play on the first message from a number she didn't recognize.

"Hey, Shortcake. You on your way or what? I been sitting out here with my thumb up my ass for an hour now. Had to borrow a phone offa"—mumbling in the background—"some chick named Carol, and she's gettin' real uppity about getting it back. Call me back."

The next voicemail was from yet another different number.

"You think you can just leave me hanging, huh?" He was practically growling now, his voice low and dangerous. "I've been out here for over two hours, Maggie. Where the hell are you?" He spat her name out like a curse.

A shudder rippled through her flesh, and an icy gust of dread fluttered over her flushed skin. How easily something as simple as a slight shift in his tone of voice used to be able to ruin her entire day.

Next.

"Maggie…" Charlie's voice was softer now, almost pleading again. "Pick up the damn phone, would ya? Look, it's okay if you don't have gas money because you got your nails for me. I ain't even mad. You still got my old man's ring? We can pawn it for..."

Next.

"Never mind. I got me a ride. I oughta be home by"—a lengthy silence, during which Charlie presumably did the heavy lifting of basic math—"six o' clock. I sure hope you're there waiting for me."

This sounded more like a threat than a wistful wish.

"What the fuck, Maggie!" Charlie bellowed at the beginning of the next message. "I just walked in on some old broad in the shower. Where the fuck are you? And where the fuck is all our stuff?"

Every rational cell in her body screamed at her to hang up, to delete these vile messages and put a continent between herself and this dark specter from her past. But she couldn't stop until she knew everything there was to know.

Her curse, always.

"You know I can find you, right, Shortcake? You always did love your games. But just remember, baby doll, I got the better team. Always have, always will."

By *team*, she assumed he was referring to the pack of pathetic self-styled petty criminals and con men who sat around Italian restaurants trying to convince themselves they were in an episode of *The Sopranos*. They'd never been the most capable bunch, but frequently what they lacked in mental acumen, they made up for in bravado and surprisingly effective police connections.

Maggie took a sip of water, willing it to loosen her aching throat.

The last three messages were the most disturbing by far.

By the muffled quality of the sound, she could tell Charlie had the phone tucked in some pocket on his person. She heard the rustling of material, and a low hum of background noise. Then the sound that sent shivers coursing down her spine: a woman's voice, roughened by decades of a pack-a-day habit.

Her mother's.

Charlie had gone to her parents' house in Long Island to try to figure out where she'd gone.

She made out a few words, "Boston" and "business" among them.

In the next message, Maggie could hear a shriller edge in her mother's voice.

In the last, Charlie was back, this time his words dripping with the smug self-satisfaction that had always made Maggie's fingers itch for a Louisville Slugger.

"Maggie, Maggie, Maggie," he cooed into her ear, pouring a sickeningly sweet, paternal poison down the line. "Never figured you for a Pacific Northwest girl, what with all those hippie-dippy granola types." His low chuckle gurgled in her ear like a drain threatening to overflow. "But I think a little travel will do me good. I owe yas a second honeymoon. I'll see you soon, Shortcake."

The line went dead, Charlie's trailing laughter lingering ominously for a moment longer before being swallowed by the silence.

Maggie's heart hammered in her chest, her fingers remaining frozen into a claw when she let the phone slip from her hand and clatter to the counter.

He knew.

Some-fucking-how, he knew where she was.

And he was coming to find her. Here, in Townsend Harbor.

A cold wave of terror washed over Maggie, cementing her in place as she grappled with the fact that Charlie knew where she was. She could practically see him swaggering into town, his sneer turning every warm, welcoming smile cold. The thought of him interacting with the people she had begun to care for made her stomach lurch.

Vivid pictures began to paint themselves in her mind like a horror movie on fast forward. Charlie at Sirens, his boisterous laugh filling the space, his hand too low on Chris Stone's back as he ordered a beer. Charlie in Nevermore Bookstore, the ever-present toothpick making its constant journey from one side of his thick lips to the other, sucking his teeth at the very idea of wasting your time doing something as useless as reading. Charlie at Bazaar Girls, his ragged fingernail catching on a bright knot of yarn as he snorted his scorn at all fanciful feminine pursuits.

"Everything okay?"

Maggie leapt at the sound of McGarvey's voice, her entire body sizzling with a hot bolt of adrenaline.

She clutched a hand to her chest, whirling around to find him leaning against the doorframe in a sexy slouch, boxers riding low on his lean hips, eyes hooded with sleep.

"Jesus," she wheezed, trying to arrange her face into playful scorn. "You shouldn't sneak up on me like that."

His luscious lips twisted into a smirk. "I, uh, flushed the toilet and cleared my throat."

"Oh," she said, folding her arms beneath her breasts and willing her hummingbird of a heart to slow. "My bad. I just came out to get some water."

He sauntered to the fridge and pulled out a water for himself. "Good idea," he said before snapping off the cap and chugging several healthy swallows.

Maggie watched the muscles in his back shift and flex as he bent to examine the contents of the fridge. The broad expanse was a testament to a man who had been through many varieties of trials, endured, and emerged stronger.

Strong enough to bear the full weight of her past?

Maggie didn't know. But for the life of her, she couldn't bring herself to ask him to.

Swallowing hard, she watched as Trent turned around, leaning against the counter with a puzzled expression etched on his handsome face. The intensity in his eyes made her heart pound harder in her chest. "So, what were you doing out here all alone?" he asked, eyes slightly narrowed. "And why did you sneak out of bed all catlike and quiet?"

Maggie tried for a saucy giggle but landed closer to a constipated chuckle. "I just thought that after all that activity, you might could use some rest."

McGarvey's brows lowered as he tipped his chin down, all seductive smolder.

"On the contrary," he said, coming around the counter. "I woke up very ready for another round."

Maggie's eyes widened as she noticed for the first time the slitted head of McGarvey's cock just visible above the waistband of his boxers.

And damned if her mouth didn't water.

Her breath hitched as he came around behind her, pressing his arousal against her lower back, big arms sliding around her ribcage and pulling her back against the warm wall of his chest.

Maggie tipped her head backward against his sternum as his chin came to rest atop her crown like he'd held her this way a thousand times before.

Her eyes fell closed as a wave of unexpected emotion washed over her. The scent of him, a mix of lingering cologne and the musky remnants of their passion, proved a potent comfort.

"I like seeing you in things that belong to me," Trent rumbled against her back, a finger tracing the edge of the bathrobe against the swell of her breast. "Like my bed."

Desire pooled low in her belly as his hand slipped beneath the flush fabric, finding her already achingly stiff nipple and pinching it lightly between his fingers.

Maggie bit her lower lip as his other hand began sliding down her stomach.

Just as she felt her resolve beginning to crumble, her phone buzzed on the counter, its screen lighting up with the same number Charlie's final voicemails had come from.

Maggie lunged for it without thinking, her slick hands fumbling to silence it before turning it facedown on the counter.

"Sorry," she said, extracting herself the rest of the way from McGarvey's embrace. "Goddamn telemarketers."

He tilted his head, furrowing his brow thoughtfully. His dark eyes were like an x-ray machine, scanning her for the truth she was trying so hard to hide.

"Which reminds me," she said. "I owe Chris a call. I'm just going to throw my clothes on and give her a shout."

"Whoa," he said, reaching out for her elbow. "Hey. Where you going all of a sudden?"

"It's not sudden." Maggie laughed, wiggling out of his grip and striding toward the laundry closet. "I've been here for hours. It's almost Roxie's dinnertime, and—"

He blocked her path, resting both hands on her shoulders. "Take a breath. Your clothes aren't even dry yet."

Maggie ducked out from beneath them, wrenching open the dryer drawer and grabbing the still alarmingly damp items before they'd even finished their tumble.

"Dry enough for the short walk home," she said, already padding away.

"You could borrow some of my sweats," Trent called out after her as she disappeared into the bathroom.

Maggie gave a dry chuckle as she got her bra and panties. "Aside from issues of physics when it comes to your narrow hips and my not-narrow ass, making my official walk of shame in clothing different than what I came in is the *last* thing I need after your little parade leader act earlier."

McGarvey was waiting outside the bathroom, following after her as she strode toward the foyer. "How about I come with you? I was excellent at feeding Roxie, if you'll remember."

Maggie turned around, meeting his earnest gaze and offering a small, rueful smile. "I remember, Trent," she said softly, reaching out to cradle his cheek for a moment. "You are excellent at many things." She dropped her hand and took a step back, her defensive walls rising again. "But I really need to get working for notes on my podcast, and with you around, something tells me I'd be doing a lot of *not* writing."

She winked at him as she stepped into her boots and shrugged into her coat, a measure of the ache in her chest easing as she saw his eyes soften.

"Gotta go," she said, leaning in to plant a quick peck on his lips that Trent foiled by taking her face in both hands. They threaded into her hair as his tongue teased the seam of her lips, the brief squeeze against her scalp enough to send fresh goosebumps cascading down her body

"I'll call you later," he said, releasing her.

"Not if I call you first." Tears blurred Maggie's vision the second she pushed through the door and threatened to spill from her lids by the time she hit the bottom of the stairs and shoved through the door to the street.

Running directly into Gabe and Gemma in the process.

"Whoa," Gabe said, catching Maggie by both shoulders and helping her catch her balance. A knowing smirk lifted one corner of his mouth as his eyes moved from her hair to her mouth to her eyes. "I'd ask you where the fire is, but I have a feeling I already know."

"Shut up, Gabe," Gemma scolded, but her grin betrayed her own curiosity. "Maggie's in a hurry, that's all."

Maggie wanted nothing more than to crawl into a hole and hide from their prying eyes. Her mind raced, searching for a sassy retort or a quick deflection, but all she could do was stammer out, "Right. Well, I...um...need to check on my dog. Because she's blind. And deaf. And hungry. And blind."

"You said that already," Gabe said, arching an eyebrow.

"Uh, yeah, well, that's because she's...uh...*very* blind," Maggie said, her cheeks flushing with embarrassment. "Anyway. I always cock—uh—cook her dinner myself and...and okay, fine!" Maggie suddenly blurted out, tears welling in her eyes. The emotional turmoil had finally bubbled over, and she needed to get it all out. "We totally fucked! Is that what you want to hear?"

Gemma and Gabe exchanged shocked glances, neither expecting such an outburst from their usually composed friend.

"Whoa, Maggie, we were just teasin'," Gabe said, his expression softening. "No need to get all upset about it."

"It's fine." Maggie sniffled. "But I'm going to go now, okay? Away. Like, now. Right now."

And for no reason she could think of, Maggie found herself sprinting, tearing down the street like a woman possessed, feeling her past gaining on her even as the frigid winter air chilled the tracks of her tears.

FIFTEEN
"FIDO"

AN ACRONYM USED BY POLICE OFFICERS THAT MEANS "FORGET IT, DRIVE ON"

TRENT COULDN'T HELP BUT ADMIRE THE WAY MAGGIE'S vibe seemed to catch the very essence of Valentine's Day as they strolled through Townsend Harbor's Love Fest. The town square was alive with crimson and pink streamers, heart-shaped balloons bobbing in the chilly breeze, and the laughter of couples clinging to the festive spirit like it was their love's own lifeline. Music swirled around them—a blend of peppy pop songs and classic love ballads that made even Trent's cynical heart twitch in rhythm. True to cliché, the scent of cotton candy and popcorn beckoned, lending a sweet note to the crisp air that'd just dipped about twenty degrees once the sun disappeared.

Maggie's soft red sweater peeked from beneath her black wool peacoat, teasing the strawberry notes in her hair and advertising her scarlet quilted leather Gold Coast Kate Spade bag. Trent had taken the fact that his crimson pocket square sort of matched as some kind of cosmic sign the night would go well.

That *they* would go well...

Together.

Slow your roll, McGarvey.

"Know what I learned last year?" he began, his eyes flicking toward the distant lighthouse with its scarlet light shining like a beacon. "That the first Ethan Townsend bought the red light-house Fresnel lens from a special glassmaker in Antwerp. It's written in the town bylaws that it be used every year on Valentine's Day to light the Love Fest." He glanced at Maggie for her reaction, curious to see if this little tidbit of local history would pique her interest.

"Really?" she asked, her voice lacking its usual spark. She looked at the lighthouse too, but her gaze seemed unfocused, distant.

"Yep," Trent continued, trying to engage her. "He wanted it to be seen all the way from the Canadian fort on Victoria Island, especially from Lonely Cove. He wrote that it was his way of sending friendship and fealty across the sound."

"Interesting," she said quietly, but her distant look remained.

A pang of concern lanced Trent through the guts.

The aroma of fried donuts and kettle corn twisted his stomach, and he tucked Maggie under his arm. "I'm hungry. Want anything?"

She hummed noncommittally beside him, her usually vibrant eyes dulled, as if the crimson pall of light from the lighthouse cast a shadow rather than its intended warm glow. She was there, but not quite present, her mind meandering through some internal maze.

He gave her shoulders a squeeze. "You've been quiet all night. What's going on in that beautiful mind of yours?"

"Just thinking." She rubbed her arms. "It's nothing."

Liar. Maggie couldn't hide from him any more than he could mask the concern gnawing his gut. "Come on. I'm not buying it."

She sighed, tearing her gaze from the lighthouse to meet his eyes. "Or maybe I'm thinking about everything? I don't know."

"Like what?" he asked cautiously, trying to understand her internal struggle. They had been moving fast since their initial attraction to each other; maybe she was starting to doubt their compatibility. Maybe she was worried about her job. Her performance on the podcast.

What happened *after*?

That was where his thoughts kept snagging. What happened to them when her show was finished?

"It's hard to... I haven't figured out how to put words to it just yet. Is that okay?" Maggie's voice was a whisper lost to the wind.

Trent grimaced. He supposed they *were* an odd pair—she a tornado of curiosity and defiance, whisking through life's conventions; he a man who ironed his socks and arranged his books by color. Then subcategories like alphabet, chronology, and, of course, series.

It was hard not to notice how Maggie's attention drifted back to the lighthouse, how her fingers fiddled with the hem of her vintage coat instead of tapping along to the beat of the music.

"Imagine being so sure about something, you'd want it to outlast you," she mused, her gaze unfocused. "To know that *this* isn't a part of your life, but you are a part of *their* life. That's something..."

Trent watched as she absent-mindedly twirled a lock of hair around her finger. He knew he had to do something to lift her spirits, and fast.

A mischievous grin spread across his face as an idea struck him. "You know, Ethan Townsend used to be the sheriff before— Uh—well, anyways..." Now didn't seem like the time to bring up his boss. "His full name is some ridiculously olde-world white-boy shit like Ethan Reginald Haverford Aristocratic Butthole Townsend the Fourth."

That seemed to pull her from the deep lake of her thoughts to the surface.

"That's not his real name." She chuckled wryly.

"No, but the fact that he was the *fourth* Ethan Townsend is exactly the point. The first Ethan Townsend being of *this* lighthouse fame. Ethan Townsend, the *first*, was more than a man who owned half this town once upon a time. He was a romantic. Why else would he install the red lens into the lighthouse and father this February festival in the winter off-season?"

"A shameless grab for tourist dollars during the most dismal month on the coast?"

Who was the cynical one now? Trent frowned. He didn't like this change in their dynamic one bit.

"Hey," he said, nudging her gently with his shoulder, "you're not already plotting your escape to Boston after this investigation, are you?"

Her smile was brief, a flicker of warmth before she masked it with a shrug. "Who knows where the wind will blow, deputy?" There it was, the nudge back at him, an echo of their usual repartee. But it was fleeting, gone as quickly as it came, leaving Trent grappling with the worry that maybe, just maybe, he was thinking long term while she was already half packed in her mind. "But I haven't even started recording yet, so I'll be here for at least a handful more weeks."

"I'll tell my men to be on alert," he teased.

"You'd better prepare them for the likes of me." She laughed deviously, the sparkle returning to her haunted eyes.

Arm in arm, they wandered through the crowd, stopping at various booths along the way. Maggie inspected handmade quilts and locally sourced honey while he debated the merits of various craft beers. Their casual banter flowed easily, as if they'd been together for years instead of weeks.

There she was. He'd done it, coaxed the devil-may-care attitude from Maggie and brought the laughter back to her every interaction.

What if he could make her laugh every day?

The intrusive thought was dispelled as they arrived at the Bazaar Girls booth, beside which Gabe, Gemma, Ethan, Darby, Myrtle, and Vee gathered around Vee's Lady Garden tent. The air vibrated with the laughter of friends and...actual vibrators.

As they approached, Gabe regaled the coterie with tales of his latest mechanical conundrum—a car that was more rust than metal and an owner with more money than sense—while Gemma finished a sale of hand-dyed alpaca wool that cost more deconstructed than a finished craft project would.

Ethan sidled up to Trent as Maggie abandoned him for the ladies. "Glad to see you two worked things out." His pale-blue eyes gleamed knowingly. "Maggie was looking a bit...stormy earlier."

Trent glanced at her, unable to stop his smile. "Skies are clear now."

"So, it's serious, then?" Ethan waggled his Viking-blond brows. "Should we be expecting a wedding invite anytime soon?"

"Whoa, let's not get ahead of ourselves." Trent held up his hands in mock surrender. "We're keeping things casual. No need to pick out china patterns just yet."

Ethan's laughter boomed, drawing the attention of the others. "You pass that detective exam?" he asked with a magnanimous change of subject.

"I didn't know you were going for detective!" Darby bopped over to them in a feathery coat that might have once covered a turquoise-assed sasquatch.

"Scheduled for the summer." Trent dipped his head, unprepared to be the center of attention.

Darby poked Maggie. "*Two* detectives in a relationship? The best part of Ethan and my relationship is that I barely know what's going on half the time, and this man has to know what's going on all the time. Oh, and that *dee-ock*!" She punctuated her appreciation for her man with a smack on his very tight (in all the ways) ass before saying, "Neither of you will be able to keep secrets from each other."

Trent glanced at Maggie in time to see her creamy skin empty of any shade but a sickly gray as she summoned a wan smile. When she might have given a witty rejoinder, she just let her smile wobble until her gaze latched on to the social distraction that was Vee and Myrtle.

"Hey, you two!" she greeted them, with a bit more brightness than he expected. "So glad to see you're out and about after your protest ordeal, Myrtle."

"Ordeal?" Myrtle's bright yellow coat and oversized orange waders made her look like Big Bird's elderly (and recently molted) aunt. "You say *ordeal*, I say *adventure*. Probably needed my new fingerprints on file anyways, so it was about time I was processed. At least this time they didn't make me squat and cough." She jabbed Trent with one broken yellow wing. "Been a few decades since I hid coke in my cornhole."

Most of the laughter Myrtle received was born of astonishment and fueled by mirth once the shock wore off.

As per usual, the validity of her outlandish claims was left open for interpretation.

Vee was a picture of elegance in a flowing, long pink wool coat over mauve slacks and buttery-looking boots. In her hands was the most realistic-looking dildo Trent had ever seen. So realistic, in fact, he had to look away as a well of undiscovered Judeo-Christian shame brought heat to his cheeks. She brandished the...*device* like Samuel Jackson trying to be a Jedi.

"What's that monstah?" Gabe marveled with a pervy smirk. "You getting your product from the Lorena Bobbitt collection? Because that looks real as fuck."

"And so it is." Vee's coy expression brought out a vision of the young, mischievous woman she'd been fifty years prior. "A perfectly rendered cast of the actual member, as it were."

Gabe made a rude noise. "I don't believe in God, but *she* blessed the owner of *that* body."

"Right?" Myrtle relieved her wife of the product, wriggling it like a spring. "Sales have been down a bit lately because kids these days buy their dildos on the line. So Vee 'n' me were thinking... know what women need? RealDick."

Trent shifted along with the other men in the vicinity. "Er, Myrtle. That isn't—"

"I mean, *I* don't. But RealDicks are the best! Tell your friends!" She eyed Ethan. First in the face, and then in the crotch.

"I know you have to have a good one with how strange this one walks sometimes." She hitched a thumb at Darby. "Wanna be part of the flagship product?"

Ethan stared at Myrtle for a full five seconds before he answered. "Are you having a stro—"

Darby slammed her fingers over his mouth. "I think this conversation needs more context, Myrtle."

Vee put her hand on her beloved's arm. "We've devised a stratagem for the consumer who would prefer a more...bespoke experience. A pleasure device fashioned after their own preferences. A lover, perhaps? Or a collection of pre-made stock cast from willing...well"—she checked over the assembled men with an assessing eye—"stock."

"Whose dick is that?" Maggie asked, grabbing it from Myrtle and giving it a little wobble that made Trent nauseated.

"This one?" Vee eyed it as if it could answer the question. "Apologies, but I promised not to tell. So, if confidentiality is your thing, know it's strictly enforced."

A customer pulled Vee's attention aside for a moment, and Myrtle plucked the product back from Maggie and turned to do her wifely duty and move some inventory.

"Come get your cock cast!" she called to the milling crowd. "Help a hetero woman get the dick she deserves without having to deal with the rest of your dumb ass!"

Vee turned to her wife with a gentle smile. "Darling, I'm not criticizing, but that's not a great marketing strategy."

"It's the truth!" Myrtle insisted.

"Exactly," Maggie muttered from Trent's side, surprising him with the vitriol in her voice. "People rarely want to buy the truth."

Vee turned to her, having heard the same note. "Mags, darling, did you update our detective on what we...discovered the other day?"

Trent's lips thinned. "Once again, not a detective yet, and the two of you should not have gone...where you did."

He was summarily ignored as the women began to collaborate and speculate.

"I want to know what you learned, you guys!" Gemma chimed in, her enthusiasm sparking the others' interest. "I love Townsend Harbor history, as it's usually better and stranger than fiction, and I would rather tear off my own face than wait for your podcast to finally finish production."

Maggie's laugh was rich and warm. "Well, in the interest of saving your awesome face, I'll tell you…"

The story she told would have been a confession had she been sitting in an interrogation room, and Trent was increasingly chagrined at the amount of leeway he'd shown her that wasn't strictly legal and was definitely against the code of conduct. He didn't learn anything new until she was winding down.

"And then Vee found the symbols of an anchor and the siren branded together down in the tunnels on a grate that had been bricked over," Maggie revealed with the ardor of a campfire story-teller, in the very voice that was making her a star in a sea of online content. "When we followed up with the city, we realized there had been a drainage pipe behind the wall that they used to use as overflow until the breakwater was built in the marina."

Gabe made an impressed sound. "Great place to smuggle goods and/or people to the water. I think you found your shanghai spot."

At that, Maggie frowned. "I'm…not so sure after what else Vee found in the library."

"Ah, yes," Vee replied with a nod, her voice infused with enthusiasm. "A ledger, if you believe it. We found it tucked away in an old desk drawer. It listed payments from somewhere, but instead of noting the source, there were just pictures of anchors next to each sum."

"Anchors?" Ethan furrowed his brow, his old investigative instincts aroused.

"Yup," Myrtle chimed in, "and the amounts were quite large for the time. Large enough to make a big-dicked whale blush!"

"Are you suggesting a collaboration between your ancestor and Madame Katz?" Darby asked her man, leaning forward with a glint in her eye.

"Can't rule it out." He shrugged. "I had a conversation just the other day with Mayor Spew—er—Stewart, because I found several personal accounts of the old-timey Stewart spending much time and money at Madame Katz's, despite hating the woman. And... I don't know... The way he wrote about her..." His pale cheeks pinkened, as the starch-shirted town hero hadn't yet learned to let all his hair down. Darby was still working on him.

"Could be more than just a business deal," Myrtle added, wading into the conversation with her usual sharp insight. "Those two could've been thick as thieves, or maybe even lovers! I'll bet they were lovers. I'll bet they were *secret fucking* lovers!"

Gabe faked a gag. "Please don't say *lovers* unless there's a *meat* before and a *pizza* after."

The group shared a chuckle, and then a knowing look, contemplating the scandalous implications.

Ethan's eyes widened as he made an internal connection. "You know, my family crest has an anchor in it."

Darby smacked him hard on the shoulder. "That's right! You were telling me the Townsends were famous seafarers since before the first Elizabeth was getting her dick sucked by Shakespeare."

"I didn't say it like that," he muttered with a boyish sense of defensiveness. "But after they settled in the Americas, they became carpenters. Built most of this fucking town—you're welcome. If you see a charming building, Ethan's brother Ryan planned the thing, and Ethan built it. That's why there are anchors chiseled all over the damn place... Ethan and Ryan wanted all their buildings to carry the mark."

"Gangster move," Gabe said approvingly.

"Really?" Maggie's eyes twinkled as the pieces started to fall into place. "Madame Katz used the siren symbol as her own. Do *you* think it's possible that your ancestor and Madame Katz might

have been working together instead of being enemies? Perhaps...
even more?"

"My family used to own the building that housed Sirens, as
well as pretty much the entire waterfront side of Water Street.
Mayor Stewart's ancestor bought up most of the other side and
made the co-op." Ethan nodded toward an imaginary line in the
distance. "It was all very Montague and Capulet back in the day
until they decided to work together on some downtown project at
the docks." He hesitated, his expression turning somber. "Unfortunately, due to the somewhat tarnished Townsend legacy, our family
has been forced to sell many of the buildings over the years. What I
do remember, though, is that Sirens Pub was created, named, and
owned by Ethan Townsend the First before anyone else."

The group exchanged glances, tension and excitement
bubbling among them. As they pondered the implications, Trent
noticed that Maggie's spirits seemed to be lifting, clearly invigo-
rated by the potential twist in her investigation. He admired the
way her intellect fired up like a vintage engine—it was one of the
things he found irresistibly sexy about her. "We could always look
deeper," he said, his voice low and determined as he enjoyed the
goosebumps he saw in response to his breath hitting her ear.
"How about we take a little trip to the lighthouse? The view is
amazing, the atmosphere romantic, and maybe you'll find some
clarity there."

Maybe they both would.

"Trying to sweep me off my feet with romantic vistas, Deputy
McGarvey?" Maggie teased.

"Guilty as charged," he replied, offering his arm with a flourish. "Besides, everyone deserves a breather—even hotshot investigative journalists and ruggedly handsome deputies."

"Ruggedly handsome, huh?" She looped her arm through his,
her laugh light and musical. "Okay, rugged man, let's see how
those Bruno Magli loafers hold up on the beach."

"Pfft, these were made to shoe the descendants of Roman

gods as they sexually harass women up and down the Mediter-
ranean. I think it'll handle Townsend Harbor's strip of rocky sand
just fine."

As they excused themselves from the group, Vee called out
after them, "You two enjoy the red light! Make some memories!"
Her innuendo-laden sendoff sparked another round of laughter
among the crowd.

With a quick wave to their friends, they set out into the night.
A cool breeze rolled in off the water, carrying the fresh scent of sea
salt and evergreens. Stars blinked to life overhead as the last sliver
of light abandoned the port.

"It's beautiful out here." She gazed up at the indigo sky, a
wistful note in her voice. "Peaceful. Makes you feel small in the
best possible way."

"Mmm." Trent squeezed her hand, struck by her observation,
as he helped her over a rocky part in the path. "I know what you
mean. There's something humbling about it."

"Thanks, my knight in shining—Armani," Maggie quipped.
She was a vision against the backdrop of the restless sea, her red
hair a fiery banner whipped about by the whims of the wind.

If ever there was a night to believe in happy endings...

They strolled hand in hand along the beach, sand crunching
under their feet.

Ahead, the lighthouse stood sentinel, its sturdy form etched
against the twilight sky like a promise. And there, casting a scarlet
hue upon the churning waters, was the red light—legendary and
unwavering. It beckoned to lost sailors and love-struck hearts
alike, its pulse a steady reminder of past devotion and present
allure.

"Wow," Maggie breathed out, her eyes alight with the reflection of the red beacon. "Ethan wasn't kidding."

"Wait until you're standing right beneath it," Trent said.

When they reached the lighthouse porch, Maggie stopped in
her tracks, gaze traveling up the spiral staircase to the top.

"Do you want to go up?" he asked. "We don't have to if you're not up for the climb."

"No, I definitely want to go up." She flashed him a determined smile. "I just...have a feeling there's something waiting for us at the top."

Trent didn't question her intuition. If Maggie sensed they were meant to climb those stairs, he would follow her lead.

They made their way up the metal staircase, moonlight filtering through windows at each landing. He tried to focus on the magic of the night but couldn't keep his eyes from how hot her ass looked from this angle.

Spiral staircases. Maybe he needed to get one of these.

When they reached the top, they stopped to let their blood thrum and their breath catch up.

Trent felt the shift in Maggie's mood again as they threaded their way along the coastal path, the salty tang of sea air mingling with the earthy scent of damp soil. The Love Fest's jubilant noise was a distant melody now, usurped by the symphony of crashing waves that seemed to cheer them on with every thunderous applause against the rocks.

They shared a look then, charged with the energy of their conspiracy and the unsaid words that hung between them like the very secrets etched into the lighthouse walls. At Maggie's insistence, they scoured the indoor walkway, using the red rotation of light as their guide. Only when every inch had been painstakingly checked did she lean against the stone with a disappointed huff.

"Nothing more exciting than what you'd find etched on a bathroom wall," she muttered.

Trent stood in front of her, using his wide shoulders to buffer some of the wind picking an increasing chill off the water below.

Maggie's fingertips lingered on the ancient grooves in the stone, tracing them as if they could unlock the secrets of a century-old tryst. The salt-laden breeze tugged at her hair, whipping it around her in a tempestuous halo. Trent watched, his thirsty eyes missing nothing, the glow from the lighthouse casting a dangerous red sheen over the scene and deepening the russet strands into flickering embers.

"I can just feel how close I am to answers. Can't you sense it too?" Her voice trembled with emotion. "The romance, the mystery—it's like the past is reaching out, begging us to listen, and I'm trying so hard, but..." She hissed frustration through her tight throat.

"Townsend Harbor has always had more secrets than a speakeasy, see?" Trent quipped in his best Edward G. Robinson voice. "And you, Maggie Michaels, are just the dame to crack 'em wide open, read all about it, yeah." He flicked a fake cigar.

Her laughter bubbled over her irritation, genuine and rich, and for a moment all the aloofness that clouded her earlier melted away, leaving behind a woman whose passion for history was decorated by the curves she wore so confidently.

"How about you cut yourself a break?" he suggested, pulling her from outside into the insulation of the indoor walkway, where the window ledges were just wide enough to lean against. The man-sized red light turned and turned on well-oiled axles at shoulder height, making them appear as disembodied torsos standing above a black void. "You've uncovered more truth about this town's past in a couple weeks than anyone could have in a century. Just because you didn't find an answer here, doesn't mean you won't follow your impeccable nose to where it hides."

He pressed his lips against the tip of that nose, if only to warm it.

And damned if the sprightly woman didn't turn the innocent gesture up to ten.

As her lips met his, Trent felt a shiver run down his spine. Her soft, luscious mouth was supple as velvet against his own, electrifying every nerve ending in his body. He couldn't help but deepen the kiss, hungrily exploring her mouth with his tongue, seeking out hers in a passionate dance. His heart raced in his chest, thudding erratically against his ribcage as he lost himself in the moment.

God, he loved everything about the feel of her against him. The way her plump thighs pressed against his, the softness of her stomach as it conformed to his hard abs. He felt more alive than he had in years. Trent knew then and there that he was falling for her, but he pushed those thoughts aside for now, focusing instead on the intoxicating feelings coursing through him.

Tentatively, Maggie reached down toward his pants, caressing him through the fabric. He couldn't help but moan into her mouth as she began to unbutton his slacks with practiced ease. Her hand dipped beneath his waistband, grasping his rapidly hardening length. Trent gasped as her fingers encircled him, stroking up and down in a steady rhythm that had him seeing stars.

She broke the kiss then, giving him a sultry look as she sank to her knees. The red glow of the lighthouse bathed her face in an ethereal light as she maintained eye contact.

"Let me taste you," she purred, freeing him fully from the confines of his pants.

Trent could only nod mutely, watching as she took him into her warm, wet mouth. Her lips stretched around his thickness as she began to move, swirling her tongue skillfully along his sensitive skin. He braced himself against the window ledge, fighting to remain upright as waves of pleasure crashed through him.

Looking down, he could just make out her silhouette in the dim light, silky hair spilling over her shoulders, full breasts pressed against his thighs. She worked him steadily, moaning around his length, the vibrations shooting straight to his core.

It was all Trent could do not to finish right then and there. He threaded his fingers through her hair, gently guiding her pace. The sight of this incredible, passionate woman on her knees unstitched something tight inside of him.

He focused on the open ocean beyond the lighthouse window, the endless expanse of water merging with the night sky along the horizon. The waves rolled and crashed below them in time with Maggie's movements.

Her lips and tongue were a perfect kind of magic, and Trent did everything he could to extend the moment. He tightened his fingers in her hair as she took him even deeper. The beam from the lighthouse swept over them, illuminating Maggie's voluptuous curves. The rapture in her expression. The muscles working in her mouth. Her lithe fingers encircling his cock, the moisture of her mouth slick down the entire length, pulling a release from as deep as the root of his spine.

Fuck. He couldn't let himself come yet. Not. Yet.

Just as he was about to reach the point of no return, Maggie slowed her pace, lightly grazing her teeth along his sensitive skin. She looked up at him with a sultry gaze and grinned wickedly.

"Maggie..." Her name was dragged from his throat in a raw plea.

Stop. Don't stop. Don't ever stop.

Don't go.

I'm falling in love with you.

Her eyes rolled away from him as if she could handle the thick cock grazing the back of her throat, but not the intensity of his gaze or the words he wasn't strong enough to say.

Her eyes widened as she looked up.

"Omph mif Gawrgh!" she struggled to declare around the thick rod of sex she'd sucked into her mouth.

He meant to pull out, but she tightened her fingers around the base, clamping her lips ruthlessly, forcing a climax to slam into him with all the force of a Japanese bullet train. All he could do was brace himself against the window ledge as Maggie's talented mouth milked every last drop from him. The pleasure was so intense, it felt like his vision whitewashed for a moment, reduced to pinpricks of red and blue as the lighthouse's rotating beam illuminated their passionate encounter.

She even. Fucking. Swallowed.

He was in so much trouble.

Rather than pull her up, Trent let the starch go all the way out of his knees and sank to kneel before her, intent on returning the favor. When he reached to kiss her, she batted his hands away, ducking beneath the window ledge. "Holy fucking shitballs!" she exclaimed, taking her phone out of her coat pocket and shining the flashlight up beneath the ledge.

Trent somehow wrestled himself together and zipped up before he dared speak, using the precious seconds to try to figure out just what the fuck had happened.

"Maggie," he panted, collapsing to sit until his thighs stopped twitching. "Christ, Maggie, I—"

"I fucking found it, McGarvey," she whispered in awe. "Proof. Here it is."

He stared at her dumbly.

"Look!" She scooted aside and pulled him lower so he could duck beneath the window ledge and gaze idiotically up at whatever had been able to distract her from the best blow job in the history of ever.

For K.R.K., my beacon amongst all storms. ~E.T.T.

For E.T.T., my secret and eternal heart. ~K.R.K.

Feb 14, 1898

"K.R.K.—Katherine Rose Katz... A beacon amongst all storms." Something in her whisper broke his heart, and Trent found himself reaching for her without thinking. "E.T.T. has to be Ethan Townsend." Maggie's eyes shimmered with unshed tears as she looked back at the inscription. "They loved each other."

"I'll be hosed," he breathed. "You fucking did it, Maggie." Trent squeezed her, feeling the excitement tense her entire frame.

"Imagine, all those years ago," she mused, her thoughts racing with possibilities. "What sort of secrets did they share? What could've brought them together? How did they even meet? How did they fall in love?"

"Guess you'll have to stick around and investigate." Trent grinned, his brain finally surfacing from a miasma of cum confusion. "But...how about we take this back to my place, and I investigate what's happening in those skimpy panties I know you're wearing?"

Her grin did something incredible to his insides. Something so warm he felt like he'd swallowed a goddamned campfire.

Screw falling—he'd done fell in it already. Fell in fucking love without even realizing it.

He wanted to say it. To blurt it. To yell it to the black swath of ocean and every creature seen and unseen.

Maggie kissed him with a playful smack and stood, reaching down to comically help him to his unsteady feet.

"It sucks to know exactly the codes to how many laws we just broke," he lamented. "This is government property."

"Stick with me, kid." She winked. "I'll teach ya a thing or two."

They descended the spiral staircase of the lighthouse together, talking excitedly about theories and timelines, their words intertwining like the threads of the intricate tapestry they were unraveling. Trent felt a surge of satisfaction at seeing some of her enthusiasm returning, her detective's mind snapping pieces together with every step they took.

The beach greeted them with its sprawling canvas of sand and sea, but the sight that awaited by his meticulously kept car drew a stark line through the idyllic setting. There stood a man—broad-shouldered, burly, and with an air of ownership that irked Trent immediately.

Maggie halted so abruptly that he instinctively reached out, steadying her with a firm grip on her elbow. Her face drained of color, and for a split second, he saw vulnerability flashing across those usually fierce green eyes. She leaned into him, subtly seeking support, and Trent's protective instincts flared to life.

"Easy, I've got you," he murmured, prepared to shield her from whatever storm this stranger brought into her eyes.

Then the man moved toward them, his steps deliberate, a challenge etched into the lines of his jaw. His voice rumbled across the space between them, heavy with accusation.

"How about you take your hands off my wife."

SIXTEEN

Bruised

THIS REFERS TO A DRINK THAT HAS BEEN SHAKEN TOO LONG AND HAS A SHABBY APPEARANCE

THERE WAS A MOMENT OF STUNNED SILENCE BEFORE Maggie's brain could put words to the sight before her. Not that relishing the taste of McGarvey in the back of her throat helped.

Charles Wiggins, leering at her with the hooded eyes that had once made her weak in the knees, but now mostly just made her want to vomit.

His black hair was slicked back in a pompadour with enough grease to fry a donut, his bulky body stuffed into a pinstriped suit that looked like a Spirit Halloween version of a *Godfather* costume.

His crooked grin widened when they locked eyes, the flash of a silver canine tooth winking from the corner of his thin lips.

Prison issue, she suspected.

"Ch-Charlie?" she stammered, her voice betraying the shock that coursed through her body.

"Hey, baby doll—long time no see," he drawled, his arms crossed over a chest that he'd added some muscle to without managing to rid himself of the former quarterback flab. "And"—the toothpick rolled from one side to the other—"it's Chazz now."

Just when she thought he couldn't get any more repellent.

"What are you doing here?" Maggie asked, her mind racing to comprehend the sudden shift in her reality.

"Can't a guy visit his lovely wife?" Chazz replied, eyes widening in feigned innocence.

McGarvey tensed beside her, but Maggie couldn't bring herself to turn to him, afraid of what she might see.

"*Chazz,*" she said, trying to load the name with the full measure of annoyance she felt. "The only reason I'm still legally your wife is because you refused to sign the divorce papers I served you with four years ago."

"And I've been thinking of you every minute of that four years," he said, his hand drifting to his chest for emphasis.

"That's funny, because I've been doing everything I can to forget you exist," she shot back, her words dripping with venom.

"How's that working out for you?" he asked, his smug smile making the toothpick point toward his bushy brow.

Maggie threaded her fingers with McGarvey's. "Before you decided to invade my privacy, it was working fucking great."

She felt a stab of vicious pleasure when his smile wilted.

"That hurts, Shortcake," he said, shaking his head. "That hurts real bad."

"Look, Chazz," she said, trying to regain her composure, "I don't know what you want, but I assure you, I am not interested. It's over."

"You say that," he said, a wicked gleam in his eye as he took a step closer to them, "but you and I know there's still something between us."

Maggie's chest tightened at the suggestion of his words.

"There's about to be a restraining order between us if you don't leave now."

"Aw, baby, you don't got to be so cold," Chazz replied with a smirk. "You know, I think it's pretty romantic that I found you all the way out here in Townsend Harbor. Shows dedication, doesn't it?"

"Romantic?" she scoffed, rolling her eyes. "More like completely delusional and downright fucking frightening."

"Your wit is still as sharp as ever." He grinned, seemingly unfazed by her sarcasm. "But really, Mags, I came all this way because I love you. You're the only thing that kept me going while I was in prison."

The bottom dropped out of her stomach as a numb silence muffled the nearby festivities.

"Prison?" Hearing this word asked quietly in McGarvey's voice made Maggie feel like someone had dropped a brick on her chest.

Now, Chazz's smirk stretched into a shit-eating grin. "Oh, she didn't tell you that, eh, pal?" When McGarvey said nothing, Chazz strutted another step toward them. "Well, if that's the case, I'm willing to bet there's all kinds of things my little Short-cake ain't told you. Like how she's the reason I ended up behind bars."

In her peripheral vision, Maggie saw McGarvey turn to her, and knew she could be a coward no longer. Without relinquishing her grip on his hand, she turned to face him. His shock was palpable, his face tight, as he met her gaze.

"What he means is, I testified for the Feds," she admitted.

"Turned state's evidence, you mean," Chazz drawled. "To avoid charges of her own."

The cold air seemed to thicken around them, freezing them both in place, refusing to fill her lungs.

"Is that true?" McGarvey asked.

"Yes," Maggie admitted.

The look he gave her then—not of anger but of disappoint-ment—cut deeper than anything she'd ever felt before.

"You have to understand," she pleaded. "I was young and totally naïve. I—I didn't know what he was involved in before I married him. And once I did..." She wrestled with a rapidly closing throat. "I was just trying to protect someone I loved."

"So you *do* love me!" Chazz crowed.

"*Loved*," Maggie corrected him, shooting him a withering grin. "Past tense."

"Kinda like you *loved* all them fancy-ass designer clothes and shoes I scored for you?" he said, plucking the sodden toothpick from his lips and flicking it away.

Maggie felt the blood drain from her face, her cheeks and forehead pricking as if infested with a thousand insects. "I... You... Those were *gifts.*"

An overpowering surge of Chazz's sinus-melting cologne enveloped Maggie, making her head go all swimmy.

"You didn't seem to be asking too many questions about how I afforded them on a plumber's salary." He leaned back against the bright red Camaro...what was most assuredly a rental car.

"They were *fake*," she spat, furious at herself for the tears she felt gathering in her eyes.

Chazz's six-o'clock-shadowed cheeks lifted in his ugliest smile yet. "Then how come you's still wearin' them?"

She clutched at the handbag, as if somehow holding it, owning it, would make it genuine.

McGarvey's eyes followed Chazz's to where her hand clung to the bag's strap before slowly lifting to meet hers.

What she read there robbed her of breath.

Pity.

The sting of humiliation seared through her skin like wildfire.

Chazz retrieved another toothpick from his pocket and pointed it at Trent before poking it between his lips. "The difference between me and this guy is that I never minded that you was a phony," he said. "In fact, I always thought it was kind of cute. Just like when you asked me and the guys to help you break into that asylum for that little radio show of yours. I noticed you never mentioned that when you was talkin' to the Feds."

Maggie felt McGarvey's grip on her hand slacken and tightened hers.

"Please," she said, hating the plaintive note in her voice. "You have to let me explain."

Just then, a group of rosy-cheeked, red-hat-wearing MILFs spilled by, tossing out, "Good evening, Deputy McGarvey," flirtatiously as they passed.

"Deputy?" Chazz burst out in his always obnoxiously loud laugh, even slapping his meaty thigh for good measure. "Holy shit. I bet you've been all kinds of useful to her since she's been in town."

"Trent, *please*," Maggie said, blinking hard as McGarvey's fingers slipped from hers. The loss shocked her more than she'd anticipated.

"Don't feel bad, buddy," Chazz said. "My Shortcake has never minded her fellas breaking the law. So long as they was breaking it in ways *she* liked. This one has always had a thing for the bad boys, but I can see she's upped her game with yous."

McGarvey took a step back.

Eyes that had looked at her in with affection, flirtation, and even passion countless times over the past weeks now looked at her with questions, doubts, and, most painful of all, hurt.

"Is that why you came to Townsend Harbor?" he asked, his voice icier than the winds whipping around them. "Is that why you...why we—"

"No," Maggie said, pouring every ounce of the truth she felt burning in her chest into the word. "Trent, everything I've said about the way I feel is true."

"Wait a minute," Chazz interrupted, his gaze flitting between Maggie and McGarvey like he were a hungry seagull eyeing a pair of unguarded sandwiches. "Have you two been fuckin'?"

"Shut the fuck up, Charlie!" Maggie roared, letting every ounce of her rage boil to the surface.

"Like hell I will," he said, thumping his barrel chest like an offended ape. "It was one thing when I thought you was just using him, but I oughta know who's been keeping my wife company while I was locked up."

Maggie clenched her fists, digging her nails into her palms as she fought the urge to scream. It seemed that no matter how hard she tried to put the past behind her, it kept clawing its way back into her life, determined to drag her down with it.

"Listen, deputy," Chazz began, his tone dripping with false sincerity, "I wouldn't be standing here if I didn't still love this woman. She's got her hooks in me deep. Hell, even after she turned me in, she kept some secrets to protect me. That's how I know she still cares."

"Is that so?" McGarvey asked.

"Absolutely," Chazz continued, undeterred. "Just ask her about the time we stole that antique clock from old man Jenkins' house. She never told the Feds about that one, did you, baby doll?"

The air between Maggie and McGarvey grew thick with tension, as if an invisible fog had rolled in from the ocean. The once-joyful atmosphere that filled the lighthouse after their passionate tryst and the Madame Katz mystery resolution was replaced by a cloud of doubt and disbelief.

"I'm not saying I haven't made mistakes," she said, gazing up with him. "But I've learned from mine, and I'm not the same person I was back then."

McGarvey was silent for what felt like an eternity.

"It's not the fact that you made a mistake that bothers me. It's that you didn't trust me enough to tell me."

His eyes flickered, and for a moment, Maggie saw a shadow cross his face. His usually warm brown eyes turned steely, and the corners of his mouth tensed. He clenched his jaw, and his posture shifted ever so slightly into something more rigid.

She stared at him, her heart sinking like a stone tossed into the harbor. His handsome face, which had so recently been alight with desire and laughter, now bore an expression of steely professionalism as he assessed the situation before him. She felt the weight of his gaze on her, and it was colder than any New England winter.

"Look," she began, desperately trying to find the right words, "Trent, I know this is a lot to take in, but—"

"Ma'am," McGarvey said, his use of the formal title like a slap in the face, "please step aside while I take him into custody."

"What? You're arresting me?" Chazz sputtered, looking between them incredulously. "For what? I ain't done anything."

"Violation of parole," McGarvey replied, his tone firm and absolute. "You crossed state lines when you left New York."

The color drained from Chazz's face. He gazed at McGarvey, horror creeping onto his features as the reality of the situation sank in. "N-now hold on a minute," he stammered, panic tingeing his voice. His eyes darted around like he were a cornered fox, seeking an escape route where there was none. "Maggie, baby, tell him!" he pleaded, his voice an octave higher. He reached out to grab her arm, but McGarvey stepped in his way, puffing his broad chest out like an iron shield.

"You don't want to do that," he growled, his eyes flashing with warning.

Chazz hesitated for a moment, sizing up McGarvey. He could bluff his way out of most things, but, staring down the barrel of the deputy's cold gaze, he decided discretion was the better part of valor.

"All right, all right," he said, holding up his palms. "I'll go quietly."

Maggie's heart ached as she watched the man who had just hours ago been her passionate lover now handle Chazz with the precision of a seasoned law enforcement officer. The intimacy they had shared seemed like a distant memory, replaced by the stark reality of their current situation.

As she watched them disappear into the night, Maggie's legs gave out beneath her, and she crumpled onto the damp grass.

The desolation that settled over her was as cold and unforgiving as the waves crashing against the nearby cliffs, the lighthouse's searching scarlet beam a mocking reminder of the safe harbor she'd found, and lost, in the arms of Trent McGarvey.

SEVENTEEN

Skate

GETTING OUT OF TROUBLE; A CRIMINAL MIGHT
SKATE FROM HIS CHARGES IF A WITNESS DIDN'T
SHOW UP FOR TRIAL

A CLOUD OF STEAM BILLOWED AROUND TRENT AS HE paced by the police car, his breath visible in the chilly air, the sound of his boots on the gravel and the pop of gum from a visiting transport deputy a symphony of impatience as they waited to whisk the Bostonian bad boy back to his concrete suite on the other coast.

Trent had always loved the rain, but today it felt like a cruel joke, adding to the weight of his thoughts. Weeks had passed since his explosive fight with Maggie, and here he was, escorting the man still legally attached to her out of his goddamned life.

"Let's hope we never see each other again," he said, his tone dripping with thinly veiled disdain. Chazz, hands cuffed, leaned against the car with an air of resignation.

"No chance of getting off for good behaviah?" he asked with a smirk, his thick accent flavoring the air with a hint of East Coast arrogance.

Trent's jaw tightened, and his fingers instinctively curled into a fist before he caught himself. He had to be the embodiment of law and order, not some lovesick vigilante with an axe to grind.

But Chazz's words clawed at him, stirring up the murky waters of his emotions.

The pink-faced fucker's smile died as he glanced up at Trent's carefully expressionless face.

"Should've treated her better," Chazz muttered. "But you know how it is, brother. Can't be lookin' soft in front of the guys. Spent too much time trying to be the king, forgot that my queen deserved better."

"Don't call me brother," Trent said.

Still, Chazz's confession hung between them, raw and unsettling. Trent stole a glance at the man who'd snared Maggie's heart once upon a time. It was almost pitiable how he clung to his machismo like a security blanket.

After three weeks in the county jail, he looked like a child's drawing of his own worst nightmare. Hair askew, skin pale, face bloated from five-thousand-calorie jail meals of mostly Spam, hot dogs, bologna, white carbs, and kitchen worker jizz.

"Chazz! You Protestant hooch-swilling, half a Scot tryna be Irish, droop-dicked, haggis-fed, black-and-tan-loving mothah-fuckah." Gabe's Southie patois put a hard edge on the rapid-fire insults, half of which Trent admittedly didn't comprehend the significance of. The ex-con's voice was a taut wire ready to snap. He stalked up to the cruiser's back door, where Chazz stood cuffed and temporarily repentant. There was maybe four inches between them both uncovered by Celtic tattoos, and Trent watched the strange generational dance they did with interest. "Next time I sees you, I'll make you wear your own intestines as a—"

"Can't threaten a man's life on actual police property, Mr. Kelly," Trent said, though he doubted any of the officers present were planning on providing Chazz much in the way of protection from insults.

Gabe's chin jutted forward, his hard jaw tightening. "This fucking guy? Please, he probably picks up his girlfriends from high school and tries to convince grown-ass men she's 'really mature.'"

Trent gave in to a derisive laugh.

"Hey, fuck you, Kelly. You set foot back in Boston and you've a lot of the old family who can't wait to meet you in a dark alley." Chazz took a step forward and ran into the hand Trent used to block him.

"If you so much as think about coming back here or even breathing in Maggie's direction, I swear I'll make those Irish mobsters look like choirboys," he murmured in a register low enough that the onlookers missed the words, but not the intention.

Damned if the asshole's face didn't crumple. Not out of fear so much as...guilt?

"I messed up with Maggie." He paused, looking away. "She's too good for me. I was running around with other women 'cause I didn't want to look whipped in front of my boys. Made her believe I was the best she could get, just to keep her around. I'm going to do better."

"You won't get the chance, you delusional cock wad," Trent said, drumming his fingers against the car door. "But I'll give you this: you're right about Maggie. She's too good for you."

"What did you do to the divorce papers, you spineless bastard?" Gabe spat, his tattoos seeming to come alive as his muscles tensed beneath them. "Four years you had to sign. Four fucking years."

Chazz spat at Gabe's feet as a transport deputy pushed his head until he relented and folded into the back seat. "Burned 'em. She wants to leave me? She'll have to—"

Trent slammed the car door shut. The window smacked Chazz in the face.

He wasn't given time to worry about the visiting deputies before their guffaws and knuckle bumps drew a satisfied smirk.

Rain dripped from the edge of Trent's hat, creating a rhythm only he could hear. He watched as Chazz was dragged off like a piece of unwanted luggage. As the car pulled away, Gabe stepped closer, shaking his head.

"That fucking cocksucker," he muttered, wiping water from his face. "Maggie had it wicked rough growing up, y'know? Shitty father. Trashy mother. You know the story..."

"Uh, no, not really," Trent admitted, surprised by Gabe's openness. "Maggie never told me about them."

"Did you ask?"

He glanced away from the Irishman's keen gaze.

No. He'd been so intent on finding out who Maggie was, he'd forgotten to ask *her*. To know her. To see her beyond what he wanted her to be.

Maybe that was why he couldn't pinpoint the moment he'd fallen in love with her—because he loved the things about her he didn't even allow himself to look at.

"What happened to her?" he asked, gaze latched on to the rear lights of the cruiser.

"Maggie learned early that she needed to look out for herself," Gabe explained, his voice laced with bitterness. "Then she met Chazz, and that whole thing happened."

"What whole thing?"

Gabe opened his mouth, scowled, then snapped it shut. "That's her story to tell you. But I'll say this... Maggie, she's like one of those muscle cars I love so much. Under all the ferocity, tenacity, and that fucking smart mouth are years of being told she's not worth much. But if you tweak a few things about how she runs...there's a classic beauty just waiting to roar."

Trent arched an eyebrow, a half-smile tugging at his lips. He liked the sound of that—a project, something he could polish until it gleamed. "She'd never mentioned wanting to divorce Chazz."

"Ah, well." Gabe exhaled, blowing out a breath that formed a cloud in the cool air. "Maggie's always been more about action than words. Tried to leave him a dozen ways before that. Mark finally drew up the papers when that lowlife got cuffed."

"Action, huh?" A chuckle rumbled deep in Trent's chest. "That's one way to say 'dives in headfirst without checking the depth.'"

"Exactly," Gabe agreed, the corner of his mouth hitching up. "She's all passion and impulse, but with a brain that doesn't quit. You get her on your side, McGarvey, and you're golden. Guess what I'm trying to say is, she deserves better than she's had so far. Don't screw it up, man. She's a fighter, but even fighters need someone in their corner."

"Thanks, man," Trent said, working up to an epic brood. He needed to speak to Maggie. Needed her to understand everything he'd said. Everything he was. Everything he'd done to make her feel like she was less was never about her. It was him.

He was the one who brought his Kentucky-fried bullshit into their interactions and then made her feel less for not accepting it.

He needed to do better.

To be better.

And he had an idea of just how to get her back.

EIGHTEEN

Top shelf

THE HIGHEST QUALITY AND MOST EXPENSIVE
BOTTLES OF ALCOHOL AVAILABLE, OFTEN KEPT
ON THE TOP SHELF BECAUSE THEY'RE NOT USED
THAT OFTEN

"Where *the* fuck are they?"

Maggie kicked a pile of clothes out of the way and stepped over the avalanche of pillows and cushions that had escaped from their encampments on the couch.

"Jesus, Magpie." Mark Kelly stood in the doorway of Maggie's bedroom closet, a glass of prosecco in either hand, and a delicately disdainful expression on his face. "You find your self-respect yet? Because I'm starving, and the selection in your fridge and pantry is downright unacceptable."

"I *know* they were in this box." Seeing a file labeled *Charlie Taxes, 2020*, she hurled it over her shoulder and reached for the next one.

"I mean, I understand you're a resident of the Pacific Northwest, but quinoa salad? Really?"

"The hall closet!" Shoving herself up from the floor, Maggie ducked under Mark's arm and pushed past him into the hallway.

"And kimchi? That shit's spicy farts that just haven't happened yet."

Wrenching the closet door open, she yanked the light bulb

string and reached up to the top shelf for a box marked *Fuck This Motherfucker* in angry marker scrawl. She dropped it to the floor and yanked open the flaps, pausing to flip the bird to the stack of files related to Charlie's trial and subsequent conviction.

"But the marinated tofu thing, you're going to have to explain to me," Mark said before tipping back his glass of prosecco.

She paused while dumping out a box of Charlie's high school football memorabilia. "You're not helping."

"All right." Mark raised one hand in mock surrender, his green eyes lit with amusement. "What are we looking for, then?"

"The divorce papers Chazz the fuckstick never signed," she snapped, tossing a stack of old birthday cards aside.

"First things first," he said. "You're going to stop, take a breath, and take a sip of this excellent prosecco I acquired for you."

She blew out a sigh, puffing her hair off her sweat-kissed forehead as she accepted the glass. The crisp, citrusy swallow made her eyes sting.

"Better?" Mark asked.

Maggie nodded, feeling her throat tighten.

She truly had been better since Mark showed up on her doorstep, a box of her favorite Italian wedding cookies in one hand and an industrial-sized box of Kleenex in the other.

Better, as in she wasn't eating, sleeping, and sobbing on her couch for days on end.

Better, as in she'd taken a shower and put on actual clothing instead of the holey sweats that had become her uniform.

Better, as in she'd traded the soul-sucking, shame-fueled sadness for a refreshingly fiery rage.

At Charlie, for thinking he could just show up and call her back to his side like a dog.

At her father, for making her think that a man like Charlie was all she could expect for herself.

At McGarvey, for telling her that she deserved better.

But mostly at herself, for believing it.

"Okay," she said, setting the glass aside to resume her search. "I'm okay. I can do this."

"The thing I don't understand," Mark said, setting aside his own drink to begin scooping everything into something resembling a pile, "is why you need those now."

"For fucking McGarvey," she spat. "I'm going to march right up to him, shove those papers right in his stupid, uptight face before flipping him off and never speaking to him again."

"Riiight," he drawled, raising an eyebrow. "And the point of doing that would be..."

"Proving to McGarvey that I was trying to leave Charlie even before his well-deserved incarceration."

"I'm just saying, that seems like a shit-ton of work for someone you never intend to see again."

Maggie used the doorframe to haul herself up and stomp over to the desk, where she began yanking open drawers.

"It's about closure, Mark." She grabbed a stack of notebooks and set them off to one side. "It's about knowing that he knows that I was trying to get as far away from that lifestyle as I possibly fucking could."

"So basically, you're saying McGarvey's opinion of you matters."

"Yes! No. Fuck off." With a disgusted sigh, she reached for a manilla folder. Seeing *Sirens* on the tab in McGarvey's mechanically precise handwriting felt like a sucker punch to the guts.

In the aftermath of Chazz's unwelcome visit, she hadn't even started laying out her notes for the Madame Katz episode of her podcast. A hot flame of irritation flickered within her chest.

One of the throw blankets that she'd hurled across the room began to move. Maggie whipped it off and scooped up Roxie. "Here, take this," she said, handing her over to Mark.

Cradling her in one arm, he walked over to the couch and set the dog down. "You know, the real tragedy here is that we haven't even gotten to discuss my latest Tinder disaster," he said. "And when I tell you that a narcissistic Manhattan pastry chef with a *crème anglaise* fetish is the new sad thing, I mean it sincerely."

"Huh," Maggie said, paging through her notes. "That's crazy."

"All right, that's it." Mark stood up from the couch. "I'm officially staging an intervention."

She looked at him, bewildered. "What?"

"You heard me," he said with a wry smile. "We're going to pregame until we're pleasantly lit, and then we're hitting the town. Or what passes for one around here."

"Mark, I don't—"

"Look, I get that you've been through hell and back. But you can't keep going like this. I'm here now and I'm taking my best bitch out. Step away from the papers, get your ass in the shower, and put on the outfit you'd want to be wearing when you see McGarvey next."

Maggie chewed her lower lip, alarmed by the sudden tightness in her chest.

"Good," Mark said. He wrapped his arms around her in a tight embrace, and suddenly Maggie found herself unable to hold back the tears any longer. They streamed down her cheeks, wetting Mark's shirt as she quietly sobbed into his chest.

"Hey, hey," he murmured, rubbing her back soothingly. "I know, Maggie. I know."

"It's..." she choked out between sobs. "Trent... He was the first person who ever made me feel like I was better than what I'd come from. Like I deserved more than just...this." She gestured weakly at the chaos surrounding them.

"Hey, look at me," Mark said gently, tilting her face up to meet his gaze. "You *are* better than this. You deserve the world, Maggie, and if McGarvey isn't man enough to see that, then fuck that motherfucker. Next."

She gave a weak chuckle.

"And, on a related topic"—he cleared his throat—"it's worth

reminding you that my family has a history of disposing of bodies."

Maggie sniffled, attempting a small smile as she gazed into her best friend's eyes. "Thank you."

"Always," he replied, squeezing her one last time before letting her go. "Now, speaking of bodies," Mark continued, "I love you, but yours needs some self-care. So, let's get you cleaned up, shaved down, and shimmy you into something that shows off that dat ass."

"Oh, we're so going in here."

They slowed in front of Vee's Lady Garden, the salt-scented air chilling Maggie's cheeks.

"Um, thanks but no thanks," Maggie said, hugging her coat tighter around her. The last thing she needed was to be anywhere connected to strong sexual memories about the man who had ma'am'd her.

"How about this? You're single now, and it's time to upgrade your toy collection." Grabbing her hand, Mark led her up the stairs toward the boutique. "Trust me, this is essential self-care."

As they entered, Maggie couldn't help but feel a mixture of curiosity and trepidation. The usually bustling boutique was eerily quiet, void of any other customers. She furrowed her brow, curiosity piqued.

"Looks like we have the place to ourselves," Mark said, waggling his brows. "Now let's find you something fun, shall we?"

Maggie rolled her eyes but followed him as he led her toward the back of the store. As they pushed through a set of velvet curtains, she gasped at the sight before her: a luxurious private shopping area filled with designer outfits in her size, displayed like treasures for a queen.

"What the…" she breathed, trailing her fingers over a silky blouse.

"Hello, Maggie."

Trent McGarvey stepped out from behind a clothing rack.

Maggie froze at the sight of him, surprised and momentarily speechless. His warm gaze seemed to map the planes of her face, lingering on her lips before finally meeting her eyes.

"Wh-what are you doing here?" she stammered, her pulse quickening.

"Apologizing," he said, lips stretching in a smile.

The words evaporated from her throat, the world around her blurring.

"Listen, Maggie," he began. "Since meeting you, my life has changed. You've brought color, laughter, and warmth into a world that was cold, rigid, and empty. But my point is, you changed my world for the better. And I want to be a part of yours."

As his words washed over her, Maggie felt a warmth spreading through her chest. It was as if something within her chest had unlocked, allowing in air and light. And maybe…the possibility that she could believe.

Her vision blurred with tears as she took a shaky breath, unable to contain the flood of emotions any longer. In a sudden burst of movement, she ran into his arms, burying her face in the crook of his neck.

His arms wrapped around her shoulders. Containing her. Anchoring her.

For a moment, they just stood there, locked in a silence that seemed to transcend time and space.

As Maggie pulled away, he held up a designer tote bag he had been clutching in one hand. "For you," he said gently, slipping the strap onto her arm.

"What is it?" she asked through her tears, her fingers trembling as she unzipped the bag.

"Have a look for yourself," he replied.

Maggie reached inside, her heart pounding as she pulled out a stack of papers. As she began to read them, her eyes widened in disbelief.

Her divorce papers.

Flipping through the thick sheaf, she could see an addendum had been paperclipped to the back of the bundle, wherein Charlie acknowledged responsibility for all debt and signed a promissory note guaranteeing her a monthly sum in restitution for the damages she suffered during their unfortunate union.

And on the last page, she found Charlie's self-important kindergarten scrawl of a signature.

"But...how?" she asked, looking up at Trent in shock.

"I may have taken some creative liberties and used my connections to track down the previous set," he admitted with a sheepish grin. "But after reviewing the terms and having a heartfelt conversation with our friend Chazz, we decided some amendments were in order."

Maggie couldn't help but let out a watery laugh, shaking her head in amazement. She could envision *exactly* how that conversation had gone down.

"You did all that...for me?" she asked.

"Fuck yes," Trent said, his eyes softening. "You're more than worth it, Maggie Michaels."

As the reality of this development sank in, Maggie felt an overwhelming sense of gratitude and relief wash over her.

Free.

She was finally free from the suffocating, toxic grasp of her past.

She looked into Trent's eyes, seeing the sincerity and warmth radiating from him, and knew there was only one way to truly thank him.

Surging forward, she captured his lips with hers in a passionate, fiery kiss that seemed to ignite every nerve ending in her body.

He wrapped his arms around her waist, pulling her closer as their mouths moved together in perfect harmony.

As they broke apart, both breathless and flushed, Maggie couldn't help but grin at the astonished expression on his face.

With a tender smile, Trent carefully lifted the designer tote bag from Maggie's arm and placed it on her shoulder. The scent of expensive leather drifted up to her as the strap settled against her skin, and for the first time, she felt it belonged there.

"Besides," Trent said, brushing tendril of hair back from her face. "If you're going to have baggage, it should at least be Versace."

"Snob," Maggie teased, letting herself melt into the warm wall of his chest.

"You love it," he rumbled, resting his chin atop her head as his big arms enfolded her.

Maggie's fingers stroked the buttery leather as a contented sigh escaped her. "I think maybe I do."

Townsend Harbor

BY KERRIGAN BYRNE & CYNTHIA ST. AUBIN

Nevermore Bookstore

Brewbies

Bazaar Girls

Star-Crossed

Sirens

About Cynthia

Cynthia St. Aubin wrote her first play at age eight and made her brothers perform it for the admission price of gum wrappers. A steal, considering she provided the wrappers in advance. Though her early work debuted to mixed reviews, she never quite gave up on the writing thing, even while earning a mostly useless master's degree in art history and taking her turn as a cube monkey in the corporate warren.

Because the voices in her head kept talking to her, and they discourage drinking at work, she kept writing instead. When she's not standing in front of the fridge eating cheese, she's hard at work figuring out which mythological, art historical, or paranormal friends to play with next. She lives in Texas with the love of her life and two fluffy cats, Muppet and Gizmo.

I love stalkers! You can find me here!
Visit me: http://www.cynthiastaubin.com/
Email me: cynthiastaubin@gmail.com
Join my Minions: https://www.facebook.com/groups/
Cynthiastaubins/

Subliminally message me: *You were thinking of cheese just now, right?*

And here:

Also by Cynthia

Tails from the Alpha Art Gallery

Love Bites

Love Sucks

Love Lies

Love Binds

The Kane Heirs

Corner Office Confessions

Secret Lives After Hours

Bad Boys with Benefits

The Jane Avery Mysteries

Private Lies

Lying Low

Case Files of Dr. Matilda Schmidt, Paranormal Psychologist

Unlovable

Unlucky

Unhoppy

Unbearable

Unassailable

Undeadly

Unexpecting

From Hell to Breakfast

About Kerrigan

Kerrigan Byrne is the USA Today Best-selling and award winning author of several novels in both the romance and mystery genre.

She lives on the Olympic Peninsula in Washington with her husband, two Rottweiler mix rescues, and one very clingy torbie. When she's not writing and researching, you'll find her on the beach, kayaking, or on land eating, drinking, shopping, and attending live comedy, ballet, or too many movies.

Kerrigan loves to hear from her readers! To contact her or learn more about her books, please visit her site or find her on most social media platforms: www.kerriganbyrne.com

Also by Kerrigan

A GOODE GIRLS ROMANCE

Seducing a Stranger

Courting Trouble

Dancing With Danger

Tempting Fate

Crying Wolfe

Making Merry

THE BUSINESS OF BLOOD SERIES

The Business of Blood

A Treacherous Trade

VICTORIAN REBELS

The Highwayman

The Hunter

The Highlander

The Duke

The Scot Beds His Wife

The Duke With the Dragon Tattoo

The Earl on the Train

CONTEMPORARY SUSPENSE

A Righteous Kill

ALSO BY KERRIGAN

How to Love a Duke in Ten Days

All Scot And Bothered

Printed in the USA
CPSIA information can be obtained
at www.ICGtesting.com
LVHW042325190724
785889LV00006B/1152

9 781648 396755